Thick As Thieves

By
Ken Lizzi

Aratus Scrivenery
Sandy, Oregon

Thick As Thieves.

This is a work of fiction. All concepts, characters, and events portrayed in this book are used fictitiously, and any resemblance to any persons, living or dead, is coincidental.

Aratus Scrivenery
37001 Goldenrain Street
Sandy, Oregon 97055

Second Edition May 2020

Cover art by MiblArt.

Published in the United States of America

ISBN: 978-0-578-68641-7

To Carol, and Carrol, and Livier. Thank you,
ladies, my accomplices in crime.

Contents

Chapter 1 - The Battle of Shib's Tavern

Brick held no illusions about the tavern. The place was a shithole. But a job was a job, and these days a man took what work he could get. At least the company—no, scratch that—the company was for shit too. Could be amusing, though.

"*. . . and in the torchlight we saw her tresses as a copper . . .*" the poet was saying, writing each word as he spoke it.

Chin on chest, Brick sneaked a glance from the poet to the woman behind the bar, her hair tied back with a scrap of ribbon. The lunch and early afternoon drinkers had all cleared out—with the exception of Glum Arent at his usual table near the front door.

"Hey, Brick." Glum Arent halted the scratching of the quill pen. "Would hair reflect torchlight as 'effulgence' or 'refulgence?'"

Brick tore his gaze from Livette, raised his bucket of a head and spat on the fresh sawdust that carpeted the tavern floor. "Don't know," he said. He watched a bead of black ink swell to a gobbet and, finally, drop onto Glum's lambskin parchment. "Mean the same thing, don't they?"

"Well, that's just it, isn't it? Do they?" Oblivious to the ink blotch, Glum rolled his gaunt, trimly bearded head on his thin stem of a neck. The poet working out a neck kink, hazard of the work. "I want to employ the right word. Got to convey the precise meaning to my readers."

"Fuck it, Glum. If there's a nuance there wasted on you it sure as shit is going to be wasted on your readers."

Brick rose from his three-legged stool at the tavern's front door. He upended his tankard experimentally. A forlorn dribble spattered to the floor. He grunted and sauntered to the bar for a refill. Livette, she of the beribboned hair, poured his ale while he studied the familiar debt servitude tattoo that marred her left wrist. In fading ink, blue-green links of chain encircled her wrist. Fresher red ink slashed a diagonal through one of the links, indicating completion of her servitude and satisfaction of the debt. He'd never dared ask her about it, Livette holding her past a closely guarded secret.

He returned to his seat, sniffed at the thin, sour ale like a connoisseur, and blinked in the light of the westering sun. Then, picking up the thread of his remarks, "Do you even have readers, Glum?"

"You hurt me, Brick. You know that? You wound. Of course, I have readers."

Brick laughed.

"The Four-Fold Soteriologists read me," Glum said. "The Verians are keen readers. And the Pontifical Henotics hang on my every word."

"Right. You've hooked a passel of godsbotherers and minor cultists. What about, you know, regular folk?" Brick rolled a wrist in a general, all-encompassing gesture.

"What about them? Religious types are about the only people who read. Shit, about the only people who can. 'Refulgence.' I'm going with refulgence."

"Hey, I'm regular folk and I can read," Brick said, folding his beefy arms over his barrel of a chest. He took pride in his literacy, and Glum of all people—

"Yeah, I know. I taught you. Big dumb arrow catcher comes limping into my tavern—"

"Ain't your tavern. Spending your days here scratching away and training to be a wine cask don't give you ownership."

"A man's chosen watering hole is *his* tavern, deed notwithstanding. And you shouldn't interrupt when I'm reminiscing."

"I was there, Glum. What's it matter? I already know the story."

"Tales enlighten, Brick. Even familiar tales. Children enjoy the same bedtime story night after night. Given your fundamentally childish nature you should indulge me when I revisit that fateful meeting."

"Fateful?" Brick emitted a harsh coughing laugh. "Fate steers the destiny of high priests and potentates. Fate could give a wet turd for a penniless, wine-sodden hack poet. And it damn sure ain't interested in a gimpy ex-soldier who can't get any better work than tavern bouncer."

"Don't forget you also wash the tankards every morning. Dish washing is a valuable skill, not to be disdained."

"Fuck you, Glum." Then he sighed. The little shit deserved a break. "It was magnanimous of you to teach me to read. Of course, when all I've got to read is your free verse, all that sucking up to the Electors, I find myself regretting it."

"I can teach literacy, and enhance your paltry vocabulary, but I can't teach good taste. My verse is wasted on you."

"Like rhyming is wasted on you."

They stopped bickering when a man walked in.

Brick eyed the new customer professionally. With the sun beginning its descent behind the West Hills it probably was time for the evening crowd to trickle in. This fellow smelled of dust and sweat. A canvas and leather apron covered his soiled woolen trousers and tunic. No visible weapons. A stonemason or bricklayer fresh off his shift putting up a warehouse for the Sharks, or maybe building one of their walled palace compounds.

Brick followed the man's progress to the bar, a length of varnished pine pegged down to stacks of old ale casks. The long bar dominated the taproom, that and a fireplace the only fixtures worth remark in the cramped space. The tavern wasn't an architectural wonder, just a simple stone and timber structure roofed with slate tiles that exhibited a marked propensity to leak. The taproom fronting the street allowed about thirty drinkers comfortably, fifty if they crammed in tight, filling all seven tables and lining up two-deep at the bar. Behind the taproom lay storage rooms, and above those, where the tavern rose to a second story, an office and quarters for the proprietor.

The customer reached the bar. Brick could see him scanning the offerings: casks of ale resting horizontally in cradles, the butt of wine with the ladle hanging from the side and the cloth stretched over its open top, the new ceramic bottles introduced by the Sharks filled with the sort of fortified fermentations Glum favored when in funds. And Brick could see the customer transferring his attention to the most notable feature behind the bar—Livette. She always caught their eyes. And could he blame them? She'd caught his.

In consideration of the still lingering heat of early autumn she wore her blouse only loosely laced and her floor length skirt slit halfway up her thigh. In addition to allowing a touch of cooling ventilation, Brick knew the gaps in her garments allowed access to the pair of knives she carried: a wickedly pointed bodkin sheathed between her breasts and a throat slasher of a dagger strapped to one leg.

The customer obviously couldn't see these hideout weapons, his gaze fixed on a point about a foot below Livette's narrowed gray eyes.

"He's making a move even before buying a drink," said Glum, watching as keenly as Brick. "Nervy son of a bitch."

Brick couldn't hear what the customer was saying, but he could tell from the tilt of Livette's head and her barely repressed sneer that the man was making a pass. None of Brick's business. He'd no claim on her. The occasional after-hours fuck in the storage room or in Brick's rats' nest of an attic hardly added up to marriage, common law or otherwise. She'd made that abundantly clear. Customers made a play for her all the time. Most of the time it didn't bother him, though on occasion it stung, feeling something like rejection. He wondered about that sometimes, thinking of asking Glum's opinion, but not willing to put up with the expected ridicule.

But something about this guy . . . Maybe because he was the first patron of the evening. Or maybe, as Glum had said, because he'd not even waited to buy a drink before coming on to Livette. Whatever the cause, Brick felt anger stir within him, a simmering heat commencing in his chest and rising to flush his cheeks.

He took a step forward. Livette lifted her head and looked at him, her expression saying, *Relax, I have the situation under control.* And, the look added, *don't be a stupid, jealous asshole.*

Brick halted. He buried his face in his tankard. The ale quenched the rage and he felt only a touch chagrined by the time he lowered the empty mug. "She's got a very expressive face," he muttered.

"Careful, big fellow," said Glum. "Drinking on the job is my shtick. Could get you fired."

Brick nodded and set down the tankard on the nearest table. He glanced over at the bar. A wine cup now rested next to the customer's elbow. Livette was wiping down the bar at the opposite end of the varnished expanse, a quiet smile stretching her generous lips.

Fine. Livette had managed as usual.

"You ever feel unneeded?" he asked Glum. "Like you're just taking up space, not providing any really essential service? Wait, sorry. Look who I'm asking."

"Your mood's for shit, isn't it, Brick?" Glum sounded peeved. "At least I don't spend my days tossing belligerent drunks out on their ears. At least I don't take my orders from a godsdamned Shark."

"Sorry, Glum. I was only fucking with you. Art, poetry, history. The spread of culture and information. Invaluable." Brick snagged a nearby stool and sat. "But lay off Shib. He's a decent boss."

"For a Shark, you mean. Why do you have such a soft spot for them? Shit, Brick, I didn't fight the fuckers and *I* hate them. You *did.* Fought 'em in the fucking war. Not very successfully, mind you. Big dumb ox, too clumsy to dodge an arrow. But doesn't that piss you off? Does not your blood boil, your heart rage, your mind churn with thoughts of revenge?"

"No."

"Well. Okay then." Glum contemplated his fired clay wine cup. "Can you spot me a couple bits for a refill? I'm expecting a commission from the Archtheosite of the Burgeian Order."

"Sure you are, Glum. You'll be rolling in coin within the week." Nonetheless, Brick dug out a couple of thin copper bits from the pocket sewn into the inside of his leather vest. Shib required him to wear the vest: black, form-fitting leather studded with iron rivets, cut high at the shoulder to show his arms off to full advantage. Brick thought it made him look like a rent boy for johns who liked the rough stuff. But if it did give a potential troublemaker second thoughts then it was probably worth it. And a good half-inch of boiled leather and strategically placed iron studs could come in handy if some drunk pulled a knife.

"Forgive my previous remarks, Brick. They were contumacious and ill advised. You are not a bumbling ex-soldier. You are a gentleman." Glum took the coins with a bow and a flourish that almost overbalanced him.

"Right. This is from my pay. So—second-hand at least—Shib is buying you a drink. Sure you can stomach a glass a Shark paid for?"

"I'll have you know I find such racial slurs appalling. 'Shark' is a term of belittlement. Wine is a great leveler of cultural divides and I for one will happily raise a glass of it to the honorable Haptha whose coin is paying."

"I admire the depths of your convictions, Glum. You slut."

But Glum appeared not to have heard, already on his way to the bar, his steps unsteady but his course unwavering.

Brick grunted, amused more than annoyed. The half-assed poet—more paid letter writer for the illiterate and, from what Brick had heard, occasional informant—had established his priorities. Glum would set aside a deep-seated racial grudge for two coppers worth of a throat-scouring red that most cooks would refuse to marinate onions in. Brick didn't get the hatred. The Haptha weren't exactly human and the ink on the peace treaty had only been dry for about five years now, but in Brick's experience they weren't any worse than anybody else.

As if summoned by his thoughts, Shib emerged from the door behind the bar. Brick tilted his head, taking a look at his boss. As always, he could see why people hung the Haptha with the tag 'Shark.' Shib was in some respects a less than representative example, but even he possessed the distinctive Haptha skull, the abrupt ridge jutting up and arcing back in a sweeping, narrowing curve. Wasn't much to it, the skull ridge amounting to little more than the width of a man's hand. But small or not, the ridge evoked a shark's dorsal fin. The slang term for the Haptha was inevitable.

Shib stood shorter than the average Haptha. Brick could look him directly in the eye without doing more than rising up on his toes, although Brick knew himself no ordinary specimen, reaching six-foot-five, six and a half in his boots. He was used to sidelong glances and half-mocking, half-fearful comments about his size. He could imagine what the Haptha endured daily here in the city.

Shib made his way across the taproom, Brick watching his fluid glide. Cat-like, Brick thought. Graceful. Of course, most anyone looked graceful in comparison to Brick. The Haptha arrow had missed any arteries, but the four-edged, slightly curving blades of the arrowhead had chewed up the muscle of his left thigh and the wound had never healed properly. The leg was nearly as strong as the right one, and he could still put on bursts of speed for short distances, but he was left with a permanent hitch in his gait. His incapacity to maintain pace for long marches led to his involuntary mustering out of the Army of the Clackmat Confederacy. One more disabled soldier discarded on the streets of Kalapo.

Brick didn't bitch and moan about it. He'd seen too many brothers-in-arms left with more debilitating injuries: missing limbs, blind, disfigured. And too many hadn't come back at all. He considered himself lucky to be mostly whole and at least marginally employable.

Shib seemed to think so, anyway. Employable, that is.

Shib shimmied up, that smooth glide of his deceptively fast. It looked sedate, a languid dance step, a pavane, or some such shit. But blink, and godsdamnit, there he was.

"Boss," said Brick. Shib liked the honorific. And he was, after all, the boss.

"Slow evening, Brick." Shib measured out his words, giving each one space to breathe.

"It'll pick up. Construction laborers are just getting off shift."

"Well, until they begin gracing my establishment with their presence, please refrain from bullying the one customer we have."

Shroud's dried tits. Son of a bitch missed nothing. Brick hadn't even done anything, he'd only been considering dislocating the horny customer's jaw. And perhaps an arm.

"I'm graciousness personified, boss. Consider each ass personally smooched."

"This must be another human custom I'm not yet familiar with. I have witnessed women of a certain social standing kiss each other upon the cheek. Under what circumstances do you apply your lips to the nether cheeks?"

Deadpan.

Brick took a beat to be certain Shib was having him on. It could be hard to read Sharks. Their faces were essentially indistinguishable from humans', so Brick figured the body language difference was probably more cultural than racial. For all the good that little nugget of insight did him. He still couldn't always tell when Shib was being serious and when he was taking the piss.

But Brick was pretty sure Shib was having fun this time, bullshitting with the help. So he said, "It's hard to explain, boss. Best learned through experience. I'll let you know when to drop to your knees and pucker."

"Most kind of you, Brick. You're a valued employee and I'll be sure your willingness to advise me is reflected next payday."

Shit. Slicker than greased ice, this one. Brick conceded the match.

But, Shib, it seemed, hadn't yet finished scoring points. "Paying you is simplified when you return the coin directly into my coffers." The Haptha nodded toward the bar where Glum leaned, sipping at the cup Brick had spotted him.

Brick bit back an oath. How in Shroud's Thousand Hells did Shib do that? He missed nothing. It was spooky, like he had eyes—and ears—on all sides of that ridged dome of a head. Saw all, heard all.

But no. No point in getting paranoid about it, assigning supernatural cause to what could be explained by the man being observant and asking the right questions. Probably Livette mentioned it to him when he came out from the back. That big softy of a bouncer was letting his wino friends soak him for drinks again. That was probably it.

Still, best to keep his guard up around Shib.

"Might as well keep the circulation local, boss," Brick said. "And what better way to spend a copper bit or two then on the happiness of a friend?"

A growing rumble and clatter outside forestalled whatever rejoinder Shib intended to make. Hoof beats drummed an easy rhythm against the packed, crumbling dirt of the street. Harness rattled. Wagon beds creaked on leather suspensions. Iron-rimmed wheels cut into the earth churned up by the dray beasts.

Then a crack, like an underachieving thunderbolt, momentarily drowned out the other noises. Shouts followed, and the sounds of the wagon train slowed, then ceased.

Brick walked outside to investigate.

The sun loitered, a fat orange thumbnail above the western ridgeline. About a dozen mule-drawn wagons clogged up Highmark

Street. The third wagon back canted at an angle, leaning on its front right axle. As Brick watched, the wheel finished its wobbling deceleration, the jagged splinters of the shattered hub clearly visible as the wheel's angular momentum brought it to a gyring stop.

Highmark Street gawkers looked from front doors or opened the shutters of second story windows to take in the show. The cooper's shop across from Shib's Tavern boasted an actual balcony and Brick wondered if the rickety wooden structure could take the weight of the staring apprentices clustered upon it.

Muleskinners cursed their teams, hauling hard on the reins to keep the mules in check. That fit Brick's recollection from the army, of the supply train and its levy of the godsdamned, cantankerous, four-legged bastards. It took forever to convince them to move. Then once they got going they would stop when it pleased them. Not a moment before, not a moment later.

An advance guard reined about and a rear guard fanned out, a pair of them nudging their horses around to face back the way they'd come. Brick approved. Good security, a competent team of caravan guards.

None of this was Brick's business though. He couldn't stand around rubbernecking. He went back into the tavern and took up his stool near the door. Might be an unexpectedly early crowd tonight and he should be at his post.

But the press of thirsty muleskinners didn't materialize. Instead only three representatives from the mule train entered: one man, one woman, one Haptha.

Brick took the man for the wagon train master. His high boots, woolen trousers, and tunic matched the attire of the other wagon drivers but looked to be cleaner. Boots a fine muleskinner would save a year to purchase.

The woman interested Brick more, and not simply because she was a woman. And a looker at that. No, it was more than that. For one thing, she was armed. A woman, openly armed like any soldier. Not something one saw every day on the streets of Kalapo. A long thrusting dagger hung at one hip, counterbalancing the short sword on the other. And she was armored in fine chain beneath hardened leather sewn with iron plates.

Brick would have given a great deal to possess armor of such quality back when he'd been carrying spear and shield for the Confederacy. His sergeant told him to consider himself lucky they'd been able to find a gambeson large enough to fit. A shield, that padded jack—a linen and canvas and leather overgarment quilted with wool—and an ill-fitting steel helmet provided his only protection during the Mercantile War, as the more cynical soldiers termed the Leyvan Campaign.

And that was another thing. Apparently, it wasn't sufficiently strange to see an armored woman waltzing into Shib's Tavern. No. She had to be a Leyvan woman, just to up the novelty factor.

Brick took stock, observing appreciatively. He took both a professional interest as a tavern bouncer and a nostalgic interest as a veteran of the Leyvan Campaign. The woman was tall, lean, and wide at the shoulder, though iron pauldrons strapped to the chain armor exaggerated the actual dimensions. Like all Leyvans her hair and complexion were dark, and her eyes bore the characteristic cant and faint narrowing at the outer edges.

Kalapo had seen an increase in the population of its minuscule Leyvan enclave since the peace. Most of the war had been fought on Leyvan soil, the Clackmat Confederacy and its ally, the Leyvan Hierocracy, deciding to meet the Haptha ultimatum there. It was probably inevitable that many refugees and displaced Leyvans found themselves in the Confederacy, most ending up in Kalapo.

So, all right. A Leyvan. Why not? Brick liked them well enough. Tough, smart fighters. And a woman. Well, again, why not? She'd come in with the Haptha and the Sharks viewed such things differently. Which meant she probably worked for the Shark. Brick turned his attention to him.

The Haptha easily stood seven and a half feet in his socks, at the upper end of the range for Sharks. He wore the latest in Kalapo fashion, his doublet pleated, padded, and parti-colored, his trousers tight, reinforced with leather along the inner thigh to ease saddle chafing. Kalapo haberdashery actually suited him. The shapeless felt hat—flopping to nearly cover the left eye and bearing a garish red feather pinned along the right side—was voluminous enough to minimize the characteristic Haptha ridge. If not for his height he could almost pass for human. A sword was his only visible weapon. The sword was of the slim-bladed pattern preferred by the Haptha, its furniture chased in silver. A pendant, a spindle-cut amethyst, hung against his chest on a silver chain.

Brick could not be certain, but he judged the Shark to be in his early middle-age. Say, eighty or ninety years old. He appeared vigorous enough, pausing only a moment to gaze about the taproom and then—upon spotting Shib—crossing the sawdust strewn floor between the two Haptha with only a couple of long strides.

"An unexpected pleasure, encountering a countryman here," the Haptha said.

Shib replied in a burst of sibilants and long vowels. Brick recognized the Haptha tongue but still didn't know more than a word or two, mostly profanities. The only word he caught this time was "Shib."

The other Haptha interrupted. "Please, Shib. Let us speak Clackmat. Our trading privileges we acquired with a . . . certain degree of unpleasantness. I would imagine some hard feelings remain, treaty or no. So, let us speak the language of our new host and trading partner."

"As you say, sir," said Shib. "Care for a drink . . .?" Shib let the question trail, fishing for a name.

"Vawn. I am Trader Vawn. And yes, I could use a taste. Brandy if you have it. It seems we may be here awhile, presuming on your hospitality. Oh, and a glass for my companions, if you please."

Brick saw Livette climb a step ladder for one of the seldom opened ceramic bottles, moving even before Shib turned to place the order. He also watched Glum taking a seat at a nearby table, situating himself within easy earshot of the conversation, but angled so that while his attention was obvious it wasn't comically so.

"Welcome to Shib's Tavern, Trader," said Shib, Brick thinking Shib understood ass-kissing well enough. "May I assume the spot of excitement outside brings you here rather than the fame of my establishment?"

The Trader laughed and sat down at the nearest table. He tugged at his doublet as it bunched about his slim torso and he adjusted the angle of his hat. Brick noted that, while the Shark had ordered refreshments for the wagoner and the guard, he hadn't invited them to sit with him.

"You assume correctly. This shipment covered a thousand miles, across the Strait and overland through—from what Bredrick Fines here tells me—bogs, storms, and bandit attacks. And it reached Kalapo without a hitch, without the loss of a single mule or crate of merchandise. No driver so much as caught a cold.

"Yet, not an hour after I ride out to meet the shipment a wheel snaps off. One hesitates to say that the streets of Kalapo are in worse condition than the rest of the Confederacy's highways and byways, but . . ."

The Shark talked like he was reciting lines from a play. Like one of those florid pieces Glum was always starting between poems and epigrams then discarding before he'd finished Act One. Brick decided he liked it, liked the earnest theatricality of Trader Vawn's speech as much as he did Shib's glib patter.

"You are overly considerate, Trader Vawn," Shib was saying. "Kalapo is a nice enough town. It has a rustic appeal. But as cities go . . . well, it's hardly Port Weir. Paved streets. Municipal sewer. Public wells and aqueducts. You are not going to find them. Still, the locals seem rather proud of it."

20

"There is a barb on that honeyed tongue, Shib," said Vawn, taking a glass from the tray Livette carried. "To be fair, there is great potential in Kalapo, indeed in the entire Confederacy. Abundant natural resources. Skilled craftsmen. I consider myself fortunate to have received an appointment to trade. We like to consider that we emerged from the Leyvan Trade War in a favorable position, but—oh, excellent brandy. Wisterian? What was I saying? Right. In truth, the Treaty allowed issuance of only a limited number of credentials to Traders. At least in the Confederacy. The Hierocracy is more or less a free-trade zone now. Trading there is hardly a mark of distinction. Here we failed to achieve such concessions, despite force of arms."

Brick watched the Leyvan take a birdlike sip of brandy. Bangles and charms affixed to a bracelet worn on the wrist of her drinking hand shifted and tinkled, a faintly audible musical cascade. Her face betrayed no response to her boss slagging her homeland.

The sounds of the stalled wagon train had by now become no more than background noise to Brick. It took raised voices—stepping up the aggression range from bickering to insult to yells—to draw his attention.

Bredrick Fines set down his brandy glass and went outside. Brick followed him through the doorway. Brick folded his arms across his chest and leaned up against the outside of the tavern next to the fading paint of the wooden signboard carved into the shape of a tankard. An angry drunk with a hatchet had hacked out a wedge from the tankard's rim some years back, providing the tavern its semi-official name: The Chipped

Mug. But the regular drinkers and the staff all referred to it as Shib's Tavern.

Trouble was brewing outside Shib's Tavern and a good show seemed likely.

The wagon with the busted wheel rested level now, propped on stacked crates and a few strategically placed chunks of firewood. Tools lay scattered about in the street below the bald end of the axle. A new wheel leaned against the wagon box. But no repairs were underway. Instead the teamsters—now joined by Brederick—stood in a skirmish line, facing off against a growing number of shouting, gesticulating men, most wearing red tunics of varying shades, age, material, and quality.

One step in front of the rank of red-tunics was a man who could afford a better tailor. Or so it seemed to Brick, though he was no discerning judge of fashion. At any rate, the man's outfit approximated Trader Vawn's more than it did that of the crowd at his back.

"That's Cester Bailick Faren," said Glum.

Brick turned. There slouched Glum, wine cup in hand. Brick figured the possibility of watching a good scrap outweighed Glum's interest in the conversation of the two Sharks. Then Trader Vawn and Shib emerged from the tavern, trailed by the Leyvan. Glum wasn't missing anything after all.

"Cester Something Something. That name supposed to mean anything to me?" asked Brick.

"Ought to, Brick. He's head of the Clackmat Drayage and Cartage Guild. And one of the Electors. By all accounts a string-puller. Has the ear of the Magistrate."

"What's he doing brawling in the street?"

"He's not brawling yet," said Trader Vawn. "Nor should he. The Treaty is abundantly clear that Credentialed Traders are exempt from the Confederacy's organized labor regulations and may employ such workers as they like."

"Why don't you tell him that?" said Brick. "He might not have read the Treaty. If he can read."

"I will do just that," said Trader Vawn. "I'm sure he would not want to instigate any Treaty violations. Being the cause of sanctions—or worse—can hardly be in the best interests of a politician. I will explain the matter."

With that the Trader stepped out into Highmark Street.

Brick admired the Shark's brass. Confronting a mob of angry men convinced you were taking work from them wasn't the act of a coward. Brick could almost smell the reek of ill-considered aggression. He was curious to see how this turned out.

The Leyvan bodyguard didn't share his curiosity. She hurried to the Trader's side, requiring almost two strides for every one of his. She put a hand on his arm. He turned to face her, still about a half-dozen paces from the two opposing lines.

"Sir," she said, "please keep clear. These men are not interested in your explanations. Right now, you could explain that the sun is setting and those men in the red would call you a liar. Or even if the sun is setting, it is your fault. Come back into the tavern. Finish your drink. Let the gods sort this out."

Trader Vawn laughed. "The gods, Dahlia. Stupid of me, failing to leave trade disputes to that august commercial tribunal, the

thousand Leyvan gods. Or is it a thousand
and one? I find it hard to keep track."

From his vantage Brick could not see the
Leyvan woman's face. Dahlia, was it? But he
could see one hand rise to the bracelet on the
opposite wrist and begin fingering the dense
assortment of charms.

"Sir . . ." she said, then stopped when
Trader Vawn raised a hand.

"Still, you are probably right, Dahlia," he
said. "You cannot reason with an angry bull.
He's going to charge you even if you deploy
irrefutable syllogisms proving that it is
against his best interests to do so. Let us
hope this ends without bloodshed."

The Trader walked back into the tavern,
hand resting on the hilt of his sword. Brick
heard him say to Shib in passing that, "I
don't want the blood of any of these
guildsmen on my hands. They are armed
with nothing more than cudgels. It wouldn't
look good."

Brick knew well enough that cudgels
could kill as easily as a sword. A bashed-in
skull would do for you the same as a gut-
thrust. And, unlike the trader, he couldn't
give a shit about appearances.

The rhetoric in the middle of Highmark
Street was growing more heated. From a
tunic pocket one of the guildsmen produced
a brickbat and winged it, hitting one of
Trader Vawn's wagon drivers. That put an
end to the formal debate portion of the
proceedings.

Glum drifted back into the tavern to
reappear behind one of the open shutters.
Dahlia had sword and dagger drawn, all in
one slick, practiced maneuver.

The guildsmen charged. The
muleskinners fell back, but only to take up

defensive positions alongside the wagons or between yoked mule teams. It soon became apparent that the red tunic coalition did not have a monopoly on weapons. Trader Vawn's men produced cudgels of their own along with staves, whips, and knives. Brick wasn't surprised. A caravan didn't cross the vast, half-civilized expanses between settled areas of the Confederacy with unarmed teamsters. Not even a guarded caravan like this one. At least, no successful caravan did.

Brick heard a piercing whistle from Dahlia's pursed lips: three short bursts and one long trill. It sounded like a signal. Sure enough, a moment later the mounted caravan guards urged their steeds into formation, forming a line at the rear of the wagons. So, not riding into the fight to support the teamsters. What then? Dahlia stood, blades at the ready, by the tavern entrance. Trader Vawn's well-being assured. That left the other priority—the cargo of imports—in need of looking after. The guards wouldn't involve themselves in the brawl unless it threatened to damage the shipment. Interfering in labor disputes did not appear to be on their list of responsibilities.

Neatly contained violence, an evening's entertainment for the Highmark Street locals—at least until the Kalapo Horse Guard could be roused from their barracks on Ash Way, just south of Leyvan Town, and ride to quell the disturbance.

It didn't look neat or contained to Brick. Maybe none of the combatants wore armor, and he saw no long blades catching the last light of the westering sun, but the two sides went at it in earnest. The rutted, hard-packed surface of the street was gouged and turned by hard-soled boots pushing and straining for grip. Blood began to moisten the churned dirt, as if part of some primitive plowing ceremony, a sacrifice to ensure the following year's yield.

Then a flung cudgel—about a two-foot length of stout oak—whipped past Brick's ear and shattered the slats of one of the tavern's shutters. He heard someone yell "the fucking Shark is in the tavern." And a group of red tunics detached from the scrum and came his way.

"Brick," said Shib, peeking out from the ruins of the shutter, "take care of this, please."

Right. From his relaxed position Brick pushed himself off the wall and straightened up. He'd often found that simply breathing deeply, expanding to his full dimensions, and stretching a bit could curtail violence before it began. It required a brave man to tackle someone his size. A brave man or a drunk man.

Or, as in this case, simply a whole bunch of men. There had to be a half-dozen of them, all in red tunics. Well, a range from maroon to crimson, Brick noted as they drew nearer.

He wondered if there was any compelling reason to side with the guildsmen instead of the trader's teamsters, but couldn't see it. He'd spent too much time looking for work after the army dismissed him to have much sympathy for a group of men who'd begrudge other men a job simply because they didn't wear spiffy red tunics. The Clackmat Drayage and Cartage Guild hadn't offered Brick work when he'd been desperately searching. So fuck 'em. He had his own job to do now.

Brick took a step forward to meet them, placing himself before the door, and feeling a certain comfort knowing that the Leyvan woman stood at his back with her sharpened steel. He didn't care for the twinge in his leg, but he figured it wouldn't give out right away, and once he got warmed up it shouldn't trouble him.

"That's far enough, boys," he said, stretching out both arms as if blocking the way and—once again—swelling up, flexing his arms and the muscles of his back. He could hear the leather of his stupid black vest squeaking in protest. He recognized the posturing as a simple exercise in intimidation, but it worked sometimes and maybe in the waning light they hadn't caught a good look at him the first time. If he could keep anyone from getting hurt then he considered that worth the risk of someone scoffing at his display.

It still didn't work.

"Get the fuck out of the way, freak." The leading red tunic reached out and prodded Brick—rather scornfully, Brick thought—in the midsection with the tip of his cudgel.

"Don't," said Brick. He felt the advance hints of the Fury, a faint haze of red specks at the edge of his vision. The jab with the club was insulting. And the tavern, and the safety of the people within was his responsibility. His job. He tried to keep anger at bay, though not in great earnest. He recognized the dangers of surrendering to rage, but he liked the Fury. It is what had made him a good soldier. It is what had allowed him to ignore fear—not dismiss it, not conquer it, but ignore it. It is what let him tear gaps in enemy positions, be the tip of a human wedge driving into a shield wall. He recognized the disadvantages in civilian life. Slipping the leash from impulse control could be a problem outside a war zone. So, he kept the

Fury tightly reined in. But he missed it. And if this punk ass guildsman jabbed him again . . .

The punk ass guildsman jabbed him again.

The Fury descended like a curtain of crimson sparks. Pent up frustration spewed from Brick like wine from a punctured goatskin bag. He batted aside the cudgel and grabbed the wrist, yanking the man towards him. Brick squeezed and twisted, hearing tendons pop and little bones grind together. At the same time, his other hand shot forward and gripped the guildsman below the armpit of his red tunic. Brick lifted the man, continuing to twist and pull on the wrist. The guildsman screamed as first elbow and then shoulder dislocated.

Brick shoved the broken man away, slowing a couple of his trailing companions. Then Brick stooped to pick up the dropped cudgel.

Two more darted in, scissoring him. Brick parried a blow from the man on his right and took a club in the gut from the man on his left. An inch higher and it would have fractured one or two of his short ribs. It hurt bad enough just bouncing off his leather-padded abdomen. But he managed to grab his assailant's arm and swing him bodily into the man on his right. The two tangled limbs and struggled to remain upright. Brick swarmed them, hearing the crack of fracturing bones.

Those two were out of the fight, arms hanging limply, retreating up Highmark Street. The other three hesitated. Given a moment they'd figure out the spacing, come at him as a group. That should concern Brick, tell him to retreat to the shelter of the tavern's doorway or at least put his back to the wall. But, enveloped in the red glow of the Fury, that concern was weak sauce, an insignificance compared to the burning rage, to the compulsion to hurt and keep on hurting. Brick waded into the trio, cudgel swinging.

He felt a ringing joy, a freedom, devoid of care. One man dropped, his collarbone shattered. The other was down, and Brick loomed over him, cudgel raised, about to crack open the man's skull, hatch his brain.

"Don't do it," came a voice from behind him. Dahlia.

Brick paused, club still held aloft, and glanced behind him.

The third red tunic was poised to uncork a wicked blow to the back of Brick's skull. Dahlia's sword point dimpled the guildsman's tunic, below the shoulder blade. Perhaps he figured he could take Dahlia out of the picture quickly then get back to bopping Brick on the head. After all, she was just a woman. Perhaps that explained why he tried batting aside her sword blade. She dropped her sword out of line, let the cudgel swipe through empty air, then stepped in, the dagger in her left hand digging into his armpit.

"Don't do it," she said again and the red tunic finally seemed to acknowledge the wisdom of her admonishment. He took off running after the first two.

Brick turned back to unfinished business to find that all six had now scarpered off. He looked with hunger at the skirmish still underway around the wagons. But with the immediate cause of the Fury dispatched he recollected that his job was to safeguard the tavern. Charging into the fray would mean leaving his post.

And the Fury dissipated.

Sometimes that happened. Instant calm, the Fury washed away like riverbank detritus after the first substantial autumn rain. Other times the anger ebbed only slowly, so many coals cooling to ash. Or like the sun lowering itself behind the hills, its light fading away—as was happening now, shadows falling upon Highmark Street. He liked that analogy, might mention it to Glum. No, Glum didn't know about the Fury. Wouldn't understand it anyway.

Brick returned to the tavern door.

"Thanks," he said to Dahlia, who'd resumed her sentry duty. He liked the smile he received in return.

The battle appeared to be winding down, devolving into so many isolated wrestling matches, though it was becoming harder to make out the action. From the north came the sound of distant hoof beats.

"The Guard," Brick said. "As usual, right on time. That is, late."

"Let's go back inside," Dahlia said.

Brick followed her in, feeling the pain of the blow to his stomach. He imagined he'd have a livid purple mark there come the morning. For that matter, he'd have another on his left shoulder. He'd taken a shot there he'd not even noticed at the time. And reaching up he dabbed away blood oozing from over his right eyebrow. One of them must have scratched him. Scratched him? What kind of fighting was that? Gouging, sure. But scratching?

"All sorted out, Dahlia?" Trader Vawn asked.

"Horse Guard is coming, sir. And the fighting is nearly over."

"Who won?"

"I'd call it a draw," she said. "The guild toughs couldn't take the wagons. Then again, your drivers couldn't push them back."

"That means the Trader won," said Brick. "His troops held the strategic objective. That's a win."

"Brick retired from the Confederacy on a General's pay," said Shib. "He works for me out of sheer boredom."

Brick liked Shib's wit, even when its sharp point was directed at him. He laughed, as did Glum, who maintained his viewing position at the window while still within earshot. But Trader Vawn said, "Don't discount the wisdom of the rank-and-file infantryman. He may not be privy to the grand campaign, but he knows whether or not he's advancing, retreating, or standing his ground the same as any officer moving counters on a map."

Shib didn't respond. Brick couldn't imagine Shib would care for the lecture, the man used to getting in the last word in his own establishment.

"Sir," said Dahlia, "perhaps we should be going. Before the Guard arrives."

"I've no reason to fear the Guard. In fact, it will serve my interest to be the first to explain the situation to the Guard captain. We can wait a few more moments to return home."

Dahlia nodded. The trader clicked his tongue and went on as if he hadn't already made his point. "My apologies if you must delay your prayers of gratitude, Dahlia. I imagine thanking each god individually for seeing you through the fracas unscathed will require a substantial time investment."

Trader Vawn looked at his empty glass, squinting an eye. If Brick was any judge that was not the Trader's first empty of the evening. "If we've time before the Horse Guard rides to the rescue I could use another glass. In fact, Shib, I'd like to stand you all to a glass in recognition of your assistance."

"A fine sentiment, sir," said Glum, moving away from the window and insinuating himself into the group.

Livette brought another round, shooting a sidelong glance at Dahlia as she handed her one of Shib's precious glass drinking vessels, some apprentice glass blower's first effort, warped and uneven and clouded with air bubbles. She hesitated before handing Glum a glass, but did so upon Shib's nod of assent.

"To this stalwart fellow, General Brick," said Trader Vawn, hoisting his glass in salute. "And to my redoubtable bodyguard, Dahlia the Pious."

Brick drank. The stuff burned, reminding him of the liquid fire he'd once seen a conjured war demon vomit forth. He'd never been sure which side had summoned the monstrosity, and it hadn't seemed to matter as it rampaged indiscriminately through the ranks of both sides. Still, he now had an idea why Glum coveted brandy. He could feel the warmth roil through him immediately.

The growing drumbeat of hooves announced the imminent arrival of the Horse Guard. Brick set down his unfinished glass with some reluctance and moved to the front door. Trader Vawn moved faster, preceding him, one hand adjusting the fit of his sword belt, the other reaching up to stroke the amethyst dangling from his neck.

Fine. Brick would just as soon let this Shark deal with the Horse Guard, those overpaid layabouts. If their captain held his hand out for the usual Guard baksheesh he'd have better luck with Trader Vawn's deep purse than with Brick's empty one.

Brick took up his usual seat by the door. He spared a glance at Dahlia, noting in passing that Shib had disappeared. Dahlia appeared placid enough, though stone-faced might be nearer the mark. He wondered what she really felt behind that mask. Trader Vawn seemed a decent sort, but he didn't show much consideration for his bodyguard's faith. What was going on there?

None of his business, probably.

A beautifully armored Horse Guard captain dismounted just beyond the doorway. Trader Vawn's tall form blocked much of Brick's view, but he guessed that just the silk-lined cloak, draped over the chain and half-plate armor, cost more than Shib paid him in six months.

"Captain, good of you and your men to come," said Trader Vawn.

Brick smirked. He liked that the Trader got in the first word and wished he could see the Guard captain's face. Probably sour at seeing the wealthy Haptha and knowing he couldn't get his kicks browbeating him for rousing the Guard from their cozy barracks. No fun harassing a civilian who had no need to fear you.

"What's the story here? This your wagon train blocking the street?"

"Yes, Captain. Terribly sorry about that. I am Credentialed Trader Vawn, and—as you note—this is my caravan. We stopped to effect repairs and then found ourselves embroiled in some sort of labor dispute. Certain gentlemen attired in red tunics asserted the proposition that I must hire them instead of men of my own choosing. This demand, as a man in your position is no doubt aware, runs afoul of the Commerce Rights Treaty."

"So you say, Trader." Brick thought the captain sounded distinctly uncomfortable now. "I suppose this calls for taking statements, comparing stories, hauling the culprits to prison. Said culprits might have to include your teamsters, on charges of disorderly conduct and riot."

"Indeed. You are to be commended for your diligence, Captain. In fact, I will commend you to the Magistrate when I discuss this breach of Treaty protocol with him. Your name, Captain?"

"*Might*, I said, Trader. *Might*. The ruckus seems to have ceased. Doesn't appear anyone was killed. Could be it was all a misunderstanding that your boys dealt with in a lawful manner. Still, there remains a mess to be cleaned up."

"That is true. Cracked heads, broken limbs. The sort of mess that calls for an efficient and organized corrective. The Horse Guard being an exemplar of efficiency and organization. Should an enterprising captain see to delivering the wounded—of both sides, mind—to such surgeons and apothecaries as can be found at this hour of the evening, why I think I would be obliged to him."

The rattle of silver punctuated the statement. And with that the Trader and the Captain completed their negotiations.

The Horse Guard captain left to attend to the wounded. Brick liked that Trader Vawn had bribed the Guard to care for the guildsmen as well as Vawn's teamsters. Sure, the Trader probably had some ulterior motive, polishing his image perhaps. But whatever the reason it seemed the decent thing to do.

Shib reappeared as the captain left. A neat trick.

"Well, Trader Vawn, thank you for an eventful evening," Shib said. "You livened up the place more than we're used to this early. But at the risk of sounding like a poor host, may I suggest you take your leave before the rubberneckers and neighborhood gossips begin to pour in?"

"The advice is as excellent as your brandy, Shib. Come along, Dahlia. Guide me safely home. To which home, by the way, I invite you—Brick, is it not?—to come someday soon and receive some token of thanks. I'll have to think of something suitable. That was quite a display you put on: Brick's lone stand at the Battle of Shib's Tavern."

Glum said "The Battle of Shib's Tavern," in a meditative tone, then asked, "Do you mind if I use that line, Trader Vawn?"

"Hmm? No, go right ahead."

Trader Vawn adjusted his attire and accouterments one more time. He shifted to face Brick directly. The deep lavender of the amethyst pendant took on a darker purple gleam as it caught the flickering red glow from the oil lanterns Livette was lighting behind the bar. "I am serious, Brick. Stop by the compound sometime this ten-day."

Brick nodded. "Protecting the tavern is my job. But thanks. I'd be a damn fool not to accept a gift freely offered."

"I'll be sure the door warden knows to expect you," Dahlia said.

"Thanks again for watching my back," Brick said. Dahlia nodded to him, then preceded Trader Vawn out the door, taking with her Shib's parting gift of the remnants of the brandy bottle.

"You're spending enough time watching *her* back," said Livette, bussing up empty glasses.

Brick felt grateful when Glum spoke, relieving him of the obligation to respond to Livette.

"The Battle of Shib's Tavern. Now that ought to pick up a few readers. That Trader Vawn's an interesting character. Always fingering that gem around his neck. What's the deal with the necklace, anyway?"

"What? Oh, the Panaegic Periapt, you mean? I'd heard rumors it might be in Kalapo," said Shib levelly. "Surprised to see it worn openly."

"The Panaegic Periapt?" asked Glum. "Care to elaborate, Shib?"

Brick coughed. Fucking with the help was one thing. He and Livette were used to it. Playing games with a drunken poet simply wasn't sporting.

"Surely you've heard of it, especially here in the capital of the Confederacy. Why its power is famed—" Shib cut the sentence short as the first trickle of neighborhood busybodies came in, eager to hear more about the battle. They mingled with the expected shift of off-duty laborers, reaching their nearest watering hole right on schedule.

Brick got to his feet. Looked to be a busy night.

Chapter 2 - After Action Review

Dahlia Azhak led Trader Vawn into the hum of activity disturbing the usual evening tranquility of Highmark Street. Dismounted Horse Guardsmen bustled about by the uncertain light of freshly lit torches. A pair of them completed repairs on the crippled wagon. Others assisted the wounded onto the wagons tasked as ambulances. Bredrick Fines conferred with the Captain, no doubt coordinating the operation and ensuring that the wagon train reached Trader Vawn's warehouse. Whatever the faults of the Horse Guard, once its palm had been properly greased it earned the bribe.

Dahlia was pleased to see that Bredrick had come through the battle unharmed. He was a competent, easy going sort. She didn't know him well but got along with him, one of the few of Vawn's employees who did not seem bothered that she was a woman. That probably just meant he wanted to get inside her armor, but his attitude was nonetheless a refreshing change.

Their horses remained tethered to the rear wagon under the eye of one of the caravan guards. Mercenaries to a man, the caravan guards. Not the sort Dahlia would normally feel comfortable entrusting her mount to, let alone the safety of a valuable train of cargo. But Trader Vawn paid in unclipped Haptha silver and plenty of it, those little lozenge-shaped coins about the size of the tip of her little finger, called Petals from some presumed resemblance to flower petals. That was about the best assurance of loyalty available. Besides, who was she to judge? What was she but a mercenary with a cushy billet and steady pay?

She offered, as always, to assist Trader Vawn to mount. As always, he refused. She tried not to consider that, had he been human, he'd be old enough to be her grandfather. But he was Haptha; tall and graceful and still in his prime. He did not need her cupped hands to hoist him atop his horse. She noted that he wobbled a trifle as he settled into the creaking leather of the big gelding's saddle.

Dahlia climbed aboard her own mount, a placid mare, one of the gentlest from Trader Vawn's stables. She snatched a flambeau from its bracket behind the driver's seat of the nearest wagon and ignited it from one of the Horse Guard's torches. Trader Vawn had already urged his horse into motion. Dahlia applied some heel pressure, encouraging the mare to catch up.

She felt elated. No, that wasn't quite right. She felt elation ebbing. The thrill of the battle, the rush of her tussle with the guildsman, and the heady elevation of the brandy had all peaked. Dahlia still enjoyed the rush, but was easing back to her usual state. She considered taking a pull off the brandy bottle then discarded the notion. She was on duty and needed to stay sharp. This early in the evening they were unlikely to encounter any of Kalapo's dangerous nocturnal characters, but her employment was predicated upon the chance of the unlikely occurring. Besides, the bottle was a gift for Trader Vawn.

"Sir, compliments of Shib," Dahlia said. She took the reins in her teeth, freeing up a hand to pass the Wisterian brandy to the

Shark. Not that she figured he needed any more.

Trader Vawn, however, disagreed.

"Thank you, Dahlia," he said, accepting the proffered bottle and taking a swig. "A handsome gift. Or, more likely, payment for silence."

"Sir?" Dahlia tugged at the reins, navigating onto Orison Street, beginning to work west and north toward Trader Vawn's compound.

"Dahlia, our recent host is not what you might consider a documented immigrant." Vawn sniffed at the bottle, preparatory to another drink. But his gelding had declined to follow the mare on to Orison, thus demanding that he concentrate on something other than the brandy. Dahlia looked back to see Trader Vawn sawing on the reins, reminding the horse who was in charge and forcing it back to the desired route.

"The Treaty prescribes a limited number of Credentialed Traders authorized to import goods into the Confederacy." Vawn rode up next to Dahlia, picking up his discourse with such easy nonchalance that Dahlia could not decide if it was affected or not. With Vawn she never knew if he was really that smooth or if the whole thing was a performance. "We are distributed amongst the cities of the Confederacy, the majority here in Kalapo. The Treaty also allows a number of registered Haptha to establish non-importation businesses within the Confederacy."

"Are you suggesting that Shib is not registered?"

"Let us face facts, Dahlia. I intend no offence, but record keeping standards among human civilizations—even the Leyvan Hierocracy with its vast priestly bureaucracies—leave much to be desired. And the Confederacy is hardly up to Leyvan standards of documentation." Vawn put the bottle to his lips and swallowed twice, then released a long, contented sigh.

Dahlia rode on in silence, listening to Vawn smack his lips. She figured he was working up to the point and she did not want to nudge his thoughts off the track. Meanwhile their own route zigged and zagged, switching streets to follow others that led their intended direction. They began to ascend, climbing the lower slopes of the West Hills.

Trader Vawn belched and took another sip. Dahlia admired his careful enunciation as he said, "My 'credentials,' for example, are nothing more than a bit of jewelry—a chunky brass and gold medallion. Admittedly it is a pretty example of the engraver's art and the casting was destroyed after the allotted credentials were minted, presumably to ensure authenticity. But it is crude."

"We are still talking about Shib, right? The tavern owner?"

"Patience, Dahlia. One would think the worship of a gazillion gods would teach patience. Bear with me. I'm getting to Shib. You see, many Haptha saw fit to exploit the Confederacy's record keeping laxity. Many more of my countrymen than the allowed quota are operating here, and most of that extra-legal sort were happy to get quit of Haptha territories."

"You think Shib is one of these? Skipping out of Haptha territories one step ahead of the law?"

"Looking for greener taverns, yes."

The streets steepened, leveled, then rose again. The buildings they passed increased in size while the number of structures simultaneously diminished. Trees rose to unguessed heights in the early night sky. Farther upslope the buildings were set back, behind decorative gardens or evergreen copses. Walls fronted the street. Covered gutters carried household effluvia downhill to runoff in the nearest creek wending its way down to the Mette River. Confining the sewage to boarded over runnels along the edges of the street did little to alter the typical ambiance of Kalapo, but it did tend to improve the footing.

Torches and lamps picked out windows and the occasional guard post flanking a gate. They rode through one of Kalapo's more affluent neighborhoods. Ahead lay the new construction of the Haptha Enclave. Merchants' Reach some called it. Others termed it Shark March. Dahlia had heard other, less complimentary names, even some displaying a surprising degree of wit.

Trader Vawn indulged again. "Well, if Shib meant to buy my silence, I consider my lips sealed and the price more than fair. I haven't had brandy this good outside Port Weir."

They rode by the vague outlines of scaffolding and building equipment, marking the site of the future compound of one of Trader Vawn's colleagues. Or competitors. Dahlia wasn't entirely sure what relation the Haptha Credentialed Traders held with respect to each other.

Past this point they crossed the swelling brow of a hill and rode across level ground. Farther on the West Hills continued their rise, but here lay a flat stretch and Trader Vawn's compound sprawled within high, spike-topped walls.

A door warden and a groom met them at the front gate. Trader Vawn revealed a hint of a stumble on his dismount and took another swig of brandy, perhaps on the theory that a touch more would restore, rather than further retard, his equilibrium.

"Who has the duty tonight?" he asked Dahlia as they crossed the courtyard to the main house.

The boss was talkative tonight. He could hold his liquor, she'd give him that. The amount of brandy he'd taken in would put most men down. But Dahlia supposed Sharks metabolized alcohol faster than humans. Could just be the greater height, more mass to absorb the booze. A question for her father, should she find herself on speaking terms with him again. The point being, the impaired balance, tripping over his own feet, less than expert horsemanship, the uncharacteristic nattering on with the help— the boss had a snootfull. A gap in the Haptha armor. What might he reveal?

"I am, sir," she said. "Scottile Brugeon is sick, so the rest of us drew straws to see who took his shift." She was pretty sure the other bodyguards had rigged the draw. But so what. Let the boys mess with the Leyvan bitch. This underhanded crap only showed they were too chickenshit to give her grief to her face. Besides, night watch was easy duty and she'd request bonus pay for pulling a double shift.

"Excellent. Let's continue our evening's revelry. Finish this bottle and gossip like housewives and soldiers."

Trader Vawn's chambers occupied half of the upper floor of the main house. His custom required a bodyguard to sleep in the bedchamber, stretched out before the door on a mattress of linen stuffed with pelts and scraps of fur—a bed his bodyguards all admitted they found surprisingly comfortable.

Dahlia had taken her share of night watch in Trader Vawn's room in the months she'd worked for him, dozing across the doorway, blocking the entry of any potential assassin. She'd stopped finding it strange after the first couple of weeks. Haptha, it seemed, had no sexual interest in humans. She might as well have been sharing the bedroom with one of the castrati priests of Bulugai the Tempestuous.

Trader Vawn allowed his body servant to unbuckle his sword belt and divest him of clothes. Both men—both Sharks—indifferent to Dahlia's presence. The Trader poured a measure of the remaining brandy into a stemmed goblet, the glass pure and flawlessly rounded. He took a sip before allowing his body servant to drape him in his nightclothes.

Dahlia let the body servant—an aged Haptha, pushing two hundred years if his own account could be credited—exit the bed chamber before dragging her mattress to block the door. She loosened the straps of her armor and began the laborious process of uncasing herself from leather and mail. That sort of thing went a lot faster with help. But she'd long since learned to make do on her own.

"That bouncer of Shib's is quite a specimen," Trader Vawn said, lowering himself onto the cushioned seat of a massive wooden chair, a magnificent piece that had probably required four men to haul it up the stairs. "He fights with anger. I half expected him to bite the ear off one of those hapless guildsmen."

Dahlia thought about him, liking the memory. "Yes, sir. He uncaged the rage. I suppose someone like Shib, if he is what you say, might find Brick a useful sort to have around."

She thought Brick looked to have kept his skills from the Leyvan Campaign intact, as well as some discipline, despite his battle recklessness. Dahlia recalled a night some six or seven years back when she'd encountered some discharged soldiers who had lost that discipline.

***

Dahlia Azhak preceded her father from the apothecary shop, then waited in the street while he locked up. Forskolin Azhak dropped the key—a length of brass longer than his middle finger and nearly as thick—into the pocket sewn into the cuff of his sleeve. Folded back, the cuff reached almost to his elbow, the rough silk of coat lining a lighter blue against the smoother, dark blue silk of the exterior.

Dahlia thought he looked distinguished. In the twilight, a touch of gray at his temples remained visible in the still thick, black hair, cut in the same conservative style she imagined her grandfather had worn before emigrating from the Leyvan Hierocracy. The short sword cased at his side lent him an air of formality, even authority. A look she'd begun to suspect he cultivated.

Dahlia herself felt the lack of a sword at her side. Wearing it within the high walls of the family home had accustomed her to its weight, as her father had promised it would. But a woman—and a Leyvan woman at that—toting a weapon in the streets of Kalapo simply wasn't done. Not for the first time she questioned why Forskolin carried on the training, still unsatisfied with his argument that it would be up to her to pass along the tradition of Leyvan swordsmanship to her future son.

Once again, she shrugged it off. Even with the split skirt, her dress would hamper any real sword play. Let it go. Besides, her father was probably right. He usually was. The smartest man she knew. The best apothecary in the Levyan Enclave, which also meant the best apothecary in Kalapo.

Nonetheless she fingered the stone pestle she'd secreted up the wide sleeve of her green silk blouse. It simultaneously provided a sense of comfort and unease. Comfort because she'd taken to holding the pestle as a mock sword hilt during downtime at the shop, practicing her sword forms when her father wasn't looking. Stepping through the forms always carried with it a calming, centering focus. Unease because she'd forgotten to return the pestle before Forskolin informed her it was closing time and she did not want him to catch her with it.

"Come, Dahlia. Let us see what delights your mother has prepared for us," Forskolin said. The same thing he always said, with that little, forced smile of his. As a rule, Aster Azhak did have something delightful prepared. Meaning her father was correct. As always.

They started along the pounded-earth street toward home. A street sweeper raised his broom in salute as they passed. Dahlia thought she recognized him, the man a recent arrival in the Enclave, a refugee from the warzone. Forskolin stopped, offered him a copper coin. The Leyvans taking care of their own.

A left turn, west, away from the river, onto their own street. Nearly home. An alleyway to the right led to a wine shop, a place Dahlia had only seen once. And that had been as a child, in the daylight, while exploring the Enclave. Her mother had paddled her with a serving spoon when she'd heard and her father refused to speak to her for a week. Respectable Leyvans did not frequent that place.

Three men emerged from the alley. Three Clackmat natives.

"Well, a pleasant evening to you," the leading man said. He looked at Dahlia. Looked her up and down. "And fuck me, if it ain't even more pleasant with your presence."

"Give it a rest, Chucker," one of the other two said. "You were always spouting that shit in the Hierocracy. Never any point to it. The girls in the brothels didn't need you sweet talking them."

"Money did all the talking I ever needed," the third of the trio said. He seemed to think he'd said something clever and started laughing.

"A pleasant evening to you," Forskolin said. "Now, please excuse us." Dahlia admired the control in her father's voice. Polite, without a trace of either fear or disrespect. And in truth, she felt only a twinge of misgiving. Her father remained fit. He stood as tall as any of these three men. And he was armed.

Still, there were three of them. One of them belched. A stinging whiff of alcohol reached her. She blinked away sudden tears.

"Always so polite, you Leyvans," Chucker said. He wore the filthy remnants of quilted armor. The dagger hilt at his hip matched those of his two friends. "I liked that part about serving in the Leyvan Hierocracy, fighting your war for you. Other parts I liked too." The last he offered with an exaggerated leer Dahlia's way.

"Remember those temple prostitutes in Ghazfor Ri?" the third man asked, stifling his laughter. "Sure liked that part. Hey, when you think you Leyvans gonna build a temple on Priests' Promenade to that god?"

Dahlia bridled at the disrespect to Revered Khelik. These savages had no conception of the true role of Khelik's priestesses. Her right hand crept to her left wrist, caressing the bracelet of prayer bangles there in a sort of atonement for the sacrilege.

"Least you could do," Chucker said, "considering all the killing and dying we did for you."

"I mean no disrespect, nor do I wish to contradict you," Dahlia's father said. "However, as a purely factual matter, the Clackmat Confederacy fought on its own behalf. As the Haptha Council delivered identical ultimata to the Confederacy and the Hierocracy, the two powers allied in the war. Neither fought for the other, but for its own interests."

"Yeah, then how come we was fighting over there in Leyvan land, instead of here on Clackmat soil if we wasn't fighting for you?" the third man asked.

"Two points, sir," Forskolin said, maintaining the lecturing tone he used when walking Dahlia through the sword forms or instructing a customer in the dosage and application of a decoction of roots and herbs. "First, my daughter was born in Kalapo. I myself have lived here for over twenty years. One might consider it inaccurate to assign the term Leyvan to either of us in any possessive or dispositive sense, though we remain proud of our heritage."

The second man coughed while the first shuffled his feet, his increasing frown evident even in the fading light.

Get on with it, Dad, Dahlia was thinking. At the same time, she wondered if these drunken assholes didn't have at least a bit of a point. They'd been over in Dahlia's ancestral homeland, fighting for both the Confederacy and the Hierocracy. What had she been doing? Playing with swords? Learning to sort herbs by smell and color? And what had Forskolin been doing? Tending his shop and turning his nose up at these crude, unlettered soldiers. Now these men were trickling back into Kalapo, more and more of them every month as the conflict appeared to be winding down. Some crippled, some suffering from illnesses unfamiliar in the Confederacy. Others, like these, unemployed and usually drunk. What was home like for them now, after all they'd witnessed? For that matter, what was the Leyvan Hierocracy like after a decade of war? Dahlia knew it only through her father's vivid descriptions. She ought to feel more curiosity about it, some concern over fire and blood and devastation. But while being Leyvan was central to her identity, somehow she couldn't work up a great deal of concern over the homeland itself.

"Second, while I am no general," Forskolin was saying, "I imagine the war was fought primarily on Hierocracy soil because it is several hundred miles closer to the Haptha homelands than is the Confederacy."

"You sassing us, Leyvan?" Chucker asked. "You being . . . sarcastic?"

"No, sir, he's not," Dahlia said, regretting it even as she opened her mouth. "My father is not a humorous man. No offense is intended."

The look her father shot promised words later. It was out of all bounds of propriety for her to trade words on the street with these savages. She had no business usurping her father's role, nor speaking for him.

Well, too late now. So why stop? "And if he were offending you, I doubt you'd catch it anyway."

"Shit, Chucker," the second man said, "bitch has got a mouth on her, like her old man."

"Fuck this," Chucker said. "Man says he's been living here twenty years, then we did fight his war for him, one way or the other. Got the stones to talk to us like that?"

"Needs to learn some respect," said the second man.

The three spread out, blocking the street. Dagger blades reflected a fading, rosy glow.

Forskolin unhooked the sword from his belt, keeping the blade sheathed. Dahlia understood. A Leyvan shedding the blood of Clackmat veterans within the Enclave would create trouble for them all. Still, she didn't like him giving up his one advantage. There were, after all three of them.

Chucker said, "Get him." The three of them moved in and Forskolin flowed into action. From first position, he brought the sheathed sword smoothly into line for a perfectly executed stop thrust, planting the brass drag at the base of the scabbard into Chucker's throat, dropping him gagging to the street. Forskolin stepped immediately to his right, over Chucker, sweeping the short sword in a compact arc that terminated against number two's head, the dagger thrust intended for Forskolin's chest never getting within a foot of him.

But there were three of them to begin with. And number three had worked his way behind Dahlia's father while he dealt with the first two. Number three was stepping in behind Forskolin for a kidney thrust when Dahlia let the pestle slip from her sleeve into her hand. She swung the pestle up in a full-armed diagonal blow, striking number three right behind the ear. She felt the crunch of impact. Number three folded up and collapsed like an empty tunic discarded for the maid to pick up in the morning.

Dahlia wondered if she'd killed the man. Then she wondered if she could hide the pestle before her father saw her. But he was too quick, spinning about before she could tuck it back into her sleeve.

The glare he gave her both chilled and angered her.

"Dahlia, this is unseemly. I have other words for you on this matter. But not here in the street. Come, we will discuss this at home." He turned on his heel and stalked off.

Dahlia nodded and followed. Yes, they would discuss it. They would discuss many things that had been tumbling about in her head for some time. His treatment of her had long confused and irritated her. Her passive acceptance of that had come to an end.

She would have words with her father.

***

"Yes, I imagine Shib finds Brick a useful presence," Vawn was saying. Dahlia blinked, focusing on the now, and her employer, and her job. "Shib was almost certainly a member of the criminal class back home, and he's unlikely to have reformed upon arrival in Kalapo. The very act of running that tavern is likely a violation of the Treaty, and I would wager the place is merely a front for more lucrative activities. He is almost certainly unregistered. A man like Brick watching his back is likely a comfort." Trader Vawn spoke with precision, but thickly, seemingly unaware of his retreading conversational ground. He sipped from his goblet, then stood, wobbled, and walked with exaggerated care to the clothes press. He opened it, moved aside a stack of tunics, revealing a stout, iron-banded cabinet built into the back of the clothes press. He unlocked the cabinet with a small brass key and removed a medallion on a chain of gold. "And he most definitely does not have one of these. Look at it. Pretty enough in a somewhat vulgar fashion. Odd that my prestige and position depend on such an arbitrary token. But, it is what your Confederacy stipulated. And as concess. . . concessions go it is innocuous. Credentials. Credentials for the credulous."

To Dahlia he sounded contemptuous, reminding her of her father dismissively commenting on his Kalapo customers' ignorance concerning the tinctures, reductions, herbs, salts, and ointments they purchased from him. She heard the same note of condescension, that of a resident guest feeling superior to his host.

Trader Vawn placed the chain about his neck then admired himself in the silver backed mirror hung next to the clothes press. From her position near the door Dahlia could see his slightly distorted image staring back at him. The trader muttered something in the

Haptha tongue. Then he removed both the medallion and the amethyst pendant from his neck and placed them in the lockbox.

Chat over. The boss was going to bed. Time for the bodyguard to take up her pallet by the door.

***

Glum Arent left Shib's tavern rather later than Dahlia. Early, as far as he was concerned. There were still a half-dozen drinkers throwing 'em back when he called it a night, tossing Brick a salute and stumbling out into the darkness.

Early enough that he wasn't too worried about bumping into any of the night predators: the throat-slitters, strong-arm bandits, rapists, and street gangs that ruled the streets between midnight and dawn. Glum seldom worried about them much, what with liquid courage buoying him up and his rather obvious poverty rendering him an unattractive target.

He paced north, weaving slightly. But the cool night air, the breeze rolling up from the Mette River, and the exercise all combined to blunt his glow, insert a note of sobriety into the tumult of his thoughts.

Glum was riding a high of excitement, a feeling that he was onto something grand, a big score. It was hard to put his finger on precisely what the score would be or how he'd earn it. And the wine didn't help in sorting it out, but it did contribute to the glowing certainty. Somehow, he was going to parlay the Battle of Shib's tavern into a victory for Glum Arent.

He'd write about it. Went without saying. But for all his talk and his self-identification as a poet, Glum didn't earn the pittance he lived on by his pen. His income came primarily from the sale of information. And as he wended his way north he tried to focus on what precisely he'd picked up tonight and which buyers might be most interested in which pieces. And what could he sell more than once?

Highmark Street jogged to the northwest and became Garment Street. The neighborhood grew even darker, the buildings nearby mostly retail shops, emptied of merchandise for the night to frustrate burglars, and shuttered and locked to keep out transients. Few late-night candles or cook fires peeked beneath doorways or through windows. No one was home.

North of what passed for Kalapo's downtown retail district, and just south of the Horse Guard Barracks and the adjacent ethnic enclave of Little Leyvan, stretched the widest thoroughfare in Kalapo, commencing at the river's edge and driving razor straight west, rising to peter out among forested parcels of the West Hills. The Boulevard of the Heavens—or as it was more commonly known, Priests' Promenade— was Glum Arent's destination. For one thing, he lived there. More importantly, so did many of his clients. The factions, subterfuge, scheming, and petty jealousies rife among the sects, temples, priests, stargazers, and philosophers infesting the Boulevard of the Heavens made an ideal customer base for an information broker.

The presence of Cester Bailick Faren at the battle, and his role as an instigator, ought to prove of some value if Glum could find a buyer soon enough. Information, like dairy products or fruit, possessed limited salable life. A number of the churches wielded influence over certain Electors. For that matter, a handful of churchmen also served as Electors in addition to their ecclesiastical roles. The High Vicar of the Serpent Ascendant, for instance, tended to oppose the Cartage and Drayage Guild during elections. But the man gave Glum the shivers, with his cold, reptilian eyes and surgically altered, forked tongue. Best consider him an alternative market.

Perhaps Curate Alophonse Freyen Daven of the Pontifical Henotics. He'd bought a titbit or two from Glum and had no love for Cester Bailick Faren.

Yes, good. But only good, not ... tremendous. Not glorious. The Battle was newsworthy, sure. Glum would keep the wine flowing for a week or two with this, but it wasn't the big score. No. The answer tickled at the back of his mind, tantalizing. Maybe he'd had one glass too many. Or maybe he needed one more to float the answer to the surface.

Glum turned onto Priests' Promenade, the road surface transitioning from dirt to paving stones—here those paving stones consisted of alternating blocks of limestone and granite. Glum found himself tripping on the gaps between pavers, despite the superior lighting along Priests' Promenade. Further up the boulevard cobblestones took over. Each church installed and maintained the boulevard along its frontage. The larger and more prestigious the church, the greater the length of its stretch of the boulevard and the more extravagant the paving material. If a church could lure enough worshippers it would probably pave the street with diamond.

Diamond. That was it, that dislodged the tickle from the back of Glum's mind. The Panaegic Periapt. Not a diamond, but just as beautiful, just as intriguing. As soon as Glum had heard Shib name it he'd felt a thrill suffuse his entire body. This would be the big score. Shib had been cagey, but he'd let slip it was a thing of power. This was the kind of scoop Glum would be able to peddle for more than the price of a few beakers of brandy. This would be glorious. He could feel it.

Now who'd be interested? No, wrong question. Who wouldn't be interested to learn the Panaegic Periapt had appeared in Kalapo?

To Glum Arent's right the Eternal Flame of the Enlightened Geometers burned in the portico at the top of a short flight of stairs, casting dancing shadows across the marble facade of the temple. He turned his steps that way. As good a place to start as any.

Chapter 3 - Dawning

Brick rolled out of bed shortly after the rooster finished clearing his throat, warming up for the daily solo. Brick figured he'd been down for four, maybe five hours. About his standard. He didn't sleep much. He didn't like the dreams.

Brick boarded with a baker who allowed him a cramped attic room for a pittance. Another early riser, the baker. They got on well enough.

Brick took the creaking steps downstairs, nodded to the baker who was already dusted in flour. The baker's wife slapped down a warm loaf, a pat of butter, and a couple of fried eggs on a wooden platter. She got on with Brick less well than did her husband.

After he ate Brick walked out back and levered the axe free of the chopping block. Then he set to turning a jumbled pile of log rounds into a neatly stacked pile of firewood. The baker went through a lot of wood.

Brick clenched and unclenched his fists, tight from gripping the axe haft. He stretched, feeling good. Chopping always worked up a good lather. But he still had energy to burn. He grabbed a couple of empty pails and wandered down to the river, the easy pace concealing the extent of his limp.

The baker's place was south of Shib's tavern by about half a mile, a modest stone and timber building situated on Lower Nimbus Lane, a couple blocks nearer the river than Highmark Street. Brick filled up the buckets from a creek, just upstream from where it emptied into the Mette. Then he stripped off his sweat sodden tunic and waded into the river for a swim.

Brick was dry by the time he returned to the bakery, the morning sun warming his skin and the damp tunic he'd soaked in the river. His arms, shoulders, and back burned from the toting the two full buckets uphill. Though still a bit stiff from the blows he'd absorbed the previous evening he felt good, ready to get to Shib's Tavern and start washing tankards.

The sawdust cart was pulling up when Brick reached the Chipped Mug. He let the boy in, helped him sweep up the old layer and scatter the fresh. Brought back memories, doing it. He'd worked similar jobs as a boy, shoveling chips and dust from lumber mills into carts like this one. Brick's father swung an axe for one of Kalapo's lumber magnates, one of the few hired men on a crew of mostly the indentured. Brick's mother cooked for the timber crew. If he'd not joined the army Brick probably would have ended up like his father, taking down trees until one took him down with it.

Brick was up to his elbows in suds when Livette came in, giving him a look that could have meant anything but probably meant she was pissed at him. Steamed at him for checking out the Trader's bodyguard more than likely—was easy to tell sometimes with Livette. Like that first night he'd seen her, newly hired on, uncertain what was expected of him. Shib saying to watch the door then taking off without another word of instruction. Brick taking up a position near the front, looking around, trying to get his bearings. That's when he saw Livette, behind the bar, a tray of tankards balanced on her palms. The woman looking right back at him, locking eyes, and it was like she was talking to him, asking what Shib was pulling this time. Clear as a summer afternoon.

Brick had pushed himself away from the front, muscled through the drinkers in his way, and reached out for the tray.

"Which table?" he'd asked.

"Over there," she'd said with a jerk of her chin, but hooked her thumbs over the edge of the tray when he'd tried to lift it from her. "No you don't, bruiser. Get back to the door. These boys don't want to be served by a guy looks like a recruiting sergeant." Putting him in his place immediately.

That was all right with Brick. He'd been trying to figure out his place from the moment Shib hired him.

That morning, after Brick bodied the last drunk out the door—a talkative little guy, didn't want to let go his chipped clay wine goblet—he'd met Livette's gaze once more. And got busy clearing tables without a word spoken. They worked quietly together, bumping hips in the tight quarters of the taproom, Brick growing increasingly aware of the woman, of her scent, the sway of her in that skirt slit all the way to here.

He deposited the last empty tankard on the bar and turned to find her looking up at him. He cleared his throat.

"So what now?"

"You know, you spend way too much time thinking about what you should be doing. Too much thinking, not enough doing. You'll miss your opportunities." She swayed closer to him.

He didn't ask any more questions but reached out and pulled her to him.

The next morning, they learned each other's name.

Now Brick said, "Morning, Livette," wondering if he'd had her in his arms for the last time. And if that bothered him much.

He'd positioned a pair of wide wooden washtubs on the bartop and had settled into his routine: soap, rinse, dry. The stack of clean and dry tankards now surpassed the dirty. Shib didn't prioritize uniformity of drinkware. Earthenware mugs from a dozen different potters. Wooden tankards, oak and maple, some varnished only on the inside, some cracked or splintering. A few leathern jacks, prone to mildew. Even a couple pewter mugs, though Shib didn't care to stock them. Customers tended to pilfer anything metal.

Livette said nothing, only coming around the bar to stand next to him, taking over rinsing and drying.

They worked in silence for a few minutes, Brick beginning to think he wasn't on her shitlist after all.

"I'm surprised you didn't follow your little warrior woman home last night, try to get under all that metal fetish gear," Livette said without preamble.

So, shitlist then.

"She had a horse. I couldn't keep up," Brick said.

Livette doused him with a tankard full of rinse water. Well, he'd not spent much of the day dry anyway.

"Pig," she said.

"At least you know where to get sausage when you want it," Brick said.

Livette turned her head, but Brick knew she was trying to hide a smile. Maybe their occasional fooling around had run its course, but it appeared they could still work together comfortably. Good. Livette mad could give Shroud bitch lessons.

Shib could hear Brick and Livette bickering in the taproom. He stood in one of the backrooms taking inventory. But not inventory of kegs, bottles, or salted hazelnuts. A latch on one side of a shelving rack allowed the entire unit to swing open on hinges affixed to the other side. This particular shelving rack, along with the others flanking it, stretched from floor to ceiling and was backed by a false wall. Behind was concealed another stack of shelves built into the true wall. The contents of these shelves were the object of Shib's inventory.

The tavern ran at a profit. Shib couldn't abide the thought of a front that didn't pull its own weight. But the profit barely qualified as such, chump change at best. His real income—such as it was—derived from his trade in the goods stacked on the hidden shelves: silver candlesticks, gold and silver rings, chains, bracelets, religious icons, and votive figurines. Easily portable merchandise, brought in from small time thieves and addicts then sold to clients who arrived in the taproom for a quiet negotiation with Shib before meeting him around back to take possession of their purchases.

It was a modest business; the margins were small. And its continuance depended upon those involved remaining discreet. Always a risk with humans, especially the bottom feeders he dealt with. Shib wasn't going to get rich from it and he often wondered if he was going to live long enough to move on to something bigger. Or would he instead end up swinging from a gibbet, another sky dancer entertaining the crowd in the plaza of Kalapo's Retribution Square?

He thought he'd sniffed an opportunity last night, the scent of enterprise wafting off Trader Vawn. A Credentialed Trader. A man could work bold schemes if he got his hands on one of the few allotted trading credentials. The thought of it triggered a thousand half-formed daydreams, Shib seeing himself decked out like Vawn, sword swinging at his side, striding along marble halls. A concrete vault chest-deep in silver Petals. Fat human bankers calling up at him through an open window, begging to be bilked, Shib closing the shutter, letting them stew, building the greed. Yeah.

But merely having met Trader Vawn did nothing for him. It only aggravated his dissatisfaction with this petty fencing operation, like itching insect bites he couldn't reach to scratch. He could imagine himself far from Kalapo, displaying his credentials to the hayseed authorities of some anonymous, soon-to-be-fleeced Confederate town. He wanted it. He could see it, a hazy object just out of reach. It was maddening.

Shib heard a clatter of wooden tankards, a splash, and Brick's deep guffaw.

Hadn't Vawn issued Brick an invitation to visit? And Shib thought Vawn's bodyguard had let her gaze linger on Brick a touch longer than professionally necessary. Might there be a thread to tug at?

Shib eased open the door to the taproom and slipped through, cat-footed. The two humans made such a ruckus he probably could have stomped through and slammed the door behind him without them noticing. But it was good to keep up the practice of stealth. It kept his employees in awe of him, inflicted niggling fears that he possessed supernatural powers.

And it made him laugh, though he kept his mirth locked down.

"Brick," he said and enjoyed seeing the big man jump. "May I see you in my office?"

Shib left his bouncer to collect himself, returning through the open door then taking the stairs to the second floor and into the smaller of the two upper rooms.

The furnishings were sparse. One of the sacrifices a Haptha had to make living in human territories. Simple furniture for simple folk. Shib had known he'd have to give up certain amenities when he'd slipped across the border two steps ahead of Council Constables. Still, Shib had done what he could, a padded bench against one wall for the rare visitor, a more comfortable chair for himself. A locked chest for operating cash bolted to the floor, a false bottom concealing more substantial sums. A sideboard with glasses and a bottle of Wisterian brandy. Cramped, but what wasn't around here? Humans grew on a smaller scale—beasts like Brick excepted—and they built accordingly.

Creaking stairs announced the arrival of Brick, looking nervous, concerned at being called to the boss' office.

"Sit down, Brick." Shib wanted to fuck with him, the big man's worry almost too tempting a chain to jerk. But Shib restrained himself. Now wasn't the time. "Relax. You look like a fat man invited to a cannibal's birthday party. Sit. I didn't call you up here to fire you."

"That's a relief. I just bought a burial plot from the Eschaton Delvers and I still have twenty more payments."

"Don't try to slip them shaved silver that last payment. Those bastards will repossess. Dump your bones in the Mette, sell the plot to the next sucker." Shib was fond of Brick, like a well-trained dog that knew a few tricks. Not a great intellect, but he had a sense of humor and did his best to keep up.

"Right, boss. Newly minted coins only. Mind paying me in just that from here on?"

"We'll discuss it. In fact, a pay increase might not be out of the question. I've had my eye on you. You impressed me yesterday, way you handled yourself in that street brawl. Showed initiative, courage, strength. I look for qualities like that to employ in my various enterprises." He leaned forward, elbows on his knees, steepling his fingertips together. "It comes as no surprise to you that the tavern is only one of my ventures, right?"

"I'd figured." Brick was shifting in his seat. Nervous, Shib wondered? Or just wanting Shib to come to the point?

"You impressed Trader Vawn as well."

"Maybe."

"He asked you to visit. You impressed him."

"Fine. I'm impressive."

"Well, I'd like you to take him up on the invitation. Hike your impressive self to his glorious estate in the hills."

"This have something to do with a promotion? Part of one of your other ventures?"

"Exactly. I'd like you to deliver him another bottle of Wisterian brandy. It's in my interest to cultivate someone as influential as Trader Vawn. Consider part of your expanded responsibilities to include spreading goodwill."

"So, bouncer and goodwill ambassador. Sure, why not?"

"Don't forget dishwasher. Look, Brick, I'd like to see you move up. I'd like to promote from within, let you grow as I grow. But one step at a time. You don't need to be privy to high-level executive strategy. Yet. What you do need is to be polite, pay a visit to the Trader, as he requested, and give him a gift from me. You can manage that, can't you? Or was I mistaken about you?"

"I can manage. If I try hard enough I can probably keep from tracking mud on his floor, maybe keep from setting the place on fire."

"Good. It's comforting you can maintain that diplomatically deferential tone. How about you use it tomorrow? Two days from the invite; not so soon as to appear overeager, not so late as to appear ungrateful."

"Fine by me."

Shib rose. He unlocked the chest and counted out three silver Petals from the tray of ready cash.

"Buy yourself something to wear, Brick."

"Something a bit less metal studded?" Brick asked, standing to take the coins.

"Leather and metal to intimidate at the tavern. A more refined ensemble for the goodwill ambassador. Trust me. I know Trader Vawn. Or at least I know his type. My mother served as second upstairs maid for a household in one of the better class neighborhoods in Port Weir. The very house where I was born, as a matter of fact. Or close enough; technically it was the stables."

"No jokes from me, boss. We shared the shack I was born in with more than one four-legged critter."

"Your restraint is duly noted. If I may continue? Thank you. I grew up with people like Trader Vawn. Childhood playmate with the scion of the house. Inseparable for years. In fact, he convinced his parents to enroll me in his school—an expense my mother couldn't conceive of. I think she'd hoped at best to get me a few years education in one of the Council grammar schools before finagling me a position as stable boy and groom. She was thrilled at the windfall. As was I. Pay attention, Brick, I'm sharing."

"Sorry, boss. Usually by this point in one of Glum's stories there's been a murder, or an unfaithful wife, or something."

"The difference being—and this is important—that my story is true and not bullshit dredged up from an alcoholic's imagination. So, I had the privilege of attending one of Port Weir's elite schools. The first couple of years were idyllic. Let's skip them and go on to the murder of the unfaithful wife."

"Bit ambitious for a school boy," said Brick.

"Yes, well I was precocious. What happened was inevitable. Boys begin to grow up. They take note of their differences. My poverty became an object of derision. The school was to receive an official visit from a Councilman. Much excitement. Go figure. Children get equally excited by barnyard animals and politicians."

"The joke's too easy. I'll pass."

"Fair enough. The day came, the students showed up dressed in their finest. My finest was the same I wore every day. The ridicule—"

Shib stopped. He'd only wanted to impress upon Brick the importance a vacuous popinjay like Vawn would place on dress. The impact of the dredged-up memory surprised him.

"Suffice to say that was my last day at school. Spend this money wisely. Show up looking respectable. Understood?"

Brick turned to leave.

Shib stopped him at the doorway, saying, "Oh, Brick. If you happen to see Trader Vawn's bodyguard—what was her name? Dahlia? If you see her, ask if she'd mind coming by the tavern for a word with me. And be discreet. Trader Vawn doesn't need to know about the invitation."

***

Glum Arent greeted the sun climbing near to noon. He woke in his cubby hole of a room in the cloisters of the Fullers Brotherhood. The Brotherhood had begun as a monastic order devoted to solitary contemplation, so the structures within their walled grounds held numerous private cells, more than the Brothers knew what to do with after the sect's conversion to a proselytizing faith premised upon achieving unity through shared meals. Fellowship through Feasting, the Brothers called it, and the members of the order now spent most of their time catering. That freed up a lot of space and the Fullers' abbot allowed Glum a room in exchange for the odd bit of copying, mostly recipes.

Glum snagged a bread roll and a cold slice of ham from one of the refectory kitchens. Breakfast leftovers. Food never presented a problem in the cloisters of the Fullers Brotherhood. Meals weren't part of his arrangement with the abbot, but no one seemed to mind if he helped himself to leftovers now and again.

He'd endured worse hangovers. Cutting out of Shib's early and the long walk home seemed to have forestalled the more typical aftermath. The food and a pottery mug of cloister-brewed ale took the edge off. Glum felt ready to face the day.

He dug the purse from its concealment beneath his tunic, counted out the take from last night's rounds. He'd done well. The tale of the Battle of Shib's Tavern proved popular, Cester Bailick Faren's personal involvement and evident culpability intrigued a few night owls.

Glum figured he'd wrung what he could from the raw information. He began compiling mental notes for a poetic depiction, an epic in verse commemorating the battle. Something to occupy his pen that evening at Shib's tavern. Maybe talk Shib into sponsoring a recitation, or at least standing him a few free rounds for the publicity.

The letdown was his description of the necklace Trader Vawn wore, the Panaegic Periapt. His tale met mostly with inscrutable masks. Glum figured his auditors did not want to let on how intrigued they were. A few—young, low ranking priests of some of the charity oriented religions—had listened with skepticism or outright derision. Probably too junior to have heard rumors of the Periapt's power. In all, disappointing.

Glum made his way out onto the street. The paving fronting the cloister of the Fullers consisted of worn cobbles decades past due for maintenance. Glum wasn't sure what was more dangerous: the cobbles slick with rain or the ankle catching gaps where a potentially rain slick cobble ought to be. At least it was still dry out. The rains weren't due for at least a month.

Priests' Promenade bustled with midday worshippers and the usual assortment of ecclesiastics, proselytizers, beadles, and deacons. The Clackmat Confederacy could not boast the sheer number of gods the Leyvans possessed, but the Confederacy's indigenous faiths, sects, cults, and nascent enthusiasms counted in the dozens, almost all of which claimed places of worship in Kalapo lining the Boulevard of the Heavens. In fact, the Leyvan pantheon itself had begun making recent inroads, the clergy of one of the myriad Leyvan gods taking possession of an abandoned shrine and beginning construction on a new temple. The colorful garb of the Leyvans added to the chaotic rainbow of surplices, robes, cassocks, and other religious attire livening up Priests' Promenade.

Glum wormed into the crowd. It was about time to make his way to Shib's Tavern, pick up a more substantial meal, maybe a spot of wine to help inspire his composition.

He saw a familiar figure approaching, tall but slightly stooped, with the eagerness of a bird dog on a scent. Harribol Gravin, Apostolic Truthseeker of the Verians. A decent sort, earnest. Glum could tolerate him. Harribol had once purchased an epigrammatic verse from him as well as the odd bit of gossip.

"Harribol," Glum said, meeting the Truthseeker where the cobbles of the Fullers met the pitted limestone pavers of the Pontifical Henotics.

"Glum, have you heard the news?" Harribol Gravin grinned as he spoke, the expression incongruous on the man, his long face normally so earnestly serious. "Funny, me asking you if you've heard the news."

"That is funny. Positively droll. What have you got, Harribol? I can't pay you."

"The Truth is a gift to all, Glum. I've told you that many times."

"And since that would put me out of business, Harribol, I've ignored you many times."

"Well, you won't ignore this. The Panaegic Periapt is in Kalapo. One of the Sharks is wearing it. They say it allows safe communion with the very gods themselves. How's that for an eye opener?"

Glum grunted. How about that? Somebody other than Shib had recognized the Periapt, let the word out same as Glum had. Or his own report had already begun to circulate. Or, shit, maybe both.

"Sorry, Harribol. My eyes are already open and I saw the Periapt with them last night. I'd be happy to describe the event . . . if you've got the coin."

Chapter 4 - Goodwill Ambassador

Brick's new outfit chafed. Finding clothes big enough to fit him always presented problems. Shib's money was sufficient for a good set of tailored togs, but the boss was insistent he get his ass to Vawn's right away. That didn't allow time for a tailor to stitch up new duds, so he made do with the most voluminous items he could find ready made on Garment Street. Meaning too tight around the chest and shoulders. He still had money left over, so he'd get the shirt let out when he found the time.

The minor discomfort kept his mind occupied during the hike to Trader Vawn's. Brick weighed the matter carefully, and right before he reached the walls of Vawn's compound he concluded that the armor and equipment he'd worn in the army had been more uncomfortable than his new clothes.

Trader Vawn was doing well for himself. The walls encompassed about three acres of hillside, offering fine views of the Mette and the snowcapped peaks to the east and far to the north. A sentry stood at the gate, spear in hand, short-hafted axe cased at one armored hip. Decent quality armor, too. Vawn didn't stint on equipment.

"Here to see Trader Vawn," Brick said.

"Tradesman's hours are from two bells past dawn until noon," said the sentry. "And you'll need an appointment with Gurton Lantik, the one handles the estate."

"I ever pick up a trade that'll be good to know. The name is Brick. Trader Vawn invited me. To visit."

"Right, of course he did." The sentry still sounded scornful, but his off-hand crept over to grasp the butt of the spear. Brick tended to have that effect. "Probably slipped his mind. I'll tell him you dropped by."

Brick could feel a kernel of heat begin to glow in his gut, the first stirring of the Fury manifesting those little red fireflies at the corners of his eyes. He tried to tamp it down.

"Look, son, I just humped up this fucking hill with a bum leg to visit the Shark. As requested. Now, why don't you send word to the house that I'm here? As requested. Before I find out if that spear fits up your ass. Sideways."

"*You* look . . ." began the sentry, shifting his stance. But before he could complete his rebuttal Dahlia arrived, trotting up with a jingle of armor, a wave, and a "Good afternoon, Brick."

"Dahlia, you vouch for this—" the sentry paused, evidently discarding the first few descriptors that sprang to mind before settling on "—man?"

"Guest of Trader Vawn, Heareld. The boss invited him personally after watching him take down a half-dozen thugs in a street fight."

"Way I recall it you had something to do with the outcome," Brick said, watching the sentry—Heareld—try to regain his cool, worrying now about keeping his job instead of how to get rid of an oversized intruder. "Don't sweat it, Heareld. We've got to look out for our employers, right?"

"Welcome," said Dahlia, ushering him in as Heareld held the gate open. "Didn't figure you'd show up for another day or so."

She led him into the courtyard. The main house—a stone and brick fortification in its own right—bulked in the middle of the compound. Smaller structures surrounded it. They passed a fenced-in enclosure housing chicken coops. Then a cleared and sanded area. Brick saw a trio of sweating men there, taking a breather, wooden practice swords in hand.

Dahlia slowed as she led Brick by the training ground. He noticed that her armor bagged and sagged.

"Hold up," Brick said. When she stopped he set to tying thongs and buckling straps, getting Dahlia's armor properly fastened. Up that close he noted her hair hanging damp, limp, and could smell the perspiration. "Did you win?"

"Any stick fight you walk away from is a win," she said. "But I wouldn't trade my bruises for theirs."

Brick liked the easy confidence. Dahlia showing off but casual about it, making it a joke. Thinking about it, he also liked that she wanted to impress him. A good sign.

Dahlia led him to the main house, turned him over to a man she introduced as Gurton Lantik. "I'll see you out when you go," she said.

Gurton Lantik reminded Brick of some of the more competent sergeants he'd served under in the Army of the Confederacy. The man wouldn't know fun if he was rolled in it and dipped in fun sauce, but he oozed efficiency. Even without having expected Brick, Lantik took him in charge without blinking, shuffling the afternoon schedule as they walked, leading Brick into the main house to a sitting room and arranging for refreshments. There was a coldness to the efficiency. Not a man Brick wanted to share a pail of beer with, but one he could see himself respecting.

Trader Vawn didn't keep him waiting long. Not longer than a man actually involved in something needs taking care of and less than a man trying to demonstrate his importance.

"Brick, I am delighted you accepted my invitation. Welcome. I hope my staff has treated you with the respect you deserve."

"The respect I deserve? I suppose so. 'Deserve' is a loaded word, sir."

Brick rose as Trader Vawn entered the sitting room, offering the sort of deference a goodwill ambassador ought to show. Besides, he did feel a certain degree of respect for the Shark, and he was a guest in the man's house. He'd treat the trader like he would a captain who'd shown some competence and some concern for his men's wellbeing.

"Brick, you did me and mine a good turn. You helped route those misguided guildsmen and ensured the continued integrity of my skin. Though I daresay the ever-pious Dahlia would have seen to the latter in the event of any tangible risk to life or limb. *My* life or limb I should add, to avoid any unintentional ambiguity." Vawn still managing to spit out phrases like that, strung together like beads on a chain, and not sound ridiculous doing it.

"The boss—that is, Shib asked me to . . . Look, sir, you are welcome. You were a customer. Your safety was my responsibility. 'course I agree with you about Dahlia. Fast hands on that girl."

"Yes. She is gifted with martial prowess uncommon in her sex. Though she would doubtless employ the term 'blessed' instead of 'gifted.' The Leyvan in her, understand. A

Leyvan views everything through a cloud of the supernatural. And when you acknowledge a thousand gods you leave yourself ample leeway to assign any given event to a certain numinous power. Convenient, no?"

Brick grunted. Diplomatically, he thought. He'd met a lot of Leyvans during the Merchant's War. Based on his experience, tarring them all with the same philosophical brush was an error.

"But forgive me, Brick. I didn't invite you here to discuss Dahlia or any of my bodyguards. I wish only to express my thanks. Have you lunched? Come, share a meal with me."

Turning down a meal was a foreign concept to Brick and he followed Trader Vawn through the main house, then outside to a terrace still absorbing the afternoon sun and affording a view of the city below.

Brick studied Vawn, all Shark now without his fancy hat concealing that sweeping spur of Haptha skull. Despite the absence of the feathered topper, the Shark was still dressed in the height of fashion, even here in his own home, no one to impress but Brick. Could be he wanted to, but Brick doubted it. He was the one who was supposed to be impressing: Shib's ambassador.

He wondered about that, had been ever since Shib asked him to take on new responsibilities in Shib's enterprises. What enterprises exactly? He'd wanted to ask but hadn't, afraid to chance Shib changing his mind. Brick figured being in Trader Vawn's good graces might help in all sorts of businesses, but didn't have a clue which of them Shib involved himself in. Whatever they were, Brick had a feeling they weren't entirely respectable. Or legal. And that had begun to worry him. What Shib did other than run the tavern didn't bother him much so long as no one got hurt. He was just a private citizen, keeping his nose out of others' concerns. But once he stuck his nose in, it became his concern and he'd have to learn what sorts of activities he could stomach.

What Brick could stomach was lunch. Trader Vawn put on a generous spread, generosity and vanity the two traits Brick was coming to associate most with the Shark.

"This is excellent," Brick said, spearing a chunk of roasted, honey-glazed ham. "Only time I ate ham remotely this good was once in the army."

"Indeed? Tell me of this superlative ham," said Vawn.

"Was on a troop transport, off the Leyvan coast. Ship got what the sailors called 'becalmed.' Started worrying about food and water until a storm blew up, dumped rain water and—would you believe this?—fish on board. Meanwhile the quartermaster or whoever it is provisions a ship—they've got different names for everything on a ship, like you need a different language in order to float from one place to another. But the man's worried the pork's going bad, wasn't salted enough to keep or something. So all us soldiers are put to gutting, scaling, and salting fish. Same time the cooks are grilling up slabs of pork—all of it, every single scrap—and slathering it in honey, I think so we couldn't taste if it was going rancid or not. The storm blew us toward the Leyvan coast. I got the heaves fierce, never knew if it was the waves or the pork did it. But it was excellent pig, is the point. Almost as good as this."

"We were all forced to consume a measure of unpleasantness during the War," Trader Vawn said, picking at a ceramic bowl filled with candied hazelnuts and sliced apples.

"Yeah? You don't mind my asking, what sort of shit sandwich did you have to eat?"

"I captained a company of irregular cavalry—scouts, skirmishers, flankers. I've no doubt you are familiar with the breed. Unfortunately, our primary deployment during the Leyvan Campaign was the Siege of Ko Samton, a deployment hardly designed to shower irregular cavalry with glory. Our armed opponents remained secure behind high walls, leaving me to face other, less honorable confrontations. I did not find the experience salutary."

"Ko Samton. Other side of the conflict from me. I was stuck on the eastern seaboard, trying to keep from getting killed in just about every fight from Alor Bon to High Fenport. Can't say anybody came out of those shitstorms covered in laurels."

"No. An ugly business, I will grant you." Vawn crunched a hazelnut. *Meditatively,* Brick figured Glum would call it, munching away while staring off into the middle distance, not seeming to focus on anything. Brick got that. You started remembering the war, thinking about that shit, and the present sort of vanished for a while. "The eastern seaboard, you say? As I understand most of the heavy fighting occurred on that front."

"That's what they tell me. It was only heavy fighting 'till somebody started summoning demons and war gods. Then it

76

wasn't so much fighting as everybody trying to get his ass out of the way."

"War gods and demons. Yes, you Confederates, almost as much as the Leyvans, insist upon conducting your dealings with Outside Powers on a footing of worship. You conflate the otherworldly with the supernatural. It hindered your side, in my estimation, limiting control and precision."

"You may be right, sir. That sort of thing was above my pay grade." Brick felt uncomfortable talking about it. The memories remained too vivid, of rampaging monstrosities, red fogs bursting into yellow flame, of vast fields of tentacles erupting from the ground below his feet. He didn't know how to process such events with any reference other than the supernatural. But Trader Vawn was no fool. And the Sharks had won. "Might explain why we outnumbered you three to one and you still kicked our asses."

"Perhaps. I saw little of the Outside Powers in action so I must theorize applying only secondhand information. Simple brute force proved sufficient for my company. Burning crops, butchering livestock. We would torch a Leyvan temple and the faithful would simply stand there and watch, imploring their deities with wailing prayers despite their gods' ineffectuality.

"Are you beholden to any particular faith, Brick?" the Trader asked. Brick had wondered what caused his hard on for religion. Now he had at least an idea.

"No, sir."

"But you are a believer."

"Well, you want my philosophy, here it is: I grant each god the exact same respect he grants me. And ultimately it doesn't matter. In the end Shroud takes us all."

"You are a pragmatist, Brick. A warrior and a philosopher. I confess to some trepidation that my asking you here hinged upon the hasty decision making that derives from a bottle. But I am glad to discover that my judgment—though perhaps impaired—remained sound. I invited you here to discuss a reward of some sort, and it pleases me that more than your actions render you worthy of it."

Brick didn't know what to make of that. Praise made him uncomfortable. Effusive praise made him want to squirm beneath the table. But he reminded himself he was Shib's goodwill ambassador.

He looked down at the city, gathering his thoughts, letting his gaze wander across the river to the extension of the city expanding out from the east bank of the Mette. Farmers arrived there from outlying farmsteads and orchards. From beyond the far, white-tipped mountains came prospectors. The burgeoning outcrop of the city catered to these travelers waiting for the ferry into the markets of Kalapo proper. Some of the growth east of the river consisted of merchants eager to spare the farmers and miners the need to cross the river at all, buying up the cargos on the spot, taking over the ferrying and distribution. More and more this sort of innovation blossomed. The numbers of shops and manufactories increased, the beginning of the growth in commercial activity coinciding with the end of the Mercantile War and the arrival of the victorious Haptha.

The Haptha had come in quietly. Not blowing trumpets and beating drums. Just a few of them, not many of whom were obviously soldiers. To the north of Sawyer's Ferry, Brick could see the circular tower of the Haptha garrison they'd built, if "garrison" wasn't too expansive a term for at best a dozen Sharks. One of them was probably a sorcerer, capable of calling up war demons powerful enough to raze Kalapo. So, yeah. A military garrison, even if the Haptha declared it merely a legation.

And now one of these victorious Sharks was offering Brick 'attaboys and backslaps. And still waiting for some sort of response. Brick supposed he might as well accept the praise with as much grace as he could muster.

"Thank you, sir. But let's not get carried away. Shib's Tavern is concerned with the welfare of its patrons. I was just doing my job." There, that sounded about right, though Brick wished he'd asked Glum to craft a couple of choice expressions for him, something complimentary without sounding like ass kissing.

"Modesty will only take you so far, Brick. Tell me, how did Shib's Tavern deserve the fortune of discovering an employee of your talents?"

Brick grabbed a handful of walnuts, something to get him through the story. "Well, sir, it was like this. The ship ride back home, in the stinking belly of a transport crammed with casualties like me, wasn't near as much fun as the ride out, the one with the fish and the pork feasts. Specially wasn't fun with a leg wound still oozing pus . . ."

***

The invalid wagon rolled to a halt, the mule-skinner leaning back on the reins and hauling back the brake lever which squealed against the iron-rimmed wheel. The mustering out camp abutted the southwestern edge of Kalapo. Beyond the cleared field of the camp the trees thinned where the buildings thickened, the sprawl of Kalapo marching down the hills to the Mette River, a pall of smoke rising from the chimneys of homes, shops, and manufactories. A river breeze wafted up scents of cooking fires, sawdust, and fish.

It smelled like home.

Brick hopped down from the back of the cart onto the trampled grass. He grimaced as the jarring descent instigated a wave of pain spreading out from the wound in his leg, like the beat of a single, thudding drum. The bandage beneath his woolen trews still oozed if he put too much stress on the leg. He bit back a curse, thought better of it and muttered a heart-felt "Shroud's Tits." It didn't help.

He reached into the wagon and grabbed the satchel containing everything he owned, everything the Army of the Clackmat Confederacy deemed fit to leave in his possession now that they'd parted ways with the cripple. He hobbled out of the way of the remaining ex-soldiers on the wagon, all invalided out. Brick gave them another glance. At least all of his limbs remained attached, even if one wasn't working so good.

Now what? Brick supposed he'd have to get a job. But he wasn't sure how well his recent skills would translate to civilian life here in his defeated home.

Brick shouldered his satchel. Then, with frequent halts, he limped downslope onto the streets of Kalapo.

***

80

Brick was standing in the open doorway of the tavern, facing the street. Not aware of where he was, at the lip of that drift he'd been fearing. He'd run through his discharge pay and spent about a year mucking out stables, picking up any spot of manual labor his gimpy leg would allow, selling every item of value, expending every resource to avoid becoming yet another ex-soldier begging in the street. He wasn't sure what his next move was, didn't know how he'd got here, didn't remember wandering along Highmark Street in the dark.

He did notice the hands in the small of his back, the shove that failed to budge him. He turned, seeing the dimly lit confines of a small taproom, seeing a bearded man of middle years in worn workman's clothing scowling at him.

"What're you, the fucking doorman?" the man asked, Brick having to concentrate to decipher the slurred speech. "Door man." The guy thought it was hilarious, turned to repeat his joke to anyone inside who cared to hear, then turned back to Brick. "Now open, door. Door man. I want out. Or I'm a kick you open."

He punctuated the threat with a finger poke at Brick's chest, hand raised to his own chin level to reach that high.

Brick grabbed the wrist of the poking finger with one hand, tucked the other into the drunk's belt, twisted, and tossed him into the darkness, hearing him thump and slide along the hard-packed dirt of Highmark Street. Then he heard scuffling, followed by footsteps diminishing in the night.

"The man was drunk, but he wasn't far wrong," came a voice from inside the tavern.

"You do fit the doorway. Snug, like it was built for you."

Brick faced inside again, seeing a Shark glide his way. He wasn't scared. He'd faced plenty of them, all bigger than this one and all armed. Wasn't even mad at the crack about his size. Maybe a little flutter of anger was all, but he was used to the jokes.

"Yeah," Brick found himself saying, "I'm the pattern carpenters use for making alehouse doors. Got a problem with that, take it up with their guild. Unless maybe you want to take it up with me?"

He heard a laugh from somewhere, swiveled his head to follow the sound and saw a dinky fellow by himself at a table near the fireplace.

The Shark didn't seem to bridle at the threat. Hard to tell. "You display a knack for bouncing the unruly out my door. Might be I could use you. That is if you're looking for work. Don't want to presume." That last in a forced tone telling Brick the Shark knew godsdamned well the straits Brick was in.

Brick considered. Shortly after signature of the Commerce Rights Treaty the Haptha began appearing in Kalapo. Brick hadn't met one yet running a business here, but he knew they were around. Shit, why not? They'd won the war. Didn't matter to him one of them ran a bar. Especially not one offering him a job. A Shark's money was as good as anyone's, maybe better if he paid in Haptha currency.

"Could be I'm looking," Brick said. "What are you offering?"

"Come inside. Let us negotiate."

***

"Thank you, Brick. You tell a story well." Trader Vawn had listened attentively. Brick figured Glum would kill for an audience like that.

"Comes from hanging out with poets, I guess."

"Perhaps." Vawn clapped his hands together, then spread his arms wide. "Now, how may I repay you?"

"Honestly. I don't need anything. I thumped a few heads. It's what I do."

"I feel that leaves me in your debt. I pride myself upon fulfilling bargains and I do not like feeling beholden. But you have a negotiating advantage: I owe you and will continue to until you name the sum and the currency. So, let us say I owe you a favor. You may call it in at your convenience. I admit I dislike the proposal, but there you have it."

Brick could see Trader Vawn meant it. Further refusal would only insult the man. Poor work from an ambassador.

"As you wish, sir. I'll cut the protests. Someday I'll call in the favor. I suppose the head bouncer and chief tankard washer of Shib's Tavern might find himself in need of something."

"Anything, anytime, Brick. Though the usual caveats apply: Your request must be within my power and be reasonable. And for you I am willing to stretch the definition of reasonable."

Trader Vawn rose. "Now, while I thank you for providing me such amiable lunchtime companionship, I must return to work. Gurton will see you out."

***

Dahlia wiped the excess oil from the scoured and gleaming links of armor. A sour hint of her sweat still clung to the leather, but the oils she'd massaged in to maintain suppleness carried a counterbalancing sweetness. Maintenance complete, she stowed the armor away. She was off duty, no point in gearing up again.

She splashed water from a basin on her face and neck, then rubbed a damp cloth over her body while deciding what to put on instead of steel and leather. Not that she possessed much in the way of options. Her mother was mortified by Dahlia's lack of dress sense, by her near total indifference to fabric and cut and fit. By her willingness to wear whatever was comfortable and at hand, donning even Kalapo fashion instead of Leyvan.

Dahlia experienced a passing wish that her mother was here to help her selection. But what did it matter?

She grabbed a long skirt and a blouse with three-quarter sleeves, thinking the colors of the two garments were similar enough to pass as parts of an ensemble. Then she strapped on her sword belt, and chuckled at what her mother would say about that accessory. Not to mention her father. He wouldn't care about spoiling the outfit; if anything, he possessed less fashion consciousness than she did. No, he'd be fuming for other reasons.

Such a disappointment she'd been.

Dahlia met Brick as he left the main house. She was conscious that her hair was still damp, but at least this time it was wet from washing rather than sweat-soaked from sparring with two other off duty guards.

That had been a good session—those boys were improving, finally starting to learn something from her.

The bouncer slowed as he saw her. She raised a hand in greeting, her icon bracelet tinkling at her wrist. A wave of flustered embarrassment washed over her. Why hail him with that arm? Stupid. Would he read some sort of message into the gesture? Give her a load of shit for her beliefs, like Trader Vawn?

She pushed the worry aside. Why in Greyfon's Ice Hell should she care what Brick thought? The man was a bouncer at a third-rate tavern. His opinion hardly merited her concern.

Big though.

"Dahlia," Brick said, "dressed like that I can see why you carry a sword."

"Keep using lines like that you'll wish you carried one," Dahlia said. But she smiled as she spoke. The juvenile pick-up line sounded unaffected coming from Brick, a legitimate compliment.

"Never learned how to use a sword. Don't know if I could afford one. Not one worth having anyways."

"What do you mean?" By unspoken mutual consent they'd begun walking toward the front gate, strolling really, taking their time.

"On a bouncer's pay the best I could get's probably a hunk of brittle iron that would snap first time I hit something with it. Blades like you've got strapped on don't come cheap."

"Trader Vawn does take good care of his people," Dahlia said.

"I suppose so," Brick said. "Don't know if I care for how he treats your, well, y'know." The big man pointed at Dahlia's icon bracelet.

"Oh, that. Sharks tend to look down on us primitive, superstitious humans. Vawn perhaps more than most."

"And you put up with it?"

"Small price. Just barking, a dog telling you whose territory you're in. Annoying, sure, but harmless. You work for a Shark. This can't be new to you. Why do you put up with it?"

"Point to Dahlia. I surrender. Shib's a good boss in his own way. He enjoys sniping at his employees, yeah. But he's good natured about it, I think. He's clever, makes me laugh, even if it's at my expense. Which reminds me."

They were nearing the gate now, slowing to a near shuffle.

"Reminds you what?"

"Shib wants me to ask if you'd stop by the tavern. He'd like a word with you."

Dahlia stopped. Brick turned to face her. She looked up at him, tilted her head to one side.

"*Shib* wants a word with me? Don't be coy, Brick. You want to see me, man up and ask."

"Ahh, Shroud take it, Dahlia. Now, see, you've put me in an awkward position."

"Oh? I find this pretty comfortable."

"Thing is, Shib really does want a word with you. And now you're going to think I don't want to see you again, that maybe if I'm asking it's an afterthought."

Dahlia tried to read his face. Bluff, blunt, and honest could be a good front for a bullshitter. But she couldn't tell.

"Look, Dahlia, come by the tavern. Talk to Shib. Then, if you've decided I'm not an asshole, come talk to me."

Chapter 5 - Recruitment

Shib felt uncomfortable with Dahlia in his office—all that armor and sharp steel so near his stash of cash. But he played it cool, and she was the one showing nerves, one leg jiggling up and down, quivering chain rings chiming in muted rhythm with the motion.

"I'm pleased you accepted my invitation, Dahlia. Can I get you something to drink? Wine, perhaps. Or brandy?"

"No, thank you." She weighed down her knee with both hands, stilling the willful leg. A graceful enough motion, almost surreptitious. Unless one had been observing her case of nerves.

"I trust Trader Vawn is doing well." Shib leaned back in his chair, presenting a picture of ease.

"He does not know I'm here, if that is what you're asking. Brick made it clear this visit is our secret."

Shib revised his estimation of this girl. Sharper than he'd thought.

"Brick may not've been the ideal envoy," Shib said. "He's almost as blunt as his name suggests. But I can trust him to get the job done."

"He might be more subtle than you give him credit for," Dahlia said.

Shib doubted it. "Did Brick describe his meeting with Vawn?" he asked.

"No. Seemed to think that was your business."

"He would. No secret, really. I imagine Trader Vawn informed you that I was making friendly overtures, trying to establish a relationship."

"You imagine wrong, Shib." Gentle about it, not rubbing his nose in the error. "Trader Vawn doesn't confide in me. Well, he doesn't make a habit of confiding in me. I'm his bodyguard, not his daughter."

"And an excellent bodyguard. I witnessed that first hand. How are your parents, by the way? Still back home in Leyvan while you have adventures in Kalapo?"

Dahlia stirred. Her leg got away from her for a moment before she quelled it.

"My parents are both in Kalapo, immigrated here before I was born. My father is the leading apothecary in Leyvan Town, perhaps in the whole of Kalapo."

Shib thought she sounded defensive, anxious he think well of her father. He considered that and her relationship with Trader Vawn. Daddy issues? Need for approval from a parental surrogate? Maybe. Might be strings to pull there.

"You must be proud of him. I'm sure he's proud of you, employed by such an influential figure."

"For a clever man, you sure are wrong a lot." Not gentle now. Bitter and not hiding it. "'Proud' is not the word to describe my father's attitude toward my job."

"That's a shame. Excellence in whatever field deserves praise. At least you have Trader Vawn's appreciation."

"Trader Vawn is . . . an admirable employer. He pays well, he ensures I have the best equipment. But he isn't lavish with praise. He'd rather deal jibes and snide comments than kudos and 'attagirls." Dahlia shrugged. "I've got no objection—his coin is sound. That's enough appreciation for me."

Sounded like a speech, rehearsed. Like something she kept telling herself to reinforce her self-image, convince herself her role in life was one she'd selected and was content with. But Shib nodded, the sympathetic, understanding friend. "No question there. He's a decent enough fellow, for a trader. A man with his wealth can afford to be liberal with both pay and ridicule. Probably doesn't even know he offends."

He stood, poured himself a glass of brandy. "Sure you don't want one? Fortify yourself for the ride back? One on the house is the least I can do to repay you for watching Brick's back during the fight."

Dahlia shrugged again. Shib took it for acquiescence, poured her a glass that she accepted and sipped.

Seated once more, Shib said, "I mean what I said about your help in defending the tavern. This is my livelihood. It isn't much, but it is mine. You were impressive out there. Fast, confident. Just as impressive here, talking to me. Wondering what this is all about, but still confident, smart, fast on your feet. I appreciate that."

Dahlia looked embarrassed, sipped at her glass to hide it.

"So, what do I want?" Shib said. "Let's look at your situation. You've an employer you respect, but maybe don't much like. You wouldn't want him harmed. I mean you are one of his bodyguards after all. But maybe you wouldn't mind seeing him taken down a peg or two. Nothing serious, just— discomfited."

Shib watched Dahlia's reaction closely. Had he misjudged, moved too soon?

Dahlia polished off the brandy and set down the glass. She was staring off in the middle distance, focused on nothing. One hand began playing with the charms of her bracelet.

"I'm listening," she said.

***

Glum was drinking his lunch. Two cups in and starting on his third. He watched Brick wandering about the taproom, straightening chairs with one hand, the other holding a crust he was taking bites from. The bouncer looking too big for the space, like a bear in a cage.

"Was talking to this guy, about a year ago," Glum said. "Name of Drofus Bil Enestor. A priest."

"Another of your priests," Brick said, picking up an empty tankard.

"Yeah. Ought to start a religion of my own, cherry pick the best parts of all the others. Shit, I've got the litany and dogma of most of them memorized."

"Ordain me when you do. Could be a good racket. Less head-knocking involved."

"Sure, Brick. So, this guy, Cadet Cenobite of the Five-fold Monophysites—hey, c'mon Brick, they hang these labels on themselves. This Drofus guy is telling me the way to salvation is to guard the Citadel of the Soul."

"Yeah? Where's that?"

"Not a place, dumbass. It's a metaphor. Your soul, right? It's surrounded by dangers. Needs protection."

Brick winked, the big bastard fucking with him, playing the ignoramus.

"So anyway," Glum said, then took a long pull at his wine, trying to remember where he was in the anecdote. "He tells me the citadel has five gates. You've got to guard the gate of

90

the mouth: Repeat the sacred words, avoid any frivolous or profane speech."

"Check," Brick said.

"Then there's the gate of the ears."

"Shouldn't that be two gates?"

"Shut up. You've got to guard against idle and malicious gossip. Music is right out. There's the gate of the nose that might let in perfumes, make you lust for women. Or the aroma of spices might make you a glutton."

"This Drofus a skinny virgin?"

"No, a fat son of a bitch. Don't think he was much of a gate warden. He said you also had to guard the gate of touch, stick to coarse materials. Silk is too reminiscent of flesh. Finally, the gate of the eyes, got to steer clear of tempting images, beautiful women, poetic verse, and secular writing."

"Sounds miserable. I'd just throw open the gates and surrender the citadel."

"You've got that right," Glum said and raised his empty cup to waggle it at Livette. "All these afterlives they're peddling on Priests' Promenade are pretty iffy. And the sales pitches tend to be short on rewards in the here-and-now. There's got to be a way to clean up right now, right here. Rolling in wine, women, and song. And let's not forget gold."

"No, never pays to forget gold," Brick said.

Glum let him have the last word. Livette was bringing wine and he had some more thinking to do.

***

Brick heard Shib's summons while seated on his stool at the tavern entrance, munching a meat pie and watching the early afternoon traffic pass by. He stuffed the rest of the pie in his mouth while walking upstairs, then wiped his fingers on his vest outside the door to Shib's office.

"Yeah, boss?" he asked after rapping his knuckles on the door, the door ajar a couple of inches.

"Come in, Brick. Don't stand on ceremony. Make yourself comfortable."

Shib was seated on the edge of his desk, an open bottle in one hand. Two glasses sat on the surface of the desk. "Brandy?" he asked as Brick came in.

Brick's eyes narrowed. Shib didn't look drunk. Wasn't bibulous to begin with, certainly not this early in the day. What was the Shark playing at?

"Bit early for me, boss. But don't let me stop you."

Shib set the bottle down next to the glasses. "I've no interest in drinking alone, Brick. I wanted to toast to my new associate. You did well up at Merchant's Reach, earned yourself a promotion."

Brick sat on the edge of the bench, eyeing Shib. "Yeah? Associate, huh? What's that entail? And what's it pay?"

"Always practical. That's one of the qualities I admire in you. Suits you for an expanded role."

"Someone starts fattening me up, I look around for the guy with the butcher's axe."

"Practical and clear eyed. Good. If I can manipulate you too easily you're not smart enough for the job."

Brick started wishing he'd accepted the brandy. If it took so long to get to the point he was going to get thirsty. "Right, boss. Look, I don't want to sound ungrateful for the opportunity, but you mind telling me what job it is we're talking around here?"

Shib picked up the bottle again, poured three fingers in each glass. Then he sat down behind his desk, taking a glass with him. He slid the other across the surface in Brick's direction.

"Fine. For you, Brick, I'll be blunt, practical, and clear. Some of my enterprises are—extra-legal, let's say. You don't need to know all the details yet. You're to be an associate, not a full partner. But I have a certain job in mind. I want a man I can trust in the field running the operation. Someone with a hardheaded practicality. Someone level headed enough to deal with the unexpected, improvise. Someone with enough muscle in case dealing with the unexpected gets a bit ugly. Someone who's been inside Trader Vawn's estate."

Brick reached for the brandy and gulped it down. Then he stood, unsure if he should slam the glass down and walk out or wait to hear more.

"Boss. Shib. I did a few things I wasn't proud of trying to survive after the army dropped my broken ass on the streets. But I was never a strong-arm robber and I'm not built for cat burglary. And truth is, I'd feel kind of bad stealing Trader Vawn blind. He's all right. And, y'know, the hospitality thing and all."

"Sit down, Brick. Let me put your mind at ease," Shib said and then, as Brick hesitated, "Come on, sit. Let me finish."

Brick sat. Sat and fidgeted. He didn't want to butt heads with Shib. He didn't want to lose his job and he felt an intense loyalty to the man who'd given him work when no one else would. The man who got him off the streets and gave him a role to play in life once again. What other prospects did he have, other than starving on the streets, back alley mugging, or debt servitude? None of those held any appeal. He couldn't see himself submitting to the tattooing and indenture Livette had accepted, his status forever marked on his skin, even if he did live long enough to pay off his bond. On the other hand, he'd meant what he'd said about Trader Vawn. He couldn't ransack the Trader's house, make off with the gold and silver. He'd rather take his chances again on his own, Shroud take the consequences.

"I want you to breathe easy, Brick," Shib said and took a sip from his glass. "I don't want you to fight Trader Vawn's guards. I don't want you to bash him over the head. And I don't want you to clear his house of valuables. I want only one—no, two—small items of negligible monetary value. Trader Vawn might not even notice them missing and their absence would barely dent his wealth." Shib took another sip. "And Dahlia has already agreed to assist."

"You're shitting me. Dahlia? But she's—"

"His bodyguard. Yes. And she won't let any harm come to his body. She only wants a little payback for the way he belittles her, mocks her beliefs. If she thought I actually intended to harm him she'd gut me like a Mette trout."

Brick considered the idea of staging a break-in. Without inside help, sneaking into Vawn's compound would be risky. But since Dahlia would be involved . . . yeah, maybe it could be done. He found that thinking about the practical aspects of the job made it easier to accept the possibility of agreeing to it. As if he'd already leaped the moral hurdle. And if Shib was being straight with him about the value of the objects to be stolen then he

94

figured the entire heist fell into a sort of moral gray area. Gray-ish anyway.

"What have you cooked up with Dahlia? Got a plan?" he asked Shib.

"A broad outline. Details I'd leave up to you, General Brick."

"Terrific. So, what's the outline?"

"Dahlia will inform us when Trader Vawn will be away from the compound at least overnight, and when such an absence corresponds with one of her days off. Meaning she'll be in the compound instead of accompanying Vawn."

"Yeah, I follow." Brick ladled the three words with dripping sarcasm.

"Just want to be clear, Brick. Sheath your claws. So, she'll get you in—distract a gate guard, toss a rope over the wall. Whatever. That's a detail. Your department. You get into the main house—again, detail. You go to Vawn's room. You get the box open, snatch the goodies and get out."

"That's a lot of detail. I'm assuming we don't want Dahlia's part in this known. So maybe it's not a good idea for her to just leave a door unlocked or a window open. I'm no housebreaker. Prying open windows or slipping deadbolts from the outside aren't skills I've got. And you say open the box. Meaning it's locked? Again, outside my skill set. I don't know how to pick a lock."

"I said you'd be running the operation, not doing the entire job personally. I'm starting to think I overestimated you. Come on, Brick, think. Pick a team."

"A housebreaker and a locksmith. Wondering what you need me for, then."

"A team needs a leader. Someone to think on his feet, deal with the unexpected. Keep the other two in line. Doesn't hurt if the leader is strong enough to yank locked shutters from a window frame with his bare hands if needed. Doesn't hurt if the leader has seen and walked the ground personally. And if the inside man—or, in this case, the inside woman—happens to know the leader and expects him to be there, then that makes the leader that much more important."

"You make valid points, boss. Okay, a three-man team. An experienced housebreaker and someone that can crack a lockbox. I know I'm supposed to be the details man, but you happen to know anyone fits either description?"

***

"Hail to thee, criminal mastermind," Glum said to Brick, entering Shib's office at the Haptha's invitation. He saw Brick's look of surprise. He also saw the open bottle of brandy on the desk and gave it a covetous eye.

"Glum? You're a housebreaker?" Brick asked, and Glum was almost offended by the man's incredulity.

"Housebreaker? Me? No. I don't have the physique for scaling walls and clambering up to second stories. But I do have some facility with lockpicks." Glum felt a release upon finally admitting this to Brick. "Epigrams and odes don't always pay the bar bill, Brick. And sometimes neither does a bit of judicious information peddling. On occasion, I've found myself alone in a house that doesn't belong to me. Loose valuables seem to fall into my pockets. And every once in a while, valuables fall into my pockets after I loose them from a lockbox. Then I take those valuables and—for a perfectly reasonable and justifiable commission—our friend and benefactor Shib sees those valuables find a good home."

"Shroud take it, Glum, you even try to make theft sound poetic. It ain't." Then, needing to get a dig in, "And your description is about as poetic as your actual poems."

"Always the critic, Brick."

"Yeah. Critic and your new boss, looks like. When did you ever learn to pick locks, anyway?"

"Lock picking is just one of those skills a patronless poet happens to garner along the way."

"If picking the crude mechanisms you humans call locks can be deemed a skill," Shib said. "There can't be much finesse involved."

"Did you invite me up here so the two of you could take turns insulting me?" Glum grew peeved. When Shib had mentioned to him the night before that he might want to use him for a major score, Glum thought it yet another sign that his luck was changing for the better. But he was an artist. He didn't have to put up with this. "Perhaps the Haptha might not consider picking our clumsy human locks a matter for finesse. Either way it still requires practice. Do you have any practice at it, Shib?"

Glum watched Shib closely but the Shark's face remained impassive. He had no idea what that lack of response concealed. It unnerved him.

Shib shifted in his seat to face Brick. "There's your lockpicker. Reasonably accomplished for a perpetual barfly—he's brought me enough merchandise to fence that I can vouch for his ability. Leaving us with one more spot on your team to fill.

"Nahl, come and join us."

The office door eased open and another Haptha slipped in.

Shib enjoyed Brick and Glum's reactions to Nahl's entry. Nahl stood about average height for a Haptha, so a few inches taller than Shib. But he slouched, diminishing the practical difference. He had a face made for shadows, scarred and sneering. In the daylight stabbing in through the shutters Nahl made an impression, and not a pleasant one.

"Brick, Glum, please meet the third member of your team. Nahl hasn't met a wall he couldn't scale or a shutter he couldn't jimmy open. And he's an old and dear friend of mine."

That last, Shib figured, is what Glum would term "poetic license." Nahl appeared to hold a similar opinion from the look he shot Shib. "Leach and hanger-on" was a more precise description. Nahl had worked a few jobs with Shib back in Port Weir and had latched on, finding Shib a good source of illicit work and, Shib thought, someone to do his thinking for him. When life grew overly risky in Port Weir for Shib and necessitated his abrupt exodus, Nahl rode his coattails, the both of them clearing the borders with the law uncomfortably close behind.

And even here, so far from home, Nahl remained a thorn in his side. He brought in the odd load of pilfered items, usually of middling quality, and often too conspicuous to fence without altering or melting down. And he was, in Shib's estimation, too quick to stick a knife into a sleeping homeowner, too fond of the sight of blood for a first rate second-story man. More trouble than he was worth most of the time. Still, Brick's caper might require a housebreaker.

"What's the job pay?" Nahl asked, sitting down next to the other two.

Characteristically crass opening question, Shib thought. He said, "Glad you broached the subject. Straight to the heart of the matter; like any good housebreaker going right for the target without wasting time."

"Excuse me, Shib," Glum said after Shib let his last words hang for several moments, "what *does* the job pay? And" he added with a significant look at the bottle on the desk, "may I assume we co-conspirators are sharing that brandy?"

Shib fixed Glum with a stare until the poet blanched and looked away. "No, we are not sharing the brandy. My associate Brick is in charge of this job. Brandy is for management. Now, as I was about to explain, here's the deal. You bring me two specific pieces of Trader Vawn's jewelry. One, a medallion, like an oversized coin. The second, an amethyst pendant. So, nothing but a couple of gaudy necklaces, of no great intrinsic value. But I have a buyer, a collector who's willing to pay more than they're worth. Means I'm willing to pay you more than you're worth. Bring these two shiny trinkets to me and I'll pay one hundred in silver—half to Brick, the other half you two split."

Shib observed Nahl and Glum's reaction closely, but sidelong, feigning indifference. He'd selected the amount carefully, choosing a number not so high as to generate suspicion about the true value to him of the medallion but high enough to induce these two to accept the job. Glum he didn't worry so much about. Twenty-five silver would pay for a lot of wine, especially the near-vinegar, pennies-a-barrel vintages Glum swilled. But if Nahl was in funds, twenty-five silver Haptha Petals might be insufficient to tempt him.

"I get thirty. The lock picker gets twenty," Nahl said.

"Now, wait a godsdamned minute," Glum said. "I'm making a valuable contribution to this enterprise and I deserve my fair share."

Shib stifled surprise. He didn't think the skinny poet had the gumption to challenge—well, anyone, let alone someone as menacing as Nahl.

"I get thirty. You get twenty and get to live to spend it," Nahl said and stood up to glower down at Glum.

Brick rose, confronting Nahl. Shib tensed. He did not want this to get violent, at least not here, where it might draw unwanted attention. On the other hand, it looked to be an interesting contest, Nahl possessing an edge in height and probably in sheer meanness, Brick holding the advantage in strength and maintaining that glowing ember of rage that could erupt into a conflagration of violence if the man allowed it. Intriguing contest, yes. But Shib didn't want to find out what it might do to his office.

"Twenty-five apiece," Brick was saying. "You don't want it, walk now."

Nahl opened his mouth but Shib cut off his retort. "It's Brick's show, Nahl. If you've got a problem taking orders from a human, then best take his advice and walk away. No recriminations, no hurt feelings."

Nahl sat down. "When do we start?"

Chapter 6 - Brick's Caper

Glum Arent shivered during the return to Priest's Promenade that night. Even an additional glass or two hadn't entirely dulled the pricks of fear that had begun lancing his skin once he realized how close he'd come to getting knifed by that fucking Shark. He was a poet, by the Serpent Ascendant's glittering scales. He ought to know how to weigh his words—and when to employ silence.

At least his artistry had garnered him a protector like Brick, a big, snarling guard dog. Might be that Brick's proximity made him feel comfortable enough to mouth off to Nahl. He'd have to watch that, make sure he wasn't picking up a propensity to overconfidence. A poet lived by his wits and nothing blunted sharp wits as much as overconfidence. Perhaps it was time to spend less time around Brick, the source of that overconfidence. And besides, the man was becoming reliant on Glum's clever companionship, some futile effort at self-improvement perhaps, or a grasping for an intellectual counterbalance to the sort of clods and lackwits that, as a bouncer, he was forced to endure daily. Yes, he was letting Brick take advantage of him. He needed to put an end to that, firmly but kindly.

A cacophony of screams and shrieks shredded the night's stillness. The sounds of terror emanated from the fane of the Reformed Helioformic Modalists as Glum passed by. Crimson and purple lights flared through the front windows of the fane and the gap beneath the door. More screams. The lights shaded toward orange and Glum could smell smoke, sulfur, and the scent of cooking flesh. A rancid, acidic odor added a subtle, foul note to the mélange.

Glum shook his head and increased his pace. Fools. Priests' Promenade was plagued by idiots playing with powers they did not understand, summoning up gods or demi-gods, beseeching higher wisdom, or seeking to bind demons or eidolons to do their bidding. Such incidences occurred infrequently, but often enough that the priests and scholars of the Boulevard of the Heavens ought to be wary of dabbling, ought to know that calling entelechies and eldritch entities into the world was inherently perilous. Glum had heard enough stories from Brick of war demons run amok on battlefields. And, from monks and mystics deep in their cups, he had gleaned tales of conjurations gone awry. At least the numinous visitors tended to be satisfied with sucking the life from their summoners, collateral damage generally limited to the confines of the temple. Generally. It was not unheard of for rampages to extend further afield and so Glum hoofed it until he'd left the Reformed Helioformic Modalists far behind.

Fools. But so many of them, playing with fire. An entire street of fools. A man who could confidently control these summoned powers could demand any price he'd care to name from a dedicated customer base of refractory fools. And that thought sent Glum once again to speculating about the Panaegic Periapt. From the description Shib had given of the two trinkets he wanted stolen from Trader Vawn, Glum felt confident that one of them was the Periapt. What did Shib want with it? Did he understand its powers?

Something to ponder in his cell tonight while trying to forget the horrified cries of the Reformed Helioformic Modalists.

Fools.

***

Dahlia hated the waiting most of all. When was Trader Vawn going to travel from Kalapo? Two weeks had already dragged past since her interview with Shib and she grew increasingly antsy, worrying at her icon bracelet with calloused fingers. The actual job—if and when it came off—promised to induce less anxiety than this waiting. At least it should if Brick's caper fell out as planned.

She allowed some tension to ease as she remembered going over the plan with Brick, meeting him on her day off at a secluded stretch of riverbank about a half-hour's hike south of the city, a fishing spot known only to a few dedicated anglers. She'd seen two or three of them along the strand, engrossed in their contest with the fish. Mostly her attention focused on Brick and his simple, but patiently elaborated scheme for gaining access to Trader Vawn's bedchamber.

Dahlia wasn't sure what it was about Brick that attracted her. He wasn't a particularly handsome specimen. And his limp obviated any likelihood of graceful movement. He'd not be much of a dancer. He was smart enough, but not silver-tongued, even though he let slip the occasional word or phrase indicating he possessed a larger vocabulary than one would expect from a bouncer and former spearman.

What she suspected to be the reason for the attraction was his simple acceptance of her. He didn't second guess her career decision or her fitness to pursue it. Same with Shib, actually. He didn't judge her either. In fact, that lack of criticism is probably why she agreed to assist in this frankly unethical breach of her duty. Misgivings still nibbled at the back of her mind. But Trader Vawn would not be harmed, and the losses would be—per Shib—picayune. She did not want to cause her employer any serious financial embarrassment. Like Brick and Shib, Trader Vawn accepted her martial accomplishments without blinking, treating her as any other bodyguard—except for his continual needling about her Leyvan beliefs.

And for that let Brick take the Shark down a notch. He deserved it.

Now if she could just take her father down a notch or two. Maybe she could talk Brick and Shib into another heist, clean out her father's apothecary shop. Serve him right. Why couldn't he accept her like these others?

Instead he'd denounced and disowned her. She remembered her mother weeping, but turning away, refusing to intercede. The Mouth of Skali take them both. Or at least her father.

"Dahlia," Gurton Lantik said, snapping Dahlia back to concentration on the moment—seated on a bench outside the sparring ground, putting an edge on her sword with long, gliding strokes of the whetstone.

"Gurton. What can I do for you?" She looked up, trying to keep her gaze even, hide the fact that he'd caught her off balance. A bodyguard should possess better situational awareness.

"More like what I can do for you, even if you don't deserve it. I'm the bearer of tidings. The boss is off to Satell in three days, be gone a couple of days at least. Since his departure coincides with your day off the guard roster I've assigned Heareld gate duty in your place. Enjoy the break."

Perhaps counting the icons paid off. At least one of the gods smiled upon her.

***

"A guard makes a regular circuit inside the wall," Brick said, his voice rising barely above a whisper. "We should have a ten-minute window to reach the main house once he passes. Get up top, Nahl, let us know when he goes by."

Nahl nodded and shimmied up the wall. His fingers and the toes of his boots seemed to effortlessly find purchase in the mortared stone wall rising ten feet above the heads of the three burglars. One long fingered hand groped along the top of the wall, feeling—or so Brick understood from Nahl's terse explanation earlier that evening—for a spot free of embedded spikes, crockery shards, or broken glass. Gripping the top of the wall with that one hand, Nahl let the other drop from its purchase lower down. He freed a protective length of matting from his belt and swung it atop the wall. Brick watched the Shark ease himself onto the flat burlap sack stuffed with thick swatches of leather and bits of rope, becoming just another shadow.

Dark, fat clouds drifted unseen overhead, the gibbous moon and the stars managing only intermittently to peek through. Brick figured it a pretty good night for breaking and entering, so long as the three of them didn't get separated. He assumed Nahl could look after himself, but he had no intention of searching through the gloom for Glum. The man was a weak link, no getting around it. Yes, Glum was his friend, but in this situation Brick feared he'd only end up a liability. How'd he let Shib talk him into bringing a wine-sodden poet along on a heist?

A rope snaked down from above, the other end cinched about Nahl's waist. The sentry must have just sauntered by.

"Get on up, Glum," Brick said. "Probably take the both of you to haul my ass up."

"I'm not feeling tip-top, Brick. Perhaps we should consider a postponement?"

"Move, Glum. Or I'll toss you up, hope Nahl can catch."

"Fine, but don't say I didn't warn you. My stomach feels as if it's hosting a live cat, feeding on the rotting corpse of another."

"Great, now I feel sick too. I'll stand to one side while you climb, in case you lose one of those cats. Move it."

Glum took the rope, his feet scrabbling for purchase as Nahl hoisted him up. Then it was Brick's turn, thankful that Glum hadn't slickened the wall's surface with his stomach's contents. He tried to emulate Nahl, wedging his toes into any crevice he could feel through his boots, knowing that the two men above could use the assistance. He figured he weighed in about a Glum-and-a-half, maybe two.

Brick reached the top, found the other two breathing heavily from the exertion. Nahl's padded matting held two flaps that folded out on either side, providing a protective layer for both Brick and Glum to sit on. Brick could feel jagged protrusions below threatening to punch through into his thighs and buttocks.

"Let's go," Brick whispered.

He could see Nahl raise a restraining hand. The Shark produced a sharply pointed piton and a padded mallet. He drove the piton through the matting and into the mortar beneath. Brick winced, fearing a silence-shattering clangor. But the piton punctured burlap, rope, leather, and mortar with only a slight scraping, no louder than a foot dragging across gravel from a dozen yards off.

Still, that struck Brick as too much sound for comfort. He sat like a gargoyle, listening intently for any indication of reaction, feeling the sharp points of glass digging into his thighs and ass. Meanwhile Nahl secured the rope to the piton, pulled it up from outside the wall, and lowered it down the inside.

Brick heard nothing. No tramp of booted feet. No shouts warning of intruders. He opened his mouth to tell Nahl to climb down but the Haptha was already sliding down the rope.

"Team leader, my aching butt. Go on, Glum. Right behind you."

Brick felt pretty confident they'd both wait for him below. He was the only one of the three who'd ever been here before, the only one who knew the way to the main house and the side door that Dahlia promised to leave unlocked.

"It's darker than a demon's asshole in the Thousandth Hell," Glum said. "You sure you know where we're going?"

"One," Brick whispered, "be quiet. Two. It ain't that dark, and for a poet that's a shitty simile. Three. Yes. Keep close, follow me."

It *was* dark. But not so dark Brick couldn't make out the heavier areas of blackness indicating buildings. He led through the compound wondering what the fuck he was doing here, creeping about in the night, breaking into someone's house. Why?

He'd taken the job at Shib's Tavern partially to avoid the necessity of this sort of activity. His bum leg hurt, the slow and cautious steps he employed in an attempt at stealth put added stress on the leg that was already sore from the hike up the hill and the climb up the wall. He wasn't cut out for this. He wasn't sure he wanted to be an associate in Shib's varied criminal enterprises. But Dahlia had set the wheels of this job in motion. Shib would see it through whether Brick involved himself or not. And the only way to ensure it came off smoothly, without getting Dahlia implicated, was for Brick to personally supervise the operation.

Dim lights filtering through shuttered windows away to the left placed the guards' barracks. Then brighter bands of light indicated the main house. Brick gave the front entry wide berth, skirted around to the side entry opposite the high terrace where he'd lunched with Trader Vawn.

Moment of truth. He tried the door.

It opened.

"Nahl, put some tool marks along the door jamb, make it look like a forced entry. Quietly."

"Sure. Keep telling me my business."

Brick heard the threat in the whispered words, but Nahl still retrieved a prybar from his seemingly endless selection of burglary tools. The housebreaker worried at the frame, working silently.

"What are you doing? Quit fucking around and get inside."

Brick started at Dahlia's hissed words. She stood in the entry, concealing the glow of a small oil lamp with one hand. He noted that she was wearing the quilted underpadding of her armor over what he guessed were her

108

nightclothes. Above that she wore her sword belt, loaded down with cutlery.

"Is the house clear?" Brick asked, keeping his voice as low as Dahlia's hissed complaints.

"Never is. But the staff should be asleep and their quarters are in the north wing. Gurton sometimes takes a midnight ramble, keeps the maids honest. But he ought to be deep asleep by now—I saw him on the terrace with a bottle this evening."

"Fine. Lead the way. Let's do this fast and quiet."

Brick followed Dahlia along a hallway and up a staircase, wincing whenever a tread squeaked beneath his bulk. He breathed easier once they reached the upper floor. With Trader Vawn absent the second story should be completely vacant.

"This is his room," Dahlia said, gesturing toward a door, its oak surface divided into panels decorated with geometric designs. It was also secured on the outside by an iron bar slid through the door handle and through two iron brackets riveted to each side of the door frame. Two heavy padlocks kept the bar in place, the shackles running through holes drilled in either end of the bar beyond where the ends emerged from the brackets.

"Glum, make yourself useful," Brick said.

"A poet's utility is his provision of truth and beauty."

"Terrific. Rhyme a lock open then, if you can. Otherwise, try the lock picks."

Glum lowered himself to one knee. "Dahlia, bring the lamp close, please. Like Isethere, shining her inspiration on the benighted masses. Brick here standing in convincingly for the masses."

Brick stepped back, giving Dahlia room to hold the lamp over Glum's shoulder.

Dahlia said, "My mother told me Isethere is just another name for Reneda, in her aspect of Vendiya, goddess of starlight."

"You people talk too much," Nahl said.

That brought silence, broken only by the metal-on-metal scrabbling of Glum's torsion bar and rake upon the pins.

Brick was beginning to wonder if Glum had oversold his skills to Shib when the lock snapped open.

"There, child's play," Glum said, removing the padlock. "Next."

Before he could shift over to the second padlock, Brick reached out and, using the second padlock as a handle, slipped the bar free of brackets and door handle.

"Or we could do it the easy way," Glum said and rose to his feet.

Brick pulled the door open.

"The lockbox is inside the clothes press," Dahlia said. "Here, take the lamp. I'd better get back to the barracks. You don't need me any longer. But remember the agreement, take only what Shib asked for."

"Thanks, Dahlia," Brick said. For the benefit of Glum and Nahl, in the off chance that a valuable or two might happen to fall into their pockets, he repeated "Only what Shib asked for," standing hard on the 'only.'

Brick held the door open, Nahl taking the lamp from Dahlia who dithered for a moment before leaving. Brick could read the conflict on her face easily enough. He also could figure her conclusion: Too late to back out now. She disappeared from the receding pool of light—she heading one way, the lamp another—and was gone. Brick followed the other two into Trader Vawn's suite of rooms.

Thick woven rugs cushioned his feet. He couldn't make out details of the patterns in the flickering lamplight, but he got the impression of dizzying complexity. He found he had to watch his step, the rooms lavishly furnished with chairs, lounging couches, side tables, chests, and items Brick couldn't name and didn't know the purpose of. He almost took a header over a velvet upholstered footstool and he barked his shin against the andirons of a cold fireplace jutting several feet out from the wall. Should have brought more lamps. He figured he'd have to keep a close eye on the other two. Tabletops and shelves gleamed in the meager light with small, easily portable items beckoning to be pocketed. Hard to make out what any given piece was, maybe a cloak pin here, perhaps a silver salt cellar there, some sort of game token atop that open book—and, shit, he was going to have to keep Glum from filching the books.

"Over here," Nahl said. "Clothes press."

Brick limped up, rubbing his shin.

"Step aside, let me perform my wizardry once again," said Glum. He opened the door to the clothes press. He grabbed armfuls of garments and tossed them behind him, revealing the metal banded lockbox the clothing concealed.

Brick squatted down and began collecting the garments. "Pick these up, Glum. Let's cover our back trail. Then you can show off."

"We're robbing the man. You're worried about tidying up his room?"

"Glum, we're taking only two things. Unless he's got need of them immediately he returns, Vawn might not notice he's been hit for several days. Except if you leave him a fucking note.”

“Can you two shut up and get on with it?” Nahl said.

“Fine,” Glum said, kneeling to help Brick. “But you two leach the fun out of crime.”

Brick held the newly folded garments piled in his arms. Nahl raised the lamp to illuminate the lockbox. Glum produced his tools again and began probing the lock.

For long moments Brick heard only his own breathing and the scratch and click of Glum’s ministrations. This was taking too long.

“Why don’t we just wait for Vawn to return and open it for us?” Nahl asked.

“Why don’t you fucking do it? What kind of housebreaker can’t pick a lock?” Glum asked in turn, his retort a whispered splutter of frustration.

“Used to,” Nahl said. “Was better at it than you.”

The Shark switched the lamp to his left hand, then held his right close to the flame. Brick could see something odd about his fingers. They looked knobby, twisted.

“Port Weir authorities don’t much like this sort of thing,” Nahl went on. “Got pinched coming out of a house, had my picks on me, not to mention a bag full of swag didn’t belong to me. ’s why I can’t pick a lock. Not sure you can either. Beginning to think the first one was luck.”

“I need more time and less yammering in my ear.”

To Brick, Glum’s frustration sounded about to shift across an emotional boundary to panic. That wouldn’t do. He said, “We don’t have any more time, Glum. Nahl, give me that pry bar.”

Brick took the proffered tool and shouldered Glum aside.

"What was that about leaving Vawn a note?" Glum asked, the question coming half splutter, half whisper. "You're going to leave him a fucking three act play."

Brick worked the beak of the pry bar under the join where the two panels of the lockbox met, right beneath the padlock that had given Glum so much trouble. "I don't want to do it this way, Glum. But it's either this or quit."

Rocking the bar back and forth Brick felt it worm into position, snugging beneath one of the bands of reinforcing iron. He stepped back, set his feet, got a solid grip on the prybar, and pushed, putting his weight as well as his power into the motion. He felt the calloused skin at the top of his palms tighten and protest before locking tight upon the pry bar. The lockbox held firm, resisting the pressure he applied. He eased back, adjusting his grip.

He thought about Glum, the sedentary poet risking this sort of nocturnal adventure. How could Glum Arrant possibly survive discovery of this stunt? The man was no fighter, he'd never even make it to trial, falling victim to the jail scum sharing the pre-trial holding cell.

He thought about Dahlia, so motivated by the slights she felt from Trader Vawn's cavalier dismissal of her beliefs she was willing to sanction this incursion. How could he fail her? And what would happen to her if they were apprehended?

Fuck that. This box would open.

He grunted and heaved. His feet slipped, grabbed purchase, and held firm. The muscles of his back and shoulders bunched then began to burn. Brick stood fast, feeling the dense wood of the lockbox fighting against him. But nothing was going to stand in his way. He felt the panels quiver. The ends of the prybar sank in deeper. Brick adjusted his grip again, moving it farther up the bar. A bead of sweat welled up between his shoulder blades and began the trickling path down his back as he fell into a stalemate, wondering how long he could continue exerting so much pressure.

And then, to the sound of splintering wood and the protest of shearing metal, Brick wrenched the lockbox open.

Brick held out the pry bar for Nahl to retrieve, then bent at the waist, bracing his hands on bent knees, hauling in air by the bucketful.

"Glum . . . get . . . the . . . shit." Brick gasped out the words, fighting for air and fighting down both a building rage as well as a generalized anxiety. Or perhaps not generalized, more a borderline panicked certainty of imminent violence—a fear of attack that he knew to be completely irrational. The panting breaths helped quell it and he brought the episode under control while watching Glum ransack the lockbox for Shib's prizes.

"Brick, this box is an argosy. It would be a crime not to steal at least a few extra baubles. Say, one for each of us." The lamplight underlit Glum's widened eyes and lifted brow, creating an exaggerated expression of entreaty, like a child begging for one more honeyed hazelnut.

"We bring Shib what he wants, who cares if we take a bit extra for our troubles," Nahl said.

"That's not . . . the job. Take anything else . . . and I'll crack your skull . . . leave you here for the guards . . . to find."

A knife appeared in Nahl's hand. "Threat?"

Brick straightened, wind recovered, or near enough. He rolled his neck and clenched his fists to a percussive cracking of knuckles and tendons. "Promise," he said, looking up unblinkingly at the Shark.

"Fuck it," said Glum. "Shib's paying enough. You two stags butting heads will wake the entire compound. Kill each other after we . . . what's the word? Exfiltrate? Sounds professional. Or, 'make our escape'? More poetic."

Brick and Nahl harmonized "Shut up, Glum."

At least it got them out of the lockbox without taking more. And without a fight; Nahl's knife disappeared.

Brick didn't bother replacing the folded clothes. His ripping open the lockbox ended any hope of deferring discovery of the theft. Getting their asses back over the wall became his sole priority.

"Get moving," Brick said and took up the rear, watching to see that both Glum and Nahl stayed within the ambit of lamplight and that nothing else of Vawn's left the room with either of them.

They crept back along the hallway, then back down the stairs. Brick felt a tight knot of tension in his gut. Every nerve tingled, alert for any hint of late night restlessness. They were so close to getting out successfully. He dreaded bumping into Gurton Lantik up for a late-night snack or a trip to the jakes.

The knot eased when they cleared the main house, leaving the doused lamp behind for early morning blackness. The night air felt wonderful. Brick realized he bore a light coating of sweat. He'd not felt keyed-up nervousness like that since the Leyvan Campaign. Shaking that feeling came as blessed relief.

They retraced their steps through the courtyard, making for the wall and the dangling rope end. Almost home free.

Boots shuffling on gravel sounded from ahead. Brick froze. Let the guard pass and they could be on their way. He sensed Glum pause in his tracks and hoped the poet could stay calm for just a couple more minutes. He looked about for Nahl. Where was that vague shadow in the darkness? The Shark had only been a couple steps ahead of him.

He heard the gravel shifting again, this time the scuffing of more than one set of boots. A wet, punching sound. A muffled groan. Then a faint metallic tinkle.

Nahl's dim form reappeared.

"Come on," Nahl hissed.

Brick wanted to wrap both hands about the Shark's throat and squeeze. Right then, right there. Fuck the consequences. But he hadn't finished the job yet. Instead he followed Nahl to the wall and took his turn clambering up the rope and down the other side, fighting down the Fury every step.

Brick held his tongue while Nahl collected and stowed his gear. Being outside the wall provided little more than illusory safety at this point. Rope and padded sack secured, they moved away from Trader Vawn's compound. Passing by the last of the newly constructed compounds, they began the descent from Merchant's Reach, Nahl with his longer stride beginning to pull ahead of Brick and Glum. Ignoring the protests from his leg, Brick double-timed it to catch up with the Haptha housebreaker.

"You piece of shit. You didn't need to kill him," Brick said, his words coming louder than the hiss he'd intended.

"He might have heard us, called for help. There was no point in risking our escape that close to the wall." Nahl didn't slow his pace.

"He was moving away on his rounds. He wouldn't have returned until after we were gone."

"So you say. But you're guessing. Not risking my neck on your guesswork. One of us does this for a living."

"And one of us is in charge of this job."

"Yeah? Well, job's done. Fuck off." And Nahl lengthened his gait, pulling away again.

Brick slowed, his leg already screaming at him.

"I'll talk to him, Brick," said Glum, breaking into a trot. "See you at Shib's tomorrow."

Leaving Brick alone in the dark, wondering what Glum meant to talk to Nahl about.

Chapter 7 - Renegotiation of Terms

"Slow down, Stretch," Glum said, trotting downhill in Nahl's wake. The Shark would vanish in pools of darkness then reappear in striped patches of light spilling from shuttered windows long enough for Glum to perceive him growing gradually more distant.

Nahl must have heard his entreaty because Glum bumped into him in another lightless section of road. Glum emitted a squeak of terror, then clapped a hand to his mouth. The terror remained though. He realized he'd just deliberately placed himself in this vulnerable position, alone in the dark with this throat-slitting housebreaker. And carrying the valuables they'd been tasked to retrieve. He expected to feel the cold kiss of Nahl's knife beneath his ribs at any moment. Why the fuck had he left Brick?

"Do you ever shut up?" Nahl asked.

Glum let slip a relieved sigh. No murder, then. At least, not right away. He shivered. The exercise had fought away the chill, but the early morning air sliced through the artificial warmth once he stopped moving. He wanted this night to end. He wanted to get back to his cell with the goods secure. With his future secure. But first he needed to take this risk.

"Sorry, Nahl. I'm a poet. I communicate even when it might not be politic or wise."

"Meaning you never shut up. What do you want?" Nahl began walking again and Glum scrambled to keep up.

"Safety in numbers, Nahl. Figure we can keep company until we go our separate ways. And maybe talk a bit."

"I'd have to cut out your tongue to stop you."

Glum laughed. "See, I figured you were hiding a biting wit behind that grim and silent facade you put up. More going on in that Haptha head of yours than you want to let on. Probably asking some of the same questions I am."

Glum imagined he could hear Nahl thinking during the silence that followed. He started composing a farcical monologue depicting the Shark's thoughts as he processed the implications of Glum's statement and worked out his optimum response.

"Maybe," Nahl said after they'd reached the lower slopes of the West Hills. "Tell me what your questions are, and I'll let you know."

"Right. Well, the first question you're asking is 'why is Shib willing to pay so much for these doodads.'"

Nahl's chewing over that one got them farther downhill.

"Fine," the Shark said eventually. "That's one. But I already figured that one out, so maybe you're not as smart as you want people to think."

"You figured what out? You mean the obvious—that these things are a lot more valuable than the pittance he's paying?"

"To Shib, yeah. That medallion, that's an important fucking piece of ugly jewelry. But it's worth shit to you 'cause you're just a human, and it's just about as worthless to me 'cause I ain't a grifter. Shib, he's a smart one. He's got a scam figured he can use those credentials for. So, sure, it's worth more to him than the silver he'll pay. Stands to reason. But the silver's worth more to me."

Glum shut up. It didn't pay to underestimate this Shark. He hadn't given much consideration to the medallion, to what he now realized were Vawn's trading credentials. He could see Nahl's point. A token that indicated a Haptha's status as an authorized importer-exporter was about as useful to Glum as a pair of tits. Maybe less. He supposed he could try to find another buyer. But that wasn't the story he was writing. He'd never been concerned with the medallion to begin with, and he didn't intend to start now.

"Of course, Nahl," Glum said. "That's the first question in logical order. Process of elimination, right? Leads you to the important question: How stupid does Shib think we are? Does he think we don't know about the Panaegic Periapt?""

"The Panaegic Periapt?" Nahl asked.

"Exactly," Glum said, as if Nahl's question indicated insight rather than ignorance. Playing this Shark promised to be tricky, he was by turns sharper and denser than Glum expected. But Glum needed an ally. Nahl could fit the part if Glum could just find the leverage. "He thinks we are unaware of the pendant's . . . preternatural potencies. Add whatever confidence trick he's got planned with Trader Vawn's credentials to the protections the Panaegic Periapt can provide against the supernatural, and you can see the potential value to Shib is limitless."

"Sure, I can see that," Nahl said.

Glum doubted it. He tried to frame it clearly, so even Nahl could understand. "If the magi of Priests' Promenade and the summoners of the Haptha army are powerless against him, Shib can position

120

himself to do more than pull off a con impersonating a Trader. That's got to be worth more to him than a few coins. We, my friend, need to renegotiate."

"That's just what I was thinking," Nahl said.

***

Brick headed to Shib's tavern behind schedule. The streets teemed with morning business. Women returned from market with baskets containing the makings of the evening meal. Apprentices scampered through the crowd on errands, heedless whom they jostled. Workmen carried tools and supplies to job sites. Carters drove mules through the massed humanity, scattering the unwary. Kalapo displayed the bustle Brick normally liked to watch beyond the front door of the tavern. But today he barely noticed, even as he shouldered his way through it.

He'd slept poorly, even more poorly than usual. The murder of the guard preyed on his mind. He didn't know what he could have done differently, what would have prevented Nahl from knifing the poor son of a bitch, but there must have been something.

Like refusing the job when Shib offered it in the first place. But that would have left Dahlia hanging. That thought raised the obvious concern: How was Dahlia dealing with the man's death? Was there a chance some suspicion might fall on her? And if so, would she give up Shib? That would lead to Brick choking out at the end of a rope in Retribution Square. And that might well be justice.

But, shit. Not how he wanted to go. How'd he let himself get into this? He was a soldier, not a thief and murderer. Used to be a soldier anyway. Used to be.

Brick was full of shit, and they all knew it.

"Fine, Kedrun, have it your way," Brick was saying, "I am a fucking war god. But you're still going to have to kill one or two of them this time."

Brick did feel almost like a war god right then, the glow of the Fury a gentle warmth in his belly. He looked the part too, his height and heavy musculature marking him, conspicuous in the dead center of the front rank of spearmen like a full-grown oak in a row of saplings.

For all the good it would do. What they needed was an actual war god.

Across the plain of knee-high grass, a single, slender Haptha rank—flanked by the squads of archers that linked the Haptha center with its left and right wings—faced the center of the Army of the Clackmat Confederacy. One rank, that was all. The rank Brick anchored outnumbered it probably two to one. And there were three ranks behind him. But from bitter experience Brick knew one rank of Haptha swordsmen was enough to do the job.

The day didn't seem made for killing. Or dying. No clouds marred the pale blue of the morning sky, the day promising to grow miserably sticky and hot by the afternoon. The high grass offered a deceptive picture of unbroken, level ground, bordered to the left by a bamboo forest that terminated the field like a green wall, and on the right by climbing highlands that rose to distant mountains dusted with a glimmer of white at the summits. The grass hid undulations in the dry, rocky soil beneath Brick's boots, and rabbit holes added to the fun.

Brick hoped the commanders would let the Haptha come to them. Let those fuckers risk broken legs. Not that any of them would misstep. Agile as rabbits, even on legs that would put ladder makers out of business back home in Kalapo. Not one of them would end up stepping in a hole. Bastards.

Without any human troops nearby to provide scale the Haptha's size wasn't obvious. Brick no longer required any scale. The proportions of the average Haptha soldier had been ground into him from previous set-tos, Brick craning his neck to stare them in the face at spear's length. The curving morion helmets the Haptha wore to protect that freaky skull ridge lent their lean height an unnecessary emphasis. Knock that helmet off, see the bony arch rising from the hairless skull like a crest, or a fin, and they didn't appear any less intimidatingly tall. The fucking Sharks made Brick look short.

Each Haptha soldier was a whirlwind of death with a sword in his hand. A greased tornado spiked with lightning bolts. On fire. The Haptha didn't field as many soldiers in battle as did the Clackmat Confederacy or its Leyvan allies. Brick didn't know if that was because of lack of population or simply because they didn't need to. The Sharks' reach and devastating quickness compensated for lack of numbers. Something so tall shouldn't be so godsdamned fast and agile.

Brick adjusted his grip on the rough ash haft of the spear. He'd wrapped a bit of cord around a section his hand had worn smooth, and he was still accustoming himself to the feel. The butt rested against the instep of the hob-nailed boot on his right foot. The spearhead glittered, three finger-breadths at its widest, tapering to a point, the edges sharpened by countless hours honing with a whetstone. Brick's other hand clenched the woven leather strips providing the handgrip of his shield, the warboard an oblong of two layers of oak planking bolted to a central iron boss. It was heavy, but other than his quilted jack, the only protection between his skin and Haptha blades. Heavy suited him fine.

It was going to be a bitch when the afternoon heat arrived, though.

Brick's scalp itched beneath the padding of his steel helmet. A dented, antiquated kettle helmet, out of place amongst the sallet helmets the rest of spearmen wore. But it was the only nugget bucket the armorers could find big enough to fit him back when Brick enlisted.

He locked shields with Kedrun on his left. Severn Fullish, the squad's senior spearman, overlapped Brick's shield on the right. Brick felt a nudge behind him, knowing it was Grent, touching his back and Kedrun's and Severn's with an offering of pre-battle good luck. Brick could think of no others he'd rather fight beside, despite Kedrun being an asshole and Grent a little too free with others' belongings. Thieving prick, Grent, but steady in a fight. How many times had they held the shield wall together? Three major battles? No, four. And about a dozen minor engagements. The new kid—Baelot? Belat?— stood in the third rank. Too soon to know if Cohlin's replacement was worth a shit.

Looks like they'd find out soon, here on this nameless field in the Leyvan Hierocracy. Well, it probably did have a name, Brick supposed, but no one had bothered telling him what it was. Someplace close to the Leyvan midlands, the eastern coastal cities at their back, rugged highlands to the north, patches of jungle, grazing, and farm land stretching to the western and southern horizons. A reasonable spot to offer battle. Though it didn't matter much to Brick where the brass decided to turn and fight, as long he was fighting alongside his boys. After years of marching and battles, interminable stretches in hot, smelly tents, too infrequent R&R in Leyvan cities—his back against the cooling tile of a tavern wall, drinking and laughing with the squad—more marches and counter-marches, fording wide, silt-swollen rivers and pushing, teeth-gritted, through endless swarms of biting insects—after all that shit he was still content to be here, a part of him even happy. This is what he did. This is where he belonged. These were the people he belonged with.

The Clackmat center remained unengaged, but Brick could see the stirrings of the formation of Haptha infantry facing them. The right was already at it with the Haptha left, while on that flank Clackmat heavy cavalry, together with a squadron of Leyvan skirmishers, mixed it up with a detachment of Haptha light horse. A probe, maybe, the Sharks looking to see if they could turn the Confederate flank. From the looks of things, they might pull it off, even though outnumbered about three to one.

And on the Clackmat left—oh, Shrouds Tits. Not this shit again. Advancing before the left wing waddled what looked like some sort of house-sized turtle, though Brick didn't recall ever seeing a red turtle before, let alone one with tentacles. A yellow mist rose from its back. Clackmat battle mages—Serpent Ascendant priests, Brick thought—summoning up another war demon. When did that ever work out? Already he could see a cloud of bluish smoke roiling up before the Haptha right, the Sharks calling up their own answer. He wondered what sort of twisted abomination would emerge.

Could be an interesting show, but it wasn't one he wanted to be near. It didn't appear he'd have time to watch anyway. The Shark center began its advance, swords beating a fast, rhythmic tocsin against steel bucklers.

"Luck," said Kedrun.

"Luck," said Brick, watching the Sharks come on.

As always, the speed of the Haptha advance amazed him. They didn't appear to be moving that fast, merely striding forward, but the distance between the two armies shrank at a startling pace. Brick shrugged it off. Same old shit, no point goggling at it. He felt the Fury begin to close about him, could feel the rising joy from somewhere deep in his gut.

"Shroud take me," the new kid said, the awe in his voice evident even from two ranks away, "these bastards are big."

"Yeah," said Grent. "Easier targets for your spear."

"Remember to use the pointy end," Kedrun called over his shoulder.

"Shut the fuck up," Severn Fullish said. Then, "Arrows!"

Brick raised his shield to meet the breaking wave of arrows that preceded the Haptha advance. He barely acknowledged the angry, whistling flutter, the impact of arrows striking shields with the solidity of an axe meeting a tree trunk, the screams indicating arrows finding flesh. The sounds receded to insignificance. The Fury had almost fully embraced him.

And then the Fury washed away, damped like a squad's cookfire beneath a shovelful of earth. Brick looked down to see the arrow shaft driven deep into his thigh. The pain followed, blossoming like a grease fire and spreading through him. Then the leg collapsed beneath him.

"Spears!" the company captain bellowed. Brick barely heard the familiar, booming voice. Someone, Grent probably, stepped over him. Hands reached down, dragging him back through the ranks.

After that, all he remembered was pain.

***

"Brick. Brick. Wake up, man."

Brick blinked and focused on Glum. The poet walked at Brick's side and waved a hand in front of his face.

Brick frowned. "Glum? The meet isn't 'til later tonight. What do you want?"

"We need to conduct a dialogue. But not here. Come on. This way. Don't worry, I'll feed you your lines."

Brick followed Glum down an alley, one popular with mule carts, judging from the grape-cluster clumps of shit the two were forced to maneuver around. Glum gestured to the wall of a graying timber-frame house fighting a losing battle against the sag of its two stories, the structure relying on its neighbors to fend off the inevitable. Brick looked up, made sure they weren't risking an upended slop bucket from a window above.

"I'm listening," he said. "What second-rate drama you want to act out here?"

"Brick, you go straight to the heart of the matter, as always. Thing is, I'm tired of second-rate drama. I'm tired of second-rate everything. It is time Glum Arent advanced to first-rate. I've been afforded an opportunity. I've learned enough from drama—second-rate or otherwise—to know that if I don't grasp it now the opportunity will never arise again."

"What are you trying to say, Glum? I'm not in the mood. Nahl murdered a man last night and I didn't stop him. So you'll have to forgive my impatience with your usual . . . bullshit."

"'Circumlocution' is the word you're looking for, Brick."

Brick moved a half-step closer to Glum, who shrank back against the splinters of the ramshackle wall.

"Look, Brick, I'm sorry the guard is dead. I don't like it any more than you do. But it's done. We need to concentrate on what happens next."

Brick relented. The poet infuriated him sometimes, but he was the closest thing Brick had to a friend and he didn't want to hurt him. He couldn't blame Glum for Nahl's actions. It wasn't fair taking out his mad on Glum.

"I'll tell you what happens next," he said, "and that's delivering the goods tonight to Shib and getting paid."

"Not precisely," said Glum.

"Glum, what the fuck—"

Glum overrode him, speaking faster than Brick was accustomed to hearing him, his voice betraying a quaver of nerves. "What's going to happen is you're going to talk to Shib tonight. You're going to tell him the price has gone up. Tell him he's paying double. And we're keeping the Periapt."

"What?"

"The pendant, the Panaegic Periapt. We're keeping it. Shib will be satisfied with the medallion. Eventually. He can run whatever scheme he's got planned without the power of the Panaegic Periapt. Just tell him, Brick. He'll see reason."

"He'll see reason? You've lost it, Glum. The 'power of the Panaegic Periapt?' Shib was fucking with you. You swallowed the hook and he played you like a fish. It's just a shiny rock on a chain. It ain't fucking magic. Let's give Shib the stuff, like we agreed, and get on with our lives."

"Brick, your world is so narrow, so limited. You possess no vision. I have sources, contacts. You really think I'm naive enough to rely solely on Shib's say so? Give me some credit. I have independent informants. Rumors reach me. People share information with me. There's a reason I'm a poet while you're just a bouncer. The Panaegic Periapt is real and I have it. Not on me. But I have it and I've no intention of letting Shib possess both it and the medallion. He could do too much damage. Think of Kalapo, Brick. Think of the Clackmat Confederation."

"I have no fucking idea what you're talking about, Glum. And neither do you." Glum had been gulled about the amethyst pendant. That was clear. And he'd probably been misled about this medallion as well, though Brick wasn't sure. The two items were obviously of value to Shib. He had some plan to profit from them, that Brick *was* sure of. But he didn't know what the plan was and, as sure as Shroud would take them all someday, neither did Glum.

"You're wrong, Brick. My mind, my motivation, my intentions have never been more clear. You can try to stop me now, bash me over the head and drag me back to Shib's tavern. But it won't help. Shib won't get the medallion. Nahl won't release it unless I'm with him. And unless we receive double the Petals." Glum pushed himself away from the wall. He straightened to his full height, fixing Brick with a look that Brick supposed he was meant to interpret as determination. "We're keeping the Periapt, Brick. Accept it. You're our envoy to Shib. Pass along the message. Toss in a bonus for yourself if you want. Shib'll cough it up. He wants the medallion that badly."

Glum stepped forward. Brick didn't move and the poet was forced to edge around him. Brick considered wrapping one hand around his skinny throat and slamming him up against the wall. But he let him go, Glum casting one last look over his shoulder before putting on a burst of speed that took him from the alley into the traffic of Highmark Street.

***

Gurton Lantik was crouching over Heareld's body. Dahlia let the end of her sword belt dangle and her right hand rose unbidden to cover her mouth.

Morning sun lit the scene sharply, the air crisp, hinting at autumn chill to come. Heareld's corpse sprawled akimbo on the graveled promenade that followed the inner perimeter within the compound wall. The ground around Heareld's upper torso looked black, the blood from the gash ripped into the guard's throat congealing pools in the pits and runnels of the gravel walk. Heareld's eyes stared up at Dahlia, his face a white mask of mute terror.

Mute, dead terror.

Gurton looked old this morning, gray and grim. He tilted his head to stare up into Dahlia's eyes and he shook his head. Dahlia felt her dismay intensify, as if Gurton's gesture was an official pronouncement, certifying the reality of Heareld's murder.

Dahlia didn't doubt who should bear the blame for the crime: She did. She felt sick. It wasn't the corpse or the blood, she'd seen enough of both to grow inured. It was the guilt. She'd assisted, let the bastards in. It was her fault. But no one was supposed to get hurt. What had gone wrong? Who'd decided to kill Heareld? Couldn't have been the spindly armed poet. Brick? Maybe. The man was big enough and no stranger to bloodshed, a veteran of the Mercantile War. Hard to square this killing with the impression she'd gotten from their brief meetings, though. He'd seemed—well, gentle wasn't the right word, didn't capture the man at all. 'Measured' might fit better. The kind of man who'd think before acting. Then again, she'd seen he had a temper. Violence roiled somewhere beneath the exterior calm. So, yeah, it could have been Brick. Discounting the possibility based on their short acquaintance was unprofessional.

So was inviting thieves into the boss' bedroom.

She wanted to affix the responsibility to someone else, but the onus fell on her. She felt her stomach rebel, breakfast threatening to spontaneously return.

"Been dead since at least the first couple hours of his shift," Gurton said. "See how the blood's congealing?" Gurton lifted one of Heareld's arms, let it drop. It fell stiffly, like a fresh caught trout, not limply like a dead cat.

"Yeah, at least six hours. Who was supposed to relieve him?"

"Trel Minton," Dahlia said just as Trel appeared, still buckling on his sword belt.

"Late to your post," Gurton said when Trel neared.

"No, sir. Heareld and I, we always . . ." Whatever he was going to say remained unspoken. Trel saw Heareld's corpse and his mouth stopped moving, his next word refusing to emerge from his wide-open mouth.

"Too late to prevent this, anyway," Gurton said. "Then again, that can be said for all of us. This is on me. I failed to change up the guard rotation, alter the duration and timing of shifts. I failed this boy, and when Trader Vawn returns I'll turn this job over to someone younger and more responsible."

"Gurton, you're not gonna resign," said Trel, his mouth working once again. Saying what Dahlia was thinking. "Sir, no way was this your fault. Only one who should take the fall for this is the one who stuck a knife in Heareld. Oh, shit, look at his neck."

Trel turned to the side, bent over and heaved, vomit spattering and pooling about his boots. Dahlia joined Gurton Lantik helping the young guard to a bench, facing away from the body.

Trel wiped his face on the back of a gauntlet. "Shit. Heareld. Asked me to switch shifts with him last night, but I told him no, had a dice game." He fought back another round of puking as the thought hit home that the corpse could have been him. "I didn't have a game, lying to him. I just didn't want to take another night shift so soon after the last one. Thing is, even so this wasn't my fault. And it ain't yours. So why would you

132

quit, sir? How do you figure you're to blame? It's not right."

"Son, the thing you'll need to learn someday is, if you're in charge, you're responsible. Our job is to prevent unauthorized ingress. Obviously, we didn't do our job. Gonna have to check, by the way, sweep the grounds and main house, see how badly we failed to do our job. The point is, if the job isn't done right, someone's got to fall on his sword. It's a sign of a second-rate leader if he discounts responsibility, or scapegoats a subordinate. If there is a clear fuckup, and you can assign blame and fix the problem, that's one thing. Otherwise, you go to the principal, shoulder the blame, and accept the consequences. Do you understand?"

Dahlia looked at the two of them, the aged veteran and the kid. Trel must be a year or two younger than she was, too young to have seen service in the Mercantile War. Little more than a boy. Could be this was the first body he'd seen done in by violence. This being Kalapo, though, probably not. She contrasted his reaction to that of Gurton Lantik, the man willing to tender his resignation over this. A consummate professional. She admired him. Far as she knew the man despised the Haptha. But he'd accepted this post, meaning what he thought about his employer didn't signify. All that mattered was the job. He took the duty personally, took the failure personally.

Dahlia felt even worse, thinking about that. In Gurton's eyes what she'd done was the equivalent of treason. Nothing worse she could have done than this betrayal of faith. She could think of at least three Leyvan gods whose portfolios included retribution and karmic justice, and she wondered what fate awaited her. Again, the compulsion to confess pushed at her hard. But no, until she knew who was responsible she couldn't roll over, turn in the others. Wouldn't that be a betrayal as great as the first?

"Gurton, shall I rouse the rest? Get the sweep started?" She kept her voice low, pleased at the even modulation, no telltale quaver evident.

Gurton nodded. Dahlia rounded up the members of Trader Vawn's security staff remaining on the premises, none of whom expressed any appreciation at being woken early, or by her in particular. Once she'd explained the facts, however, the sweep began in earnest.

Dahlia fought to maintain a patient, composed front when an insistent part of her wanted to push on directly to Trader Vawn's suite of rooms to see if the three burglars had left any evidence of their passage. She felt a conflicting wash of disbelief and relief when Trel Minton announced the discovery of the destruction of Vawn's lockbox. Disbelief because she found it hard to credit that with all the time in the world to discreetly work the locking mechanism, these bumbling shitheads had physically torn it apart. Relief that the search could wrap up.

"You look as pale as a fresh snowbank," Gurton was saying. Dahlia realized she'd been unmoving, daydreaming, for she didn't know how long. "I've got to complete the sweep, see if we missed anything, then work up a report for Trader Vawn. None of that requires you. Take the rest of the day off. Go fishing. Fine, not fishing. Probably not your pastime. Go get drunk. Or—I don't know—go see your family."

134

The family. Maybe. Go see her family and not return to the compound, to the employer whose trust she'd abused. Yes, perhaps that was the answer.

If they would see her.

***

Brick trudged up the stairs to Shib's office, taking his time. He felt no particular urgency to deliver this piece of news. He couldn't begin to guess how Shib would react. And that reaction might determine whether or not Brick would stay on working for the Shark.

"Enter, it's unlocked," Shib said even as Brick raised a fist to knock.

Shit. Brick wished he wouldn't do that.

Inside, Shib at his desk parceling out Petals into three even piles. Silver coins always looked smaller to Brick in reality than in his imagination. Nonetheless those three piles appeared plenty large and plenty real. Maybe if Glum could see this real, existing, cold hard coin he might lose his hard on for imaginary riches and power.

Brick let that thought stew for a moment. No, probably not. Glum had latched on to a dream and wasn't going to let a paltry thing like tangible wealth shake him loose.

"Did you enjoy your night's excursion?" Shib asked, sliding one of the piles into a kidskin pouch. "As you can see I'm divvying up the wages in anticipation of rewarding a job well done."

"Yeah. About that, boss. There are . . . complications."

Shib's hands ceased counting and sorting. He looked up at Brick. "Complications? Please elaborate."

Brick noted that he'd not been invited to sit. But he'd a twinge in his bum leg from the climb upstairs, and he figured he was about to lose his job anyway. So, he planted one cheek on the end of the bench.

"First the good news," Brick said. "We got the items you requested. There ends the good news."

"So far so good. I'm pleased. I'm also experiencing some trepidation about what could diminish such good news." From somewhere beneath his desk Shib produced a short, curved dagger and proceeded to clean beneath his fingernails with the point. Effective showmanship, Brick conceded, though he figured Glum would call it hackneyed.

"Bad news is supposed to come in threes, but I've only got two bulletins for you. First, your man Nahl killed one of the guards. Murdered him before we climbed back over the wall. No reason for it, the man was no threat. So that's one. Second—and you need to understand I have no part of this—Glum and Nahl decided they want to renegotiate."

"Oh?" The dagger slipped from the underside of a nail. The tip, flecked with whitish bits dug from beneath the nail, now pointed at Brick's throat.

Brick didn't care for the implied threat. It seemed to suggest a suspicion of dishonesty on his part. He could feel the stirrings of the Fury. And the Fury didn't give a shit about a little knife like that. Brick clamped down on the rage, knowing it couldn't help in this situation, could only hurt. He described his meeting with Glum earlier that morning, finishing up with ". . . and they want to keep that stupid pendant *and* they want double the amount promised. *They* want. I'm perfectly content with what we agreed on. I don't know what the fuck they are thinking with this stunt. What I do think is your little game with Glum went squirrely on you, come back to bite you."

"Is that what you think? Perhaps so. Perhaps not. Every venture is fraught with uncertainties: war; crime; games—especially games. Or maybe they are all games. Only difference is the stakes we play for." With a flourish, Shib returned the dagger to its concealment beneath his desk.

Showing off, Brick thought. That's all he's doing here. Playing with his knife, spouting nonsense like it's profound. But he's just showing off.

"Yeah, exactly. Uncertainties," Brick said. "Stakes. So, what do we do about it? About this renegotiation?"

"We? You're still an associate, then. Good. I admit some concern that your first assignment might have soured you on the position."

Brick grunted, hoping it sounded dismissive rather than noncommittal.

Shib leaned back in his chair, interlaced his fingers behind his head, that Haptha ridge jutting up prominently at this angle. "What we do is counteroffer. I want you to find Glum, present that double-dealing little dipsomaniac with ... No, wait. This shouldn't come second hand. Tell him I want a meet with both him and Nahl. He can choose the location. I'll make my counterproposal then."

Shib sat abruptly forward, the front chair legs banging the floor. "Don't worry so much, Brick. That's one of your problems. You affect this stoic exterior, but you're a worrier. Desist. We'll emerge unscathed from this temporary setback, ahead of the game." He picked up one of the small kidskin bags and tossed it to Brick. "Here. See? You're already ahead."

***

Brick entered the taproom without remembering the walk downstairs. He felt control slipping from his grasp. No, that wasn't right. He felt a step removed from normal life, as if watching the world go by through a particularly warped pane of glass, glass so thick he couldn't be heard through it. Shout and gesticulate all he liked, he could make no impression on those distorted forms on the other side. And he could trace the feeling back to the moment he'd agreed to Shib's request to burglarize Trader Vawn. He wanted to bash through the glass, batter down this feeling, but he didn't know how.

A familiar thump and rattle of tankards in a washtub drew his attention. Livette stood behind the array of unwashed mugs, dunking and scrubbing. Brick joined her, took up a towel, and commenced rinsing and drying. The familiar motion returned some semblance of normality, brought back at least an illusion of control.

He'd always felt comfortable with Livette. There was a solidity about her. Had nothing to do with her size. There wasn't much to her really—except for that phenomenal rack. But she felt grounded. She knew who she was and what she wanted. She seemed content. Brick remembered trying to pry some hints of her past loose from her. Might as well have tried squeezing beer from a boulder. She was happy with the now and wasn't going to dredge up the past. She didn't worry, she didn't second guess. She just dealt with the present.

The last of the tankards plunked into the rinse water. Brick dunked, drained, and dried. He inflated his cheeks like a pig's bladder, then expelled the breath with a popping of lips. Livette looked up at him, a quizzical eyebrow raised. Suds dripped down her arm, partially concealing her servitude tattoo.

Brick thumped the dried tankard onto the bar top decisively.

"I'm going to find Glum," he said. "I'll be back as soon as I can."

***

Glum fidgeted, wishing Nahl kept a bottle or two in this rattrap of a squat the Shark called home. The place had been a sawyer's mill back about a century ago. Now it was an abandoned heap of stone and warped, weather-beaten boards, likely to collapse in a stiff breeze. The neighborhood didn't look much better, aged buildings once housing and catering to the loggers that cleared the area, supplying Kalapo with the logs that built it. Only stumps remained now, obstructing the streets crisscrossing this rundown neighborhood north and west of Priests' Promenade. The loggers had moved on, clearing timber higher up the West Hills, leaving this older settlement to transients, criminals, runaways, and madmen.

"Gloomy ruins of a bygone era. Picturesque. I never pegged you for a romantic, Nahl."

"You want to do any pegging, there's a cathouse 'round the corner on Mill Lane. Humans don't interest me, so keep your perversions to yourself."

Nahl sat on a pile of silk-covered cushions, the shimmery red and green fabric incongruous among the dust and cobwebs. Glum faced him, seated on a stack of hand-carved wooden serving trays. More swag the

Haptha thief hadn't been able to fence, Glum figured.

"Don't worry, Nahl, you're not my type. Or species." Glum stood, walked a couple of steps to stare out through one of the larger gaps in the plank wall. "It has been a while since my last visit out here to Stumpville. A long while. I must have been eight years old, came out here with a Brother of the Sylvanic Order, the benefactors of my second—no, third—orphanage. I remember him pointing out the stumps, one by one, as if letting me in on a profound mystery. Then he told me, 'These are the fallen, the murdered, leaving no mark of their passing save these axe-hewn fanes.' I looked around at all the wooden buildings, thinking he was full of shit, these trees had so left a mark. Maybe I spoke aloud, or maybe he could just read it in my face. I was on to my fourth orphanage not long after. And that was fine with me. A few of those Sylvanic Order types were a little too fond of marking we orphans with their little stumps, if you know what I mean."

"I know that you talk too fucking much, that's what I know," Nahl said.

"I told you, I am a poet. I communicate. Say what you want about Brick—and I've got a few complaints—the man's a good listener. He appreciates wit when he hears it."

"Brick is a fool. Anyone who likes your prattle is a fool."

"Well, you've got half a point there, Nahl. Brick is a fool. Had a chance to be part of something big—no, something monumental. Our deeds will form the basis of epic cycles for ages to come. You, at least had the wisdom, the vision, to see the possibilities of the Panaegic Periapt. With its protections, we can dare great things. We . . ."

"Go on. I'm listening."

"Sorry. Got distracted. Look. Through that gap. No, that other one. Right there, down River Drag. That man walking this way? That's Brick."

"Brick? How did he know we were here?"

"Oh, I left word with a few of my contacts on Priests' Promenade. I figured Brick would make inquiries there after Shib gave him a response to our ultimatum."

Two gliding steps brought Nahl looming over Glum. From a sheath at the small of his back the Haptha produced a poniard, its narrow blade ground to a needle point.

"You, poet, are shaping up as a shitty partner. This's exactly the sort of information partners share, so one partner don't get surprised and knife the other partner in a moment of shock."

Glum could not take his eyes from the point of the dagger. It tapered in an elongated wedge from the width of a finger to that of a human hair, then seemed to shrink further into invisibility, as if the point continued on, unseen, a blade of infinite sharpness. Glum collected himself. He needed a drink.

"Well . . ." Glum stopped, cleared his throat. "Well put, Nahl. I can learn a great deal from you. And I will take each lesson to heart."

A moment, then the poniard slid back into its sheath. Glum could breathe again.

Movement outside caught his eye. Brick nearing. A couple of flat panels, held together by nails driven through two diagonally crossing boards of mismatched length, made up the door to the shack. The assemblage hung askew from one leather hinge at the upper corner. Brick disappeared, passing beyond the gaps in the wall, concealed from

Glum's view by the relative solidity of the door.

"Glum, you in there?" came Brick's voice.

Nahl placed himself beside the entry, the dagger in his hand once more. He nodded at Glum.

Glum frowned. What did that nod mean? "We want to talk to him, Nahl, not carve our names in him."

"You are shit at this. He comes in, sees me where he don't expect me. Sees the blade. You know words, poet. Here's one you've probably heard before: Intimidation. Too fucking late now, you waited too long to answer. He'll suspect something." Nahl moved away from the door. He placed himself next to Glum, his disgust evident.

Perhaps there were nuances to this game Glum had failed to appreciate. He supposed he should acknowledge that Nahl did have more experience in this arena than he. He cleared his throat again. Then, "Yes, Brick. We're in here. Come on in. Unless you're more comfortable shouting through the door."

"This place is more air than wood," Brick said. "Don't need to shout. But I'm coming in anyway."

Footsteps creaked on the dodgy, splintered stairs outside. The door swung open on its lone hinge and promptly fell to the floor, tipping into an absence between floorboards and dropping to the dirt below.

Brick entered. He took in the room, the long, mostly empty space, and the two men awaiting him. Glum thought he looked disapproving, a tutor disappointed with a plagiarized exercise submitted by a promising student. Well, fuck him.

"You broke my door," said Nahl.

"That make me a housebreaker?" asked Brick. "You got a guild you want me to join?"

"Leave the wit to me, Brick," Glum said. "You don't have the gift."

"Maybe. What I *know* I don't have is the medallion and the necklace."

"Periapt. Necklace sounds feminine. This is a thing of power, a masculine thing."

"Right." Brick drawing out the word. "Point is, we agreed to give it to Shib."

Glum huffed an exaggerated sigh. "Didn't we already have this conversation? Nobody enjoys redundant banter more than I, but Nahl doesn't share my enthusiasm. So, let's get to it. Did you pass along our new demands to Shib?"

"Yes. I told him. He wants to meet."

"Fuck no," said Nahl. "Walk into the tavern, get jumped by a dozen hired arm-breakers. Bet you'd love to be one of them, wouldn't you Brick? He's got our terms, nothing more to be said."

"Shib just wants to talk. He says you pick the place, you pick the time. Means no tricks, no goons." Brick's stare said he didn't need assistance from a muscle-for-hire squad to take Nahl.

Glum knew Brick well enough to see anger building in him. If he and Nahl tore this place down brawling then Glum would likely never see the coin he'd demanded, let alone the amount initially offered.

"We'll consider it, Brick," Glum said, speaking fast before Nahl could respond. "Shib didn't send the Petals with you, but he didn't send you with an outright refusal either. Correct?"

"Like I said, he just wants to talk. He didn't say yea or nay."

"I don't like it," Nahl said. "He wants the medallion, he gives us what we want. No good comes of talking a thing to death."

"Talking a thing to death? That's a trick I'd like to learn," Glum said. "But there is no harm in two souls of good will engaging in friendly colloquy over a contested point. I'll convince him to see reason. Brick, did you request a bit extra? I don't want to inadvertently queer your deal. How much did you add to our demand?"

"I didn't ask for a copper bit more than agreed. 's why I already got paid and you two jackasses are out here in a pile of kindling holding a wish in one hand and shit in the other."

"Fuck you, errand boy," Nahl said and Glum noticed one of Brick's eyes twitch in response. The pot was nearing a boil.

"Let me confer with my partner," Glum said and wondered why he felt a pang at those words, a twinge of something like loss or remorse. Probably thirst, he decided, pacing carefully over missing floorboards behind Nahl as they made their way to a corner of the squat out of Brick's earshot.

"This is bullshit," Nahl said. "I say we saw off his head and send it back to Shib. Let him know we're serious."

"That's a thought. Why don't we keep that idea in reserve? First, what do you think of this?"

Chapter 8 - Prodigals

The Leyvan enclave bore a scent distinct from the surrounding Kalapo neighborhoods, its houses and shops focal points, emitting odors of spice, peppers, and herbs. Even the buildings marked the enclave as an alien transplant. Walls of glazed brick, roofs of clay tiles, and windows of lattice-work glass beads differentiated the construction from the stone and timber of most Clackmat Confederacy work.

For Dahlia, entering the enclave was stepping back in time. A short step, but affecting. These few acres had delineated the compass of her life, the confines of her father's house and the back room of his apothecary shop the two poles of her existence.

Stepping over the threshold of home once again felt like a close embrace, at once comforting and constricting.

"Dahlia, my sweet child, welcome home," her mother said. She swept Dahlia to her breast. The hug lingered until Dahlia extricated herself, gently pushing away Aster Babeyav Azhak.

"Mother," Dahlia said, the word burdened with a slurry of conflicting emotions. She felt homesick. She felt a glow of comfortable familiarity. She felt out of place. She felt weak for setting foot back in this place.

Guilt, however, remained dominant. She'd retreated to a place of refuge. But she bore into that refuge a secret she couldn't reveal. The constant awareness of that fact was poison, offsetting whatever sense of sanctuary she'd hoped to gain.

Dahlia wanted to turn and run. What she did was walk into the front sitting room. It was unchanged, the floor strewn with elaborately stitched pillows piled up about the lacquered, shin-high table, the table set with the porcelain tea service. The same watercolors on palm-sized pine boards hung on the walls, river scenes and mountainscapes painted by her father.

"Are you well, lamb?" her mother asked. Aster's expression shifted from welcoming joy to worry.

"I'm not hurt," Dahlia said. Aster wasn't buying the equivocation, so she added, "Nothing you can cure with almond-paste cakes."

"Used to be no ill of yours couldn't be cured with almond-paste cakes," Aster said, leading from the sitting room into the kitchen, the largest room of the house. A pot boiled over the cooking fire, and the aroma of sage and pork wafted from a vent in the iron door closing the clay oven. "Or, alternatively, poached pear and honey, or—for serious matters—curried goat and millet." Her mother managed a quirked smile of remembrance. That didn't last, wiped away by a saddened trembling of the lips. "My baby. My baby with an appetite. Until you began to visit the yard."

Dahlia could see the courtyard through a pattern of slots cut into the brick of the wall, the pattern serving as decoration as well as channeling in outside air. A fresh post thrust up from a gravel circle in the center of the courtyard, the post as yet showing only a few nicks. "The yard" is the term her mother always used when referring to the enclosed

146

outdoor space as it was employed by her husband. It was "the courtyard" when she tended her herb garden or took the sun.

"I remember I was happy when you first joined your father in the yard. All those almond-paste cakes were sticking to your thighs. I figured the exercise would do you good, have the boys interested in you. Now I think I'd have preferred it if you'd just gotten fat."

For a moment Dahlia thought she might have preferred the same. Heareld would still be alive if she'd stayed portly, stuffing her face with her mother's cooking and sponging off her father, waiting for a husband willing to overlook her rolls and jowls in exchange for a sizable dowry, knowing Kalapo's premiere apothecary was bound to be loaded.

"Oh, lamb. Don't cry," Aster said and enfolded Dahlia in another embrace.

Dahlia reflected that she needed to work on controlling her facial expressions.

The sound of the front door opening announced the arrival of her father. Even if she'd not heard him enter, the scent preceding him—pungent, aromatic, papery, herbal, and peppery—would have clued her in. The characteristic odors of the apothecary shop clung to his clothes and hair.

She had wondered what she would feel if she ever saw him again. Wondered if she *could* ever see him again, if the hurt and anger at being disowned by her own father would keep her away permanently. If not for Heareld's murder she might never have risked discovering the answer. The answer, it turned out, was trepidation. Suddenly this house felt alien. This was no longer a homecoming but a formal visit to an enemy.

What, she wondered, had her mother been forced to promise to allow Dahlia to darken her father's door once again?

"Can it be my little Dahlia, come to pay her doting father a visit?" Forskolin Azhak stood erect, his greeting posture formal. Yet a wry smile softened the stiffness of both his posture and his words.

Dahlia bobbed her head twice, a gesture of submission that she knew her father would recognize as token.

"Come, Dahlia, let's whet our appetites while your mother finishes the meal. I've installed a new pell. We'll see if your stay among Clackmat warriors has diluted your training." Forskolin brushed by, kissed his wife, and made his way to the courtyard door without waiting for Dahlia's response.

Just like that? No awkward chat? No recriminations? No yelling. Straight out to the yard. Fine.

Her mother offered a reassuring smile. Dahlia shrugged, then followed her father.

A pathway of colored pebbles threaded through the herb patch and the vegetable garden. The path terminated at the edge of the graveled circle. Forskolin waited within, a practice sword in each hand. Dahlia bowed and accepted the sword. She'd helped her father make the swords before, bundling the lathes, slipping three leather straps down the length at regular intervals, then wetting the leather, allowing the bands to shrink tight, binding the lathes into a single unit, light, strong, and flexible.

She stepped into the circle. Her father turned his back on her, facing the post, then assumed the first position. Dahlia took up a position next to him. And then she flowed into the familiar dance, the simulated strikes, parries, feints, and retreats of the sword exercise. She almost felt at home again.

This activity, this place—with the gravel crunching beneath her shifting feet, with the practice post vibrating from repeated blows—this commanding presence beside her, instructing her, this was home. Or had been. Every day, from the moment she'd expressed an interest in the sword exercise until the day Forskolin disowned her, Dahlia had gone through these very motions, learning them in exacting detail. Her father passing along to her the Leyvan martial traditions he could not pass along to the son he never had. Just as he'd taught her the apothecary's arts. In the absence of a son Forskolin, willing to break Leyvan tradition and train a daughter in order to see the continuance of his work.

"Again, Dahlia," he said much later. "Do not bend at the waist. You still over commit. Here, come at me."

Dahlia switched her attention from the battered post to her father, who'd taken a stance awaiting attack. She came in fast, feinting at Forskolin's neck in the accepted, restrained fashion, then—fuck it—cut low, bending at the waist and allowing her father's counterstroke to pass over her head as her stroke connected with his thigh.

"Winning demands commitment," Dahlia said, stepping back out of range. "If you don't take a risk then you're always on the defensive. All that does is delay losing."

"Or allows your opponent the opportunity to take advantage of your mistake."

"Maybe. But not this time."

"Again," said Forskolin, with, Dahlia thought, some heat.

This time Dahlia opened with a conventional shoulder cut. Forskolin parried and countered with a wrist flick slash at her head. Her sword was in position to block almost before he'd begun the stroke. Next, he would either drop back beyond sword range or circle to his left. He circled. Feint, then a thrust. Dahlia parried, skipped back. Steps to a dance. Forskolin came on. The practice swords clacked their familiar rhythm. Feint, cut, parry. The traditional Leyvan patterns following their interminable sequence. The speed increased. Dahlia felt sweat gather in beads at her hairline.

Her father feinted at her leg then followed with the expected head cut. Dahlia blocked it, but slower than she'd hoped. She felt her own sword tap against her temple. She pushed him away, grunting with the effort. He would lunge as soon as he regained his footing. Not bending at the waist. Yes, here it came. She smacked the thrust aside, again more slowly than she'd like. The practice sword appeared to be gaining weight with every maneuver. The fight was taking too long. It always did, these prescribed formulas leading inevitably to an endurance contest. As long as her father remained bigger and stronger than she, he would wear her down. Every single time.

Well, to Greyfon's fire hell with that shit.

She remembered a sparring session with Gurton Lantik. Dahlia had gone easy on him at first, not wanting to beat up on an old man, her immediate superior at that. He'd made her pay for it, for her condescension, for her assumption of his weakness.

Dahlia shuffled back, let her foot slip in the gravel. She went to one knee, seeming to lose her balance. Forskolin stepped in, beginning a sweeping cut at her left side. Then she was thrusting, driving up from her kneeling position, not off balance at all. The bound lathes caught her father high in the abdomen, forcing the air from him and throwing his stroke off target.

Forskolin stumbled back three steps. He straightened, breathing deep, each inhalation looking like an act of will.

"Again," The word wheezed. Forskolin coughed. "Again, Dahlia. This time refrain from employing mongrel tactics."

But before she could accept the challenge the door from the house opened and Aster came through, announcing dinner.

The smells wrapped Dahlia in a blanket of nostalgia. The tastes cradled her like a mother's arms. She'd not realized how much she missed peppers and spices. She'd actually begun to differentiate among the bland Clackmat offerings, even picking favorites. How could she have ever appreciated such savorless fare? Meats, baked, boiled or fried—hard to tell the pork from the mutton. Mounds of onions boiled to a glutinous mush. Gods, it was good to taste proper cooking.

They ate in silence. It had taken Dahlia some time to understand that the conversation the Clackmat customarily engaged in at the dinner table was not a deliberate insult to the cook. Given the quality of the food it had seemed a perfectly reasonable assumption. Eventually she'd grown accustomed to it, though not before creating an impression of aloofness she'd yet to overcome.

If she returned home she could eat like this every day. Or so the meal seemed to promise. And what did she have to give up in return? A post she'd betrayed, the company of men who deprecated her despite her proven skills. She could come home. That meant returning to the apothecary shop, working under her father's tutelage, enduring his condescension. He'd be insufferable about it, no doubt: She should have listened to him in the first place. Kalapo is no place for a Leyvan, especially a Leyvan woman. Don't bend at the waist, you over commit.

Still, not a great price to pay, was it? A tidy solution to her situation, sidestepping the consequences of her actions and leaving the scene behind her.

Aster brought the dinner tea service and, since Dahlia was technically a guest, prepared the small cups, poured the tea, and set out the nuts and sweetmeats. Forskolin performed the proper obeisance to the gods, thanking the appropriate deities for the meal, and asking others to aid in keeping ill-health and disease at bay.

Forskolin slurped at his tea, exhaled a theatrical sigh of contentment, and set down his cup.

"Your mother tells me you would like to return home, ask my forgiveness," he said.

Dahlia looked at Aster. "Is that what she told you?" She had wondered how her mother had spun Dahlia's hesitant request for a family dinner, a request she'd wrapped in qualifications, equivocations, and euphemisms. What Dahlia hadn't done was say she wanted to come home.

Aster stood, refilling cups that did not actually require it. "I distilled the essence of your remarks, dear. That's all."

"I see," said Forskolin. "Did your mother take liberties relaying your exact words?"

Dahlia sipped her tea, buying time to choose her words. It was good tea, but was it worth putting up with this?

"Father, I wanted to have a meal with my parents. That's all. I thought perhaps you might have . . . softened your stance. Not changed your mind, don't mistake me. But softened. Enough to at least treat me like a daughter. A wayward daughter, maybe, instead of a . . . pariah."

Forskolin rose to his feet, clipping the edge of the table and setting the cups to wobble, splashing tea. "You are under my roof falsely. I make no decisions lightly. You, both of you, should realize that. I consider my words before speaking and my intentions before acting.

"I. Do not. Soften."

"Forskolin, please," said Aster. "She is our daughter. Our only child."

"Aster, she is *not* our daughter. Such is her election."

Forskolin composed himself, made a production of seating himself at the table. Calmly, gracefully. He slurped the remainder of his tea.

"Dahlia," he began, Dahlia thinking he'd been rehearsing for months, "I placed my hopes in you. You could have carried on my legacy of healing and science, a beacon in this backwater. You possess the intelligence, the ability to learn. I even immersed you in the sword exercises, so that in the event I had a grandson the Leyvan fighting arts could descend to him. But you turned your back on all of it. If I allowed that to pass I would bring disgrace to the Azhak family name. As much as it pained me to do so, I severed you from the family. Sometimes a man must do what is best for his family, even if it means cutting longstanding ties.

"At your mother's request, I've extended this second chance. You have spurned it. You have no place here."

Forskolin set down his tea cup. He stood again and turned his back on Dahlia. Aster dropped her head into both hands, muffling her sobs.

Dahlia briefly considered snatching up the teapot and dashing it against the back of her father's head. She didn't know what to do. At least that burst of violence would be an action, some sort of response. But she couldn't do that to her father. Not even to this man who used to be her father. And it would cause her mother more anguish than she must already feel at this rupture, this gulf opening between the two people she cared most about.

Well then. So much for the option of returning home. She would continue her position with Trader Vawn, come to some sort of peace with herself. She would have to ponder what that peace might entail.

What a mess she'd made of her life. It seemed every choice turned out to be the wrong one. Dahlia supposed that at least it was an interesting life. Those who always elected the proper path must lead boring existences.

She laughed, surprising her mother into raising her tear stained face from her hands and shocking her father into spinning on his heel to look at her.

"Got to be a first," Dahlia said, the words spat out spasmodically as she continued laughing. "Disowned twice."

***

"Hey, boss, your errand boy has returned." Brick knocked on Shib's office door with his left hand, the right clutching a quarter-full tankard of ale. "'course, you already knew that."

Brick pushed open the door at the same time Shib said "Come in."

"Did you bring enough for everyone?" Shib asked, eyeing the tankard.

"I'll send down for a pitcher, you want," said Brick, shrugging off the implied crack at his drinking. It was Shib's fault anyways, getting him involved in this shit. But he set the tankard on Shib's desk, sat down on the bench with the ale at the limit of his reach. Needed to keep a level head. And—godsdamnit—this was his own fault. He'd agreed to it, eyes more or less open. He didn't want to end up one of the typical patrons of Shib's tavern, bitching into his beers about how everything wrong with his life was someone else's fault: wife; boss; the government. Shroud take that shit. Brick would carry his own baggage and not complain about the weight. He was the one packed it after all.

"Tell me the tale, Brick. Have you arranged a meeting, or have our erstwhile compatriots delivered yet another surprise?"

"Meet's set. Nahl blustered a bit. Don't think he likes me much. Seems to defer to Glum, though."

Shib nodded. "Nahl's most comfortable receiving instructions. He doesn't trust his own planning. With good reason; he's a moron. It appears your wine-soaked friend has usurped my position as Nahl's brain. That frankly comes as a relief."

"Then maybe you'll be relieved to hear the meet is in public. Nahl's new brain proposes tomorrow, high noon, in Retribution Square."

Shib sat back, thinking about it. "Not bad. Dried out, Glum can put two thoughts together and build a third. Crowds are good for this business, and Retribution Square draws a crowd around the noon hour. Lovely lot, you humans, morbid loafers hoping to hear a guilty verdict or catch an unscheduled hanging."

"Hey, now. Some of us have jobs, no time to take in an execution. And don't piss on the people providing us cover, morbid loafers or not."

"Fair point. Pretty good odds that even a bastard as short on sense as Nahl won't try to knife me with a crowd watching. At the same time, there's no chance you're going to beat the location of the goods out of Glum with so many witnesses. There isn't a chance, is there?" Shib was talking to himself now. "No, of course not. We're still at the negotiating stage. Violence can wait."

"Glad to hear it."

"Right. We can work this snag out peacefully. No need for anyone to get hurt."

"Anyone else," Brick said, thinking about the guardsman at Trader Vawn's. He watched Shib's face, saw blank incomprehension replaced by—something. What? Regret? Scorn? What did the Shark really think about the guard's murder? Did Haptha as a species lack empathy? He doubted that. Though he'd met few Haptha, they seemed to differ individually as much as did humans.

"See what I mean about Nahl?" Shib said, after a pause. "Unpredictable. He's just as likely to gut either of us as he did that unfortunate fellow at Trader Vawn's

156

compound. Retribution Square, that is the ideal location." Done with Brick now, dismissing him. "Now, please allow me some time to consider the offer to lay before our treacherous co-conspirators. I do believe there's a taproom could use your attendance."

"This what an 'associate' is? Kicked downstairs to watch the bar while the boss does the thinking?"

"If you prefer you can be a 'former associate' as well as 'former bouncer.' Or, you could hire someone to take over the more menial duties. Long as you pay him from your own wages. I can live with either. Or you could go downstairs and let me think."

Brick noted that at some point he'd picked up his tankard. The cords in his forearm rose taut against his skin. The wooden tankard creaked. Red flickers formed at the edge of his vision. He fought it back. This wasn't the time. And he didn't want a palm full of splinters and a lap soaked with spilled beer. Besides, he still liked his job. Didn't he?

"I'll be downstairs thinking about those options, boss," Brick said.

***

"Short trip home," Gurton Lantik said. "Missed our Clackmat cooking already?"

Gurton stood at the compound gate when Dahlia arrived, looking like he hadn't left the post since Dahlia set out on her abortive visit home.

"Absolutely, Gurton," Dahlia said and passed through the open gate. "No one cooks entire animal carcasses quite like here in the Clackmat Confederation. And you can't keep me away from vegetables boiled until they're unrecognizable."

"What's a vegetable?" Gurton said. He laughed. "Good to have you back. Though to be honest, I didn't expect you."

"Wasn't too sure myself. But . . . yeah. It is good to be here." Dahlia was uncertain what to make of Gurton's comments. Had he changed his mind about leaving? About taking the blame for Heareld and then resigning? And "good to have you back"? Was that an actual compliment? From Gurton?

"Interesting timing," Gurton said. "Vawn sent advance word he's coming home early. Be back within the hour."

Heareld's body no longer sprawled across the walkway. But a dark stain remained, grim evidence of his murder. Sounds from the stables and the main house suggested the tidying up of things other than bodies. The sun crept behind the West Hills, splashing an orange light across the manses of Merchants' Reach. The air hinted at evening coolness.

Maybe it was good to be back. But she still hadn't resolved how to cope with Heareld's death. How could she reconcile in good conscience remaining on the guard payroll when she'd let Heareld's murderers into her employer's very bedchamber? Not even the long walk back from Leyvan Town to the heights of the Haptha Enclave had provided time to unravel that conundrum. There must be a way to blot this stain from her conscience. A pantheon of a thousand and one gods must contain at least one deity able to grant absolution, let her live with herself. Otherwise what good were the icons tinkling at her wrist?

Was she becoming cynical? Maybe her father was right. Step outside the Leyvan enclave and Kalapo began to wear away at her upbringing, opening cracks into which doubts and mockery insinuated. Well, what if he was right? He'd scraped her off his shoe like mule shit. That in itself provided enough to crack her Leyvan upbringing wide open. A bit of cynicism seemed appropriate.

Fine. Dahlia figured she would see what Trader Vawn had to say. Then she'd decide if and how she could deal with her mistake.

By the time Dahlia finished buckling down all the points of her armor and strapping on her weapons, Trader Vawn rode into the compound. She felt better, all suited up. Dressing the part of the Trader's bodyguard helped her inhabit the role again. She belonged. This life, this position defined her, despite her error.

A groom led away Vawn's mount and his traveling bodyguard followed behind. One gave a nod to Dahlia as he passed, travel-stained and road weary. Trader Vawn managed to appear fresh, as if he hadn't spent the day in the saddle. Only the faintest trace of sweat and grime marred his attire, the Shark ready for a formal event: A ball, or maybe an Elector's council.

". . . but I'm afraid we've had trouble," Gurton was saying as Dahlia neared. "Under my watch, sir, so I'll return the keys and you can show me the door if it pleases you."

"Nobly self-sacrificing of you, Gurton," Trader Vawn said. A house servant arrived with a goblet. Vawn took it and drained the contents at a go, returned the empty vessel and nodded his thanks. "Ahh, good to wash the road from the throat. Now, Gurton, you were offering to throw yourself upon your sword for some reason, correct? Tell me about it and allow me to form my own judgment before you do anything rash."

Gurton Lantik sniffed, appeared to consider spitting, then thought better of it. "Fine," he said. "Couldn't ask for fairer. While you were gone a thief—more probably thieves—scaled the wall and killed the guard on patrol, young Heareld. Then the thieves entered the main house, got into your room, and smashed open your lockbox. And I slept through the whole thing."

Dahlia thought it a good summing up, though she considered the sequence off. She was pretty sure the bastards killed Heareld after leaving the main house. She'd noticed no indications that any of the men she'd admitted into the house had just committed a murder. Looked jumpy, sure, but not panicked. What she'd taken for a case of the nerves, the excitement of the burglary, might have been the psychological aftermath of a killing. The three of them shitting themselves, fresh from a murder and trying not to show how frazzled they were.

No. Dahlia couldn't see it that way.

"That is the report, is it, Gurton?" Trader Vawn asked. "Did Heareld exhibit signs of drunkenness, lethargy, or inattentiveness? Did you accidentally leave a rope hanging over the wall? Did you send a crier through Kalapo announcing my absence? No? None of these? Well, perhaps you committed some other act of negligence I should fault you for. Let us go to the house and inspect the damages, total the losses. Dahlia, care to accompany us? Perhaps you can help me find some dereliction I can use to grant Gurton's wish for martyrdom."

"How was your trip?" Dahlia asked as they walked. She felt a certain pride at maintaining a steady tone, revealing nothing of the anxiety roiling within.

"Tolerable, Dahlia. Profitable, though less so than my avarice craves. We had to fight a war to knock the mercantilism from the Confederacy—and the Hierocracy—and instill free trade in place of short-sighted protectionism. I had assumed it would require a longer period for the merchants to adjust to the new paradigm, a period during which I could thicken my profit margin. But these Clackmat merchants have taken to free trade like a priest to a free meal."

"In that case, I'm tolerably pleased at your success, sir."

"Thank you. Kind of you to ask, and kind of you to listen. I know I extend my remarks beyond necessity. You possess a gift for listening."

Dahlia hoped she'd not blushed. She'd little experience with praise and didn't know precisely how to respond. Arrival at the main house obviated any need to say anything. The trio trooped upstairs, Gurton explaining that nothing from the lower level appeared to be missing.

"Ahh, but was there anything downstairs worth stealing?" Vawn asked.

"Fair point, sir," Gurton said. "A few things of value to me and the others who bed there, but . . ."

"Precisely, Sentimental value does not convert well to currency."

Dahlia nodded. "We'd all be rich if it did."

"And what a mess that would be," Vawn said. "I would need to find a new measure of worth. I, for one, am content with the current system."

"Well, you would be, wouldn't you?"

Trader Vawn paused at the door to his suite, gave her a long look. Then he laughed.

"Indeed, Dahlia. I swear it by every one of your gods."

Still laughing, he crouched to inspect the open lock. The laughter faded to a chuckle, then to silence. Vawn rose smoothly to his full height and entered his rooms, carrying the picked open lock with him, and made his way to the remains of the lockbox.

"Human, I'd wager, not Haptha," he said, examining the wreckage. "Not a particularly skillful human, if I may judge from the scratches left around the keyhole of the one lock he did manage to open. And obviously unfamiliar with Haptha locking mechanisms. It appears in his frustration the burglar—or burglars, as you surmise, Gurton—resorted to a crowbar."

Vawn rummaged about in the lockbox. He muttered something in the Haptha tongue. "Ah, Gurton, I wish I could blame you. I appear to have lost an irreplaceable item, the absence of which I may come to regret dearly. Or not. Its lack might never be noticed by anyone who matters. Still, it would improve my mood to take out my anger on an erring employee. Unfortunately, you are not him."

"Sir, security is my responsibility," Gurton said. "Security failed. My error, way I see it."

"But not the way I see it. And it is my point of view that counts. If you wish some penance, consult with Dahlia. I'm sure she can suggest an appropriate god of self-flagellation and remorse. Or, you could track down Heareld's family and find out how I can best help out with funeral arrangements and any short-term pecuniary embarrassments his death might have caused. Your choice."

"I don't know, sir. The blame—"

Vawn cut in. "Blame? The prescriptive assignment of blame does not always correspond with truth. This is a rare instance that I wish humans possessed a more sophisticated control of Outside Entities. As it is you cannot rely on summoning them consistently and once you do you've little positive control. That is probably why the closest thing to a practical use for them you can find is to have your battle sorcerers conjure them. This in the hope the Entities will blunder in the direction of the enemy instead of slaughtering your own troops. The Haptha, thankfully, have achieved greater precision."

Dahlia could see Gurton wearing his smile of polite attention, wanting Vawn to get at least within shouting distance of a point.

Vawn cleared his throat. "In Port Weir, a litigant can demand an Event Audit. It is a difficult—and expensive—summoning, but it can be illuminating. Two Outside Entities are summoned. Whether they are somehow related or whether their planes of reality are wholly separate I do not know, nor do I care. One of the Entities can ascertain veracity or falsehood. Useful in a trial. The other Entity possesses a gift of capturing evidentiary circumstances of a brief moment of the past—reflections in a wine goblet or the eyes of a dying man, the sounds captured by a cupped leaf or echoing along a corridor. This Entity thus provides context with which to evaluate the findings of the truthsaying Entity."

Gurton Lantik frowned. Then he nodded. "I can see that. A man's found with a stolen loaf of bread in his hand. But it don't mean he stole it. 'Yes' or 'no' can mislead."

"A straightforward example, Gurton. An image gleaned from a puddle of water might show the loaf tumbling from the back of a cart. A satisfactory verdict is one based on a complete picture of events. There is Truth and then there is—"

"Justice?"

"Rarely, Gurton. But I like to think it can happen."

And now Dahlia did not want to leave the employ of this Shark. Who would not want to work for a man with such a sense of fair play? And did she even have another option? She'd no family to return to. She'd just have to suck it up, keep her head down and hope she'd not become implicated. And yet at the same time Dahlia felt a compulsion to confess, to clear the air. Her lips parted, seemingly without her volition. Trust the mercy of a man who believed in the possibility of justice. But, no, that same fair play she admired would force him to fire her at the least, see her hanged in Retribution Square at worst. How could it be otherwise? Besides, she no longer considered herself culpable in Heareld's death. Trader Vawn was right not to fault Gurton Lantik for something he'd not done. And she should not fault herself for an action committed beyond the scope of her actual transgression.

Blame for the theft lay at Dahlia's doorstep. Trader Vawn appeared as distressed by the loss as she'd ever seen him. So, that guilt she'd have to bear. Heareld's murder? Some other hand had held the knife. She should take the weight of his death from her shoulders. But if she could rectify matters, see the stolen items returned, could she not cleanse herself of her actual guilt? Could she then continue her duties with a clear conscience?

Yes, she decided. The answer was yes.

Chapter 9 - Tallying the Score

Brick was bulling through Retribution Square at noon, the masses parting before him. He wondered what it said about Kalapo that its most popular public space was its venue for executions. What entertainment did people find in watching men gasp out their last breaths at the end of a rope? Brick had witnessed death. During the Mercantile War, he'd gutted more than one Shark with his spear. In the possession of the Fury he'd experienced battle exhilaration, a savage sense of triumph. But it never amounted to what he'd call enjoyment. The deaths did not entertain him. He'd felt the satisfaction of victory, the kind of pleasure that came with overcoming an opponent. And, later, relief at remaining alive. But not fun. Never for a minute.

The crowds, gathered at Retribution Square to eat a midday bite, exuded an anticipatory eagerness, an eagerness to see a man die. The hope was there in the widened, shining eyes, overloud talk, nervous jackrabbiting of the knee. The bloodlust didn't limit itself to any particular type. Truck farmers taking in the city sights and pausing for a meal before returning to the farmstead. Apprentices prolonging an errand or skipping out from work. University students swilling wine from earthenware bottles. A pair of off duty Horse Guardsmen laughing and peacocking about in their armor and cloaks. Women carrying shopping baskets heaped with bread, sausage, berries, apples, corn, and other autumn produce. Acolytes from nearby Priests' Promenade mingling, pretending to proselytize.

Retribution Square filled an open space west of the Magistery and east of Electors' Hall. Kalapo's elite inn, the Governance, rose to the north, set back from a wide, brick-walled lawn strewn with sloping backed chairs from which its guests could watch the lethal proceedings without the need to rub elbows with the crowd. To the south the elaborate facade of Indenture House concealed the barn-like structure behind. The pride of Kalapo, this architecture framing the Square. The place locals showed visitors, along with the eclectic designs lining Priests' Promenade and the elegant new construction appearing in Merchants' Reach.

The hangman's platform in the Square's center served as the focal point. Despite the grandeur of the surrounding buildings, it was the gallows that drew the eye. The support posts lifted the killing stage high. Uprights stage right and stage left lofted the crossbeam even higher, a lengthy stretch of pine that could accommodate a dozen kicking airdancers at any one time.

Brick watched a trio of stevedores arrive from Wharf Street, filing past the side of the Magistery. They were munching on loaves and taking turns at a bottle. Brick grunted, feeling the Fury stir deep within him, then return to quiescence. He'd tried to get on as a stevedore after his involuntary mustering out of the Clackmat Army. But he'd not been related to anyone in the Dockman's Guild, and no Elector owed him any favors. He could have done the work, even with his leg. Wouldn't have ended up in this fucked-up situation if he'd gotten the job. People who unloaded barges seldom had to worry about throat-slitting Sharks and turncoat lock-pickers.

Fuck it. He didn't have time for regrets. He returned to scanning faces for Glum and Nahl. Shib followed in his wake, staying right on his heels.

"A ghoulish lot, you humans," Shib said. "So excited to view death, you fill this plaza every day hoping the Magistrate has passed a death sentence that morning."

Brick shrugged, Shib still harping on this. "Different back home?" he asked. Not that he cared. He wanted to encourage conversation. Shib hadn't assembled more than two sentences during the entirety of the walk from Highmark Street. Wasn't like Shib. How could he dazzle Brick with his wit if he kept his mouth shut.

"Yes. We hold a more pragmatic view of criminal justice."

"How so? Got a list of fines in the margins of the lawbook? Deposit this many Petals with the court for assault, this many for arson?"

"Not precisely, Brick, no. We have capital punishment, yes, but we don't dispense it with the free hand of your Clackmat authorities. We limit it to cases of murder and rape. And even then, we don't make a spectacle out of it. The offender is locked away without ceremony. Then one morning he wakes up to see his headless torso on the bunk next to him. I think that's the cruelest bit: the prisoner never knows when the headsman is going to visit his cell in the night."

Brick shuddered, thinking about that. The devious, subtle torture of it both impressed and horrified him. He glanced over his shoulder at Shib, then returned to

168

searching through the crowd. He noted the looks Shib received. The good people of Kalapo still did not much care for Sharks. The size and vaguely sinister presence of the Haptha provided some protection from any sort of mob scene turning ugly, but there were no guarantees. Brick taking point, shouldering through the Retribution Square gawkers, probably contributed to Shib's safety as much as did Shib himself.

"Nice bit of deterrent, boss. Creepy, though. But what do you do with pickpockets, bandits, blackmailers. Or, you know, Nahl?"

"Options, Brick. Judges have quite a menu to select from. Might snip a finger off a pickpocket, for instance. Or simply incarcerate the malefactors for various periods, dependent on the perceived severity of the infraction. The felon may opt to decrease the sentence by accepting a shorter term of hard labor, buy his way out of jail."

"So, there is a list?"

"You might say that. Though the Confederacy's jurisprudence offers a similar approach."

"What do you mean?" Brick asked. Near as he could tell the Magistrate mostly handed out either hanging or flogging.

"Over there, Brick," said Shib, pointing past the gallows platform to Indenture House.

"Shroud's tits," Brick muttered. Spotting Glum amidst the crowd spared him from having to concede a point.

Glum Arent sat on an upturned bucket, one of the many discarded makeshift seats littering the Square. He was offering a bottle to Nahl, who stood above him, arms crossed and refusing the drink. Only a few steps away, about three bodies away, stood the off-duty Horse Guards.

"Clever," Brick said.

"What's that?" asked Shib. Then, following the line Brick pointed with his chin, "Yes, about as secure a meet as one could hope for. Still, keep an eye on Nahl, Brick. He might try to perforate my kidneys, Guardsmen or no."

"Hail to thee, esteemed erstwhile comrades," Glum said, raising the bottle in salute.

"Alliteration," Brick said, "He's started early. I'd say he's about two bottles from total incoherence."

"Meaning I'm at the top of my form at this, the moment of our conclave," Glum said. He attempted a little bow and almost tumbled from his perch on the bucket.

Nahl snorted. "Get on with it. Quit fucking around."

"Nahl, you possess no instinct for theatrics. At least allow me the opportunity to greet my bosom comrade, that most fearsome of barroom brawlers, Brick."

"I don't figure you've got much standing to call me friend, Glum. Seems to me friends show a bit more loyalty than you've done."

"Well, yes," Glum said. He took a long pull at the bottle, coughed. "There may be some weight to your exegesis on friendship. Could be why I didn't use the word 'friend.' You did."

"By all means," Shib said, "let's discuss the fleeting nature of friendship, the thin edge upon which self-interest and interpersonal relationships balance. I, for one, have most of the day to devote to philosophy."

Brick noted Shib had taken up a position to his left, the two humans providing a buffer between the two Haptha. The boss wasn't kidding. He truly believed Nahl might go after him, in the bright light of the noonday sun, in a crowded plaza, not three paces from what passed for the minions of law in Kalapo.

"Nahl, our former employer has a fine grasp of sarcasm," Glum said. "Perhaps, unlike you, he possesses a flair for theatrics. At the same time, he makes a good point. While theater endures, the day wanes. So, to business."

"Maybe it's 'cause I used to enjoy it," Brick said, "but I never really noticed how much shit you talk."

Nahl snorted again. "You ain't wrong. He's like a shit fountain."

"That's about the sort of poetic imagery I'd expect from you, Nahl," Glum said. "Fine. I can read an audience. You are a simple crowd and want straightforward action. So, Shib, have you considered the revised terms of sale?"

Brick had to admire the poet's confidence. He wondered if it was due more to Nahl's presence or the wine.

Shib took the attitude in stride.

"I have considered your proposal, Glum," Shib said. "Now, come. I've been generous with you at the tavern, turned a blind eye to some fudging of your bar tally."

"With the prices you charge for drink that's two steps shy of vinegar, you ought to turn two blind eyes," Glum said.

"I imagine you've shopped the competition and know my house wine is a loss leader. Save the lies for the gullible. Your usual customers, I believe."

"No need to get nasty, Shib."

"No? I offered generous terms for the job. You accepted, then reneged. A touch of nastiness is justified."

Nahl slid forward a half step. "I'm up for nasty," he said. "Say when."

"There's no profit in it," Shib said. "My consideration of Glum's proposal is all about profit, Nahl. Added to that, any result that leads to greater distance from you is of value as well."

Glum half-laughed, half-choked on a gulp of wine. He said, "So, you admit there is benefit to derive from my renegotiation. You do get something for the additional coin."

"What's he mean by 'distance?'" Nahl asked. "Shit, Glum, I ain't said nothing about leaving Kalapo."

"Might want to consider it," Brick said and bared his teeth in what he hoped was a menacing smile. The smile faded, but not due to Nahl's unchanging expression. Behind Glum and Nahl, Brick could see a growing clump of red tunics.

"Fuck. Just what we need," he said.

"What's that?" asked Shib.

"Maybe nothing. They might not remember me." Brick didn't believe it even as he said it. He'd done enough damage to members of the Clackmat Drayage and Cartage Guild that some of them, at least, would remember him. Some would want payback.

They were pushing through the crowd, not a purposeful advance, but the conscious aggression of a united front. The bunch making a statement by their presence, announcing their group identity and importance. However, once they caught sight of Brick . . .

"Maybe we ought to reconvene tomorrow," Brick said.

"Fuck that," said Nahl. "We're settling this shit right now."

"Nothing's going to get settled if we end up in a brawl in the middle of Retribution Square."

"Who's 'we,' human?" Nahl asked.

"I think the point he's trying to make, Nahl," Glum said, "is that . . . oh, shit, they've spotted Brick. C'mon. Let's move."

Brick looked again. Glum wasn't kidding him. He counted about a dozen of them, determined looking and starting to pick up the pace, shoving out of the way anyone who didn't clear a path fast enough. Big, well-fed, the lot of them. Brick didn't see any sign of weapons, but that meant little. Each of them could have easily stashed three or four daggers beneath those red tunics.

Brick checked over his shoulder. The two Horse Guardsmen were making themselves scarce. Must be time to collect a bribe.

"Yeah," Brick said. "Let's move."

He headed left, toward the gallows and deeper into the crowd, hoping to slow pursuit. Under the shadowless noonday sun ropes hung stark and ominous from the crossbeam. Brick imagined himself swinging from the end of one, his swaying gradually decreasing until he depended unmoving like a sausage in a root cellar. He should never have gotten involved in this.

"Don't suppose we lost them," he said, parting a covey of women burdened with woven wicker shopping baskets and twine bags gravid with fresh produce.

"No. They dog our heels like the hounds of fate," Glum said.

"Shut up," said Nahl.

The wide, twin doors of Indenture House were closer now. Brick angled that way. Maybe the armed security inside might deter the guildsmen. Maybe. It was one thing for hired enforcers to convince the newly indentured of the reality of their new condition, alone, freshly tattooed, unarmed, and frightened. Might be it was another thing to face down a squad of determined guild thugs not likely to flinch at harsh language and threats.

Worth a try anyway.

The interior of Indenture House failed to match the elegant exterior. Instead of the palatial chambers and furnishing the facade suggested, the inside appeared more like a timber warehouse. Or perhaps a stable, considering the penned off sections stretching along either wall, beginning about twenty paces into the cavernous hall and extending to the far end.

Guards armed with staves flanked the doorway, armored in quilted gambesons dyed the yellow and blue of Indenture House. They did not appear to enjoy the warmth of the padded garments. Farther in and to the left a man sat on a stool, dipping a needle in an inkwell and tattooing the debt servitude links on the scrawny arm of a gaunt man in his late twenties, naked to the waist and shivering. Nearby stood another skinny loser, looked like he could be the brother of the one getting inked, just another debtor or petty criminal. He listened with slack inattention to the spiel of a gentleman who must patronize the same tailor as Trader Vawn. Finding out what he was in for if he agreed to sign away the next three-to-fifteen years of his life.

To the right assembled a cross-section of Clackmat industry. Prosperous farmers. Timber harvesters. Mine owners. Anyone who could use a supply of labor for minimal wages, payable up front to Indenture House. Indenture House would take the funds, pay off the debts or court mandated fines of the newly indentured, pocket its brokerage fee, and set aside the remaining pittance to await the poor bastard at the end of his term. Indenture House guards paraded prospects one at a time past the potential employers.

Brick thought about Livette passing through these walls. Crimson sparks flared in his peripheral vision. He took a deep breath, asserting control.

At Brick's approach, the two door sentries hitched their posture up a near immeasurable degree from slouching. "Welcome to Indenture House," said one. "Your business?" The man could barely be bothered to address them at all, let alone give a shit about their business.

"Browsing the stock," said Nahl before Brick could reply.

The first guard shrugged. The second passed them in with a jerk of his head.

Brick hustled, moving too fast to eyeball the pathetic spectacle of the caged losers on either side. It could have been him in one of these holding pens, easy. Without Shib offering him work, he might have sold off a few years of his life or been nicked for theft and given the choice between the gallows and this.

The four reached the midway point of the vast rectangular box. Little air circulated this deep into Indenture House and Brick could feel the sweat prickling at his neck. He reached back to sluice away the moisture when he heard the commotion from the front doors. Brick knew what that signified, but he glanced behind him anyway.

As he'd feared, the Indenture House enforcers hadn't provided much of a check to the pursuit. A wedge of red pushed through a line of yellow and blue, the latter putting up token resistance, if that.

"Keep moving," Brick said. "Go on, boss. You've got those long legs. Use them."

Shib didn't object. He lengthened his stride and outpaced the others. Brick figured Nahl would do the same, but he didn't. Glum, however, broke into a sprint.

Shouts followed. Brick refused to take another look behind. He attempted to summon a faster gait, but his leg throbbed in protest. The angry bellowing grew nearer. But so did the far wall and the back door, a modest exit sized to allow egress of only one at a time.

Closer. Judging from the noise, the guildsmen were closing as well. But Brick figured he'd reach the door. Then what?

"Go on, Nahl," Brick said. "I can hold the doorway." He stopped and swiveled on the heel of his good leg, then began walking backwards the remaining few steps to the door, giving Nahl a chance to squeeze by him and out the exit.

"Fuck that," Nahl said. The Shark hipped him aside, taking up a position next to him, the two of them blocking the doorway.

Brick shrugged. Standing within the doorway would be a good defensive position. But half of his back to the wall, and his left flank guarded by a murderous Haptha with a size and reach advantage over any attacker—not a bad defensive position either.

Nahl plucked a knife from a concealed sheath at his back. Exactly the sort of weapon Brick expected the Shark to have. Which was why Brick was toting the weighted baton stashed beneath his tunic, a hunk of oak as long as the measure of his elbow to his fingertips, the business end hollowed out and filled with a plug of iron.

"Don't suppose you want to talk about this?" Brick took a firm grip on his head basher, counted the opposition. Shit, ten of them. Not quite as many as he'd first estimated, but plenty to do the job.

"The Clackmat Cartage and Drayage Guild must be respected," said the red tunic in the center.

"That would be 'no' then," Brick said. On top of the dung heap he'd climbed for Shib he had to deal with this additional sack of crap? The Fury roiled in his gut and he let it. Respect? Their little club hauled stuff from one point to another. Useful, but hardly worth the high gloss shine they put on it. Self-important, overstuffed bags of shit. "Come on, let's get this over with."

Red flashes overlay his vision. He let the Fury out.

The ten guildsmen figured to overwhelm by sheer numbers, and why not? Ten against two ought to lead pretty quick to two on the ground getting stomped and kicked by the ten. But it didn't happen.

Brick caught the first man across his teeth with a swipe of his stick, the weighted end leaving a gleaming red mess punctuated with yellowish fragments. He took a wallop on his left shoulder from another guildsman and a boot to his middle. Neither blow sufficed to put him down. Brick grabbed the foot that had kicked him before it could return to the splintering plank floor. He yanked, lifting the guildsman off his feet, the man's flailing arms disrupting a pair of blows aimed at Brick's skull.

Brick pushed off from the wall at his back, lashed out left and right, then dropped back against the wall. He felt Nahl still at his shoulder, saw the flash of Nahl's reddened knife blade.

A gleam directly in front of him focused him on his own fight. Nahl could take care of himself. Clubs clattered to the floor and daggers emerged. But the guildsmen hesitated. This hadn't gone as planned.

Brick gave them a smile. One of them—the spokesman, Brick thought—pushed out a tentative jab. Brick swung, broke the bones in the man's knife hand, the blade falling to join the clubs on the floor.

The red tunic screamed, backpedaling and holding his smashed hand to his chest with his good hand. The others facing Brick glanced about, looking for direction.

At that point, the Indenture House enforcers hit the remnants of the guild squad from behind. The two lines entangled in a thrashing scrum.

"Let's go," Brick said, making for the door. He saw Nahl take the time to stoop and thrust his dagger into the back of one of the red tunics sprawled on the planks.

"Ain't true what they say," Nahl said as they emerged onto Market Street. "Red uniforms don't hide the blood."

Market Street passed along the rear exterior of Indenture House, the backside of the building plain and unadorned. Market Street ran from the river wharves up to Market Square, about a five-minute walk farther uphill from where Brick stood. He looked around for Shib and found him about twenty paces away, toward the river. Glum waited there too, though keeping a cautious distance from Shib. Not a bad idea, Brick figured. But Shib, unlike Nahl, probably wasn't going to knife someone in broad daylight in front of several witnesses.

Brick wondered if maybe he shouldn't follow Nahl's example, beat the Shark to the punch right then, right there. And realized it was the Fury talking, still wanting to lash out. Nahl happened to be nearest, so it shouldn't come as a surprise that Brick rationalized a bit of immediate violence. Instead he got a grip on his rage, removing the Fury from the reins and nudging it aside. He'd had enough violence for the afternoon. In fact, he began regretting the bout he'd just indulged in; his left shoulder began to ache and he could imagine the size of the bruise he felt swelling on his stomach.

"So, where did we leave off?" Shib asked when Brick and Nahl arrived. "Oh, yes. We were discussing Glum Arent's proposal that I pay twice the agreed amount and for half the agreed merchandise. A very tempting offer, I must confess."

Glum edged nearer now that Nahl resumed his guardianship. "You're telling the truth, sarcasm notwithstanding, Shib."

"Oh? What makes you say that?"

"Let me tell you a story," Glum said. Then, "Shut up," as both Brick and Nahl vocalized non-verbal protests. "He *is* tempted, and I've got just the parable to explain. It's a segment of a homily from the scriptures of the Four-Fold Soteriologists, likely a borrowing from the myth-cycles of the pre-Tlikalats."

"Get on with it," Brick said. Glum could talk. He seemed to have lost his bottle in the chase, and without that Brick doubted the man had anything else to do with his mouth.

"Lack of patience is symptomatic of the barbarian, Brick. So, with your permission: In the mists of antiquity, in the time of our fathers' fathers' most distant ancestors, a young man was born to poor, but noble parents. The story goes on to tell of portents and precocious doings, but that's all padding. Essentially what we're dealing with here is the archetypal third son, so you know an adventure awaits him."

"I do?" Brick said, and immediately regretted it. He did know, and even though he no longer held any thoughts of friendship for him, or even a grudging respect for what minor gift the poet did hold, he still felt the sting of the scornful glance Glum threw at him.

"Yes, you do. Or should, if you had the brains to rub two fables together. Likely you've heard a dozen stories of the same stripe. Shit, Brick, you took an arrow in the leg, not the head. Anyways, our hero tumbles along the familiar path, falls in love with the local king's daughter. They plan to get married—the hero and the daughter that is, not the hero and the king. But she worries— for obvious reasons—that her father won't grant his blessing to her penniless fiancé. Turns out not to matter so much. She's kidnapped by a fearsome ogre, for some reason or other. The king offers her hand in marriage to whomever can rescue her. Our hero searches for the ogre to save the princess. He encounters various trials along the way."

Shib coughed. "To echo my associate Brick, get on with it. You seem to have a point. Reach it."

"Are you in a hurry, Shib? I thought you Haptha prided yourself on the development of your civilization, above that of we barbaric Clackmat. Where's your patience?"

"We're loitering within sight of Indenture House. So why don't you get to your point before we're rousted for rioting? And I wouldn't mind returning to the Chipped Tankard before the afternoon customers begin to arrive. One of us here has a business to run."

"Fine. We can walk and talk." Glum moseyed riverward, taking the easier downhill option. "As I was saying, our hero faced a series of trials. The standard slate of tests of heroism, and not relevant to the point I'm trying to make, so in the interest of not boring the impatient I'll skip them. Despite their adding to the flavor, pacing, and ambience of the narrative."

Glum paused and Brick figured he was hoping one of them would ask him to please go on, expand, tell the story. No one said a thing.

Glum cleared his throat. "Jumping ahead in the tale, our hero has reached the top of a steep ravine. The castle of the princess-stealing ogre occupies the bottom of the ravine, partly built into the walls of either cliff face. A narrow switchback trail leads down to the castle. And waiting for our hero, as if he'd expected him, is Talepos, a sort of trickster demon who makes an appearance in a lot of Four-Fold Soteriologist's parables.

"Spread out around Talepos along the edge of the cliff is a variety of items, like a merchant's caravan had tipped over and spilled its cargo. Talepos addresses the hero by name—a name none of you bothered asking, I noticed—and tells him he's allowed to select any one item from the inventory. The story grinds a bit here, running through an exhaustive list. I'll limit myself to a few highlights. There's a magic sword capable of killing any manner of beast or monster, a coil of rope, a suit of impervious magical armor. There's a sack of coin, sufficient to set up the hero for life—the demon tempting the hero to abandon the quest, you see?"

They were nearing the wharves now, and the noises rising up from the river began to rival the volume of Glum's voice. Brick nudged them off south onto Cooper's Way. Glum carried on, not seeming to notice or care which direction they went.

"The hero ponders his options. It's a pretty big decision to make. But here's the point, Shib: the hero kept his goal in mind when he weighed his choices. The sack of gold would be nice, sure. But then he wouldn't get the princess. The various other choices might or might not help him. He didn't want maybes. He wanted certainty."

"What did he choose?" Nahl asked.

"What? Oh, he chose the rope. He lowered himself down the cliff, entered the castle through an upper window and escaped with the princess without the ogre ever realizing he was there. Eye on the prize, Shib, eye on the prize. You know what you need. You want the credentials. Don't bother denying it. Focus on that. The money is secondary. You'll replace those Petals in no time once you get your hands on the medallion. Same with the pendant. You have no need of costume jewelry. You can buy a stone twice as nice in a year or two, once you've scammed the good burghers of a dozen or so towns out of all their worldly possessions."

Brick was impressed. Give Glum's mouth a running start and he could manage a glibly persuasive line.

"This may come as a surprise to you," Shib said, "but not to me: You are not as smart as you think you are. I bargained for two items. I demand both of them. What I want with them is my business. Your speculations do not interest me."

"Now Shib, you've got to ask yourself if you're better off getting half of the items or none."

"No, Glum. You must ask yourself if you are better off getting paid by me, or if you are willing to risk fencing stolen merchandise yourself. Do you know many other people willing to take the goods off your hands? Even one? Or just me?"

"Hold on," said Nahl. "This is bullshit. I'm going to get paid. One way or another." Nahl glided forward a step, into easy knife reach of Shib.

Brick edged a half step to his right, trying to position himself in Nahl's blind spot. They were nearing Runoff Alley. A short southeast jog up the alley would bring them to Highmark Street. Probably too close to Shib's turf for either Nahl or Glum to be comfortable.

"Nahl, I remain willing to pay," Shib was saying. "I am a reasonable businessman. In fact, I'm willing to offer four times the original amount."

Glum grunted. "That is something to think about. Though not precisely what a Four-Fold Soteriologist prelate would counsel after delivering his parable."

"It's enough money for you to start your own religion," Shib said. "You and Nahl can be prophets of the new, true path to enlightenment."

They'd come to a stop, a few paces shy of the intersection with Runoff Alley.

"Fine, Shib. You talked me into it," Glum said, though Brick thought he sounded hesitant, and that troubled him.

"Good," Shib said. "Though understand you will have to exercise a modicum of patience."

"What's this shit?" Nahl asked. "You just said you was going to pay."

"I am. But four times the original offer is a substantial amount of money. More than I have on hand. I will need to liquidate quite a lot of merchandise. And frankly, Nahl, most of the merchandise you've provided recently is low value crap. There's not a lot of demand for second-hand silk chair cushions. So, again, patience. I will work my contacts, make arrangements, and accumulate the funds.

"Deal?"

"Deal," said Glum. Nahl did not object.

"Excellent. This isn't the outcome I originally had in mind. But as you say, Glum, 'eye on the prize.' Once I assemble the coin, we can work out where to make the exchange."

***

"Nahl," Glum said as the two thieves wended their way to Stumpville, "I think a drink is called for." He felt his fingertips trembling and hoped it wasn't evident. Nahl was too much like an untamed beast. If Nahl sensed Glum's fear or indecision he might turn on him.

Glum had dropped the bottle he'd brought to the meet during the flight from the Clackmat Cartage and Drayage Guild. A rich, fruity red, last fall's vintage. He'd filched the bottle from the Float Dreamers' cellars while lending a hand preparing for their morning devotionals. They'd paid him three copper bits for the assistance, and one brother—still in thrall to the previous evening's devotionals—had purchased a sonnet. Not even one of Glum's better sonnets.

Considering how the day had begun, Glum should be feeling positive. As it happened, he felt balanced on the cusp of despair. He missed that bottle already. A drink would buck him up, help him work through the decision he'd already half made, and give him the impetus to see it through. Positively.

"I don't know, Glum. You drink too much," Nahl said.

"Nahl, I didn't know you cared," Glum said.

"I don't give two bent copper bits. But until we get paid you've got to keep your shit focused."

"You're absolutely correct, Nahl. I need to maintain focus. Which is precisely why I need a drink."

"Fine. Just keep your shit together, or I'll shove your head into a bucket until you sober up."

"Wouldn't that simply drown me?"

"Either one works for me."

Glum figured he'd let Nahl have the last word on the subject. The thought of getting a drink eased him away from desperation. He felt magnanimous. He felt almost sorry for the Shark.

They found a shack on the outskirts of Stumpville selling a vile admixture of apple cider and the discarded lees of a proper vintage fermented into a thin wine. Glum purchased a stoneware jug with one of the copper bits given him by the Float Dreamers. He levered the wax plug from the mouth with the edge of a quill pen he'd borrowed from the Verians a couple of years back. He took a long pull, his Adam's apple bobbed up and down several times before he lowered the jug.

Nahl sniffed. "How can you drink that? It smells like dead cat marinated in dog piss."

"Yes. It's ghastly," Glum said. He took another drink and started walking. "Nice imagery by the way. Dead cat and dog piss. Beautiful."

Soon they were weaving around the eroding stumps that made navigating Stumpville's dirt lanes such a joy. Glum considered that he might be weaving a trifle more than the obstacles required. Good. His mood was distinctly tilting toward positive.

"Glum, I was wondering," Nahl said.

"Good. Curiosity is a sign of intelligence."

". . . Fuck you."

They walked on in silence.

"Sorry, Nahl. What were you wondering?"

"Why you agreed to sell the Periapt? I thought that was our big score."

"A good question with several answers. First, Shib offered a shitload of money. I'm greedy. Second, it would have been suspicious to refuse. Third, we're not going to sell the Panaegic Periapt. Shib was talking crap. Sure, he'd like to get his hands on the power. But what he really wants is Vawn's credentials. He shows up with a chestful of Petals and we show up with only the medallion, you think he's really going to walk away? Not after going through all the trouble to get the money together."

"Guess not. And if he does, I'll shank the fucker and we can keep it all."

"That's the spirit."

They approached Nahl's squat, Glum thinking he'd about seen the last of this sort of squalor. Life would be different for him starting real soon. No more cadged meals. No more hustling just to put together enough for a cheap glass of hooch. No more tolerating disrespect and inability to appreciate his gifts.

The Panaegic Periapt would see to that. And, unquestionably, the money. A lot of money.

"That was a pretty good story," Nahl was saying as he lifted aside the door to the tumbledown ruin. "The one about the hero and the ogre and the princess. Wish Shib had given you time to tell the whole thing."

"Thank you, Nahl. Glad to see a Haptha with an appreciation for the narrative arts. Here, let me get you a seat."

Glum scrounged up a splintering ladder-back chair, missing one leg. He propped it up with a crate full of stolen tin kitchenware.

Nahl gave Glum a look the poet couldn't read, but sat down on the chair, letting a sigh escape. The Shark crossed his legs before him, stretched. He hadn't said anything about it, but Glum figured he'd taken a few lumps during the fight at Indenture House.

"Here's the thing about that parable," Glum said. "I provided the moral the Four Fold Soteriologist's derive from it." Glum rummaged about behind Nahl, then loudly dragged a box toward him, scraping it across the warped and splintered floor, bouncing over the gaps of missing floorboards. "But I think they got it completely wrong. They celebrate the hero's decision, but they are praising error. He chose the wrong item."

Glum set down the box a pace behind Nahl. "The rope was for chumps." He set the point of his quill knife against the base of Nahl's skull, right below the upper vertebra, and pushed. Nahl stiffened and Glum felt a stab of panic as the blade met resistance from the cartilage. Then the blade ground through. Nahl released a series of panting breaths, his arms and legs spasming. The spasms slowed, stopped. Nahl slumped forward, his weight dragging the hilt of the knife from Glum's sweating palm. He fell with a thump that raised a short-lived misting of dust from the floorboards.

"The hero should have taken the magic sword," Glum said, taking self-conscious pleasure at the gratuitous theatricality of addressing the Shark's corpse. "After that, kill Talepos. Then he wouldn't need to choose. He could keep it all, including the money. And then he could kill the ogre, rescue the princess. It's all a question of power, my dead friend. Once you have power, no more shitty choices. You can have it all."

Glum sat on the ladder-back chair, put his feet up on Nahl's back. The surging torrent of vomit caught him by surprise. He just managed to turn his head to avoid coating his legs and Nahl's corpse with bile.

His first murder. Both easier and more difficult than he'd anticipated. He wiped his mouth with the back of his hand, then studied Nahl, his eyes locking on the handle of the quill knife jutting from the Shark's spine. Good riddance, Glum supposed. He did not like Sharks. He did not like their victory over the Confederacy. He did not like their arrogance. He did not like their calculating outlook. He did not like their irreligion.

He'd never taken up arms against the Haptha, not like Brick. Never killed one before. It did not provide the satisfaction he'd hoped. Though he did like the prospect of getting Nahl's share of payment for the robbery. Doubled, then doubled again. Worth this corpse at his feet? Nahl, dead, and far from the land of his birth, the enigmatic home of the Haptha. What must it have been like, leaving all he knew so far behind? What must have been his last thought, realizing he was going to die here, in Kalapo, in an abandoned Stumpville hovel?

No. Glum tried, but he couldn't work up any sympathy for Nahl. He'd never liked him. In fact, Glum had probably saved his own life; Nahl was likely to have slipped a knife between his ribs as soon as they got the money. This was a simple case of preemptive self-defense.

Nahl's death had been inevitable, ever since Shib had let slip that he'd recognized the Periapt. The Shark had been tight-lipped after, probably worried he'd said too much, that an information broker with Glum's connections might find out the truth if he revealed any more. Or maybe he'd said as much as he had for precisely the opposite reason, that he discounted Glum, considered him beneath notice. People had a tendency to underestimate Glum. He'd found ways to make that pay. And he was thinking he'd now find a way to make those who underestimated him pay.

Glum stood and retrieved the jug. He took a long swallow to clear his mouth of the taste of vomit. Then he searched through Nahl's clothes, pocketing what coin he found.

He sat again, counting the meager take, and pondering his next move. Despite what he'd told Nahl, Glum couldn't be certain Shib would pay up for only the medallion. The Shark was aware of at least some of the potency of the Panaegic Periapt. He might harbor schemes similar to Glum's own. And without Nahl as protection, how could he guard against treachery? How could he be sure Brick wouldn't simply smash his head against the nearest wall until his face was a red, pulpy mess?

Glum knew he couldn't count on friendship. Looking again at Nahl's corpse at his feet, he admitted he wouldn't trust himself if he were Brick. And he couldn't count on racial ties. Brick didn't share his distaste for the Haptha. Even though Brick had fought them, even though his leg was permanently fucked up due to a Shark arrow. He still seemed to like them. Or, it could just be his absurd sense of loyalty. Glum figured Brick for the kind of man who needed a master. A dog, that's what he was. The Clackmat Army used to fill the role of master, but stopped feeding him and kicked him off the porch once his usefulness ended. So, he'd taken up a new master, Shib.

No, Glum would need to take steps. This would require careful planning. He took another swallow from the jug. The stuff really wasn't that bad. He could see developing a taste for it. Jug clutched protectively against his body, he navigated the dodgy stairs to the street, leaving Nahl's squat without a second glance.

The evening sun threw long shadows along this stretch of River Drag. Glum kicked up clouds of dirt as he walked. Timber workers shared the lane with him, heading home after the day spent in the West Hills taking down trees. Some wore debt servitude tattoos. Those tended to wander by themselves. The career lumberjacks travelled in groups, disdaining the companionship of those who took up the job from compulsion. Besides, it was a perilous occupation. A high percentage of the indentured timber workers would be killed or maimed on the job. Glum could understand not feeling any particular desire to get close to someone likely to have a tree crush his skull the next day.

Still, they had their work, freeman and indentured servant alike. And they were making their way to homes or taverns for the evening meal. All considered, that was more than Glum had. More than he'd ever had. Except the tavern. No home. No steady work, bringing in only what funds he could hustle from his pen, or the sale of information, or from flat out larceny. By all the gods on Priests' Promenade, that would change.

Glum directed his steps south and east, making for the Boulevard of the Heavens. He'd need a place to hole up for the night. And not one of his usual crash pads; he might have mentioned any one of them to Brick during a moment of bibulous indiscretion. Now was the time for caution and discipline.

He passed a manor house, one of the grand edifices erected by the timber magnates who'd been instrumental in building Kalapo from a nondescript market town into the capital of the Clackmat Confederation. The centuries of expansion and accretion were evident even in the fading light. The upper story and crenellations of the original tower remained visible above wings and additions from at least three distinctive architectural periods. The tower itself was a reminder of the wild and uncertain days when the dangers of the timber business came from more than just the trees themselves. The raids, battles, feuds, and sieges of that era still formed the basis of several epic cycles that helped create Kalapo's poetic traditions. Glum found himself reciting chunks of verse as he walked, recounting the rise and demise of Ferrod Links Mandes.

The jug held only a few swallows by the time he reached the western terminus of Priests' Promenade, where the boulevard petered out into a dirt track. Priests' Promenade remained a work in progress. It would continue marching arrow straight up from the Mette so long as new religions found footholds among Kalapo's seekers after enlightenment. And there were always plenty of those, gods' bless 'em.

A heap of stone and timber currently held the distinction—and the stigma—of being the final temple on the Priests' Promenade, a roughly cubical structure, massively built, though appearing rather slipshod, more an assemblage of building material than the result of architectural design. This was the house of worship of the Third Iteration of the Entropic Order. Glum grinned, remembering his attempts to explain to several of the acolytes why he found the name "Entropic Order" so funny. With that failure, he hadn't even bothered delving into the comedic ground suggested by the question of what had happened to the first two iterations.

Nihilists. No sense of humor.

Though humor might have explained the brightly painted brick, chevroned in yellow and indigo, that made up the Entropic Order's section of the road surface. Cheerful, comfortable to walk on, and providing reasonable traction. Glum would have gone with worn cobbles, like those before the Fullers Brotherhood, and kept an acolyte with a bucket of water on duty to keep the stones wet. That'd be entropy in action.

At that moment, as Glum chuckled at his own wit, an acolyte did appear, though without a bucket. Wearing the Order's garb of black trousers and long red cassock, the man trudged down the two steps leading from the temple to the street. Glum recognized him: Aljak Vest, about Glum's own age. A gaunt figure, emaciated even. The kind of man Glum would expect to pace, stalk, or maybe even parade. But not trudge. That, however, was Aljak. A thin man with a fat man inside struggling to get out.

"Aljak, come have a taste," Glum said. He hoisted the bottle in emphasis and was surprised at how light it felt.

"Glum Arent? Is that you?" Aljak took a few more ponderous steps closer. "You might want to lower your voice. You are still on the Void Deacon's shitlist for that epigram you wrote about us."

"Hey, that was a commission. It wasn't an expression of my personal opinion. And I offered to write a riposte to the Pontifical Henotics for the same price they paid."

"He doesn't see it that way," Aljak said. Though Glum noted the acolyte eyeing the jug and making no attempt to shoo him away. Glum doubted Brick would think to search this end of the boulevard. A safe place to bed down if he could talk Aljak into inviting him to spend the night. Or at least looking the other way when Glum sneaked in.

"Yes. Well, there's an equal number of people and opinions," Glum said. "Might even be more opinions, come to think of it. We do tend to change our minds." He waggled the jug at Aljak again.

This time Aljak accepted the offer, downed a slug of the mixture. He coughed, spat. "That's awful."

"It's empty," said Glum, upending the jug to watch a final, sad bead hug the lip before dripping to the brick below. "Come on, let's get a proper drink. I'm buying." Normally what Glum meant when he thought of him and Aljak sharing a bottle or two was limited to the contents. Glum had shared none of the expense. He figured he'd contributed sufficiently as a raconteur, Aljak being the four type until about the fourth or fifth glass, at which time he developed a belly laugh, a prodigious appetite, and a gregarious bonhomie. But now was not the time for frugality. He flashed one of the coins he'd liberated from Nahl's body.

Aljak lifted both eyebrows. "Truly a sign of end times. The end is expected. You buying, however, is a mystery in need of investigating. Lead on."

Most watering holes near Priests' Promenade catered selectively to clientele of a specific creed. Glum Arent and Aljak Vest had shared a bottle or two in some of the few taverns that served indiscriminately the sundry priests, philosophers, and prophets of the Boulevard of the Heavens that were willing to tolerate each other's presence— such taverns often enough located downstairs from a brothel. The brothels tended toward the ecumenical.

They took seats at a small table in a dim corner of one of the more tolerant establishments. The tavern buzzed. The girls circulated, distinguishing the drinkers from the johns. The staff had yet to light the candles and lamps to keep the growing night at bay. The cooking fire in the kitchen contributed little out in the taproom. Glum liked the atmospheric mood of the increasing gloom, finding it conspiratorial.

"To mysteries," Glum said, lifting his clay cup of a not half-bad house red. An earthenware carafe on the table promised more.

Aljak only grunted. But he drained his cup off at a swallow and poured more.

"Little mysteries keep the world exciting," Glum said. "This coin in my possession is one such mystery. Let us say only that I am doing my part to advance entropy. Certainly, you can appreciate that."

"You never did understand the Entropic Order," Aljak said. "We do not advocate decay, death, or destruction for the pleasure of it. There are plenty who do that already. We simply recognize the hard truths of existence. Murder, disease, war, poverty. These are the inevitable consequences of life. Prolonging existence is thus prolonging misery. That is true cruelty. The Entropic Order is an instrument of mercy."

"Then to mystery and mercy." Glum raised another toast.

"Speaking of mercy, Aljak," Glum said a couple of cups later, "I don't suppose you could offer a spare cell for the night, could you? Nothing elaborate. A spot on the floor and a blanket would be a mercy."

A candle now flickered on the table. Aljak lowered his gaze, hiding his eyes from the candle flame. Telling Glum he was hiding something else as well. "Perhaps. Mercy I could probably manage tonight. Tomorrow night would be a problem. Tomorrow night is for mystery, not mercy."

"That's a good line, Aljak. Mind if I use it? Maybe you should have been a poet." Glum playing it cool, keeping his eyes on his wine, not wanting to alert Aljak that the acolyte had piqued his curiosity.

"Do you think so? I half-suspected I might have a gift. I think the wine inspires me." Aljak took another long draft, perhaps as a poetic gesture.

"Oh, absolutely," Glum said. "Wine's inspirational qualities are unquestionable." But he had to keep Aljak on this new, intriguing subject. "So what sort of mystery is afoot tomorrow night? Something suitably poetic for the Entropic Order's unrecognized bard?"

He refilled Aljak's cup.

Chapter 10 - Belief and Power

Brick jerked upright in bed, flinging the sweat-soaked blanket to one side. The bulk of the dream still floated in his imagination, like a cloud before a wind whisks it to shreds. He'd been on a battlefield. Awake he couldn't recall having ever set foot on that spot, but in the dream, it had seemed familiar. And after all, they tended to look pretty much the same from the perspective of the line soldier.

A fog shrouded valley, hills sloping gently to either side. From some trick of dream perspective Brick could see both the Clackmat army, augmented by its Leyvan allies, and the Haptha army facing off, each with its back to a hillside. Through the fog strode a colossal horror, something like a bipedal reptilian mule, the height of a watch tower. It sent a deafening bray echoing through the valley as it stalked toward the Clackmat lines.

The patch of fog near Brick took on a yellow tinge. Somehow his vantage point had shifted and he was seeing from within his own ranks. Though, oddly, from deep within the formation. Within the dream that seemed normal. In reality, Brick had always been positioned near, or in, the front line. The yellow mist blossomed orange and another monstrosity took shape within. A boar-like head swung at the end of an impossibly long neck, the neck growing from a muscular, low slung body, part terrier, part elephant.

The Clackmat summoned war demon shuffled toward the Haptha mule-lizard, head swinging from side-to-side on its absurd neck. Then the swinging stopped. The neck curved about, facing back along the demon's body toward the Clackmat ranks. The war demon huffed, a bull's angry snort. Flame jetted from its nostrils and curled up into yellow smoke. Then it charged, smashing deeply into the Clackmat formation. Brick could see bodies tossed to either side. The rush slowed, the neck raising the boar head high. Then the neck arched, the snout opened and a gush of yellow flame filled Brick's vision.

And he woke.

There were, Brick reflected, positive aspects to not sleeping much. It usually precluded dreams such as this. And he seldom felt any particular lack of sleep. He was used to it. Must have needed the rest last night. Paid the price for it, though.

Brick demolished a pile of logs to feed the baker's ovens. He barely tasted the meal he gulped down from the platter the baker's wife clattered onto the breakfast table. The dream stuck with him, frustrating his efforts to shake free of it. His leg throbbed, and he took his time walking to Shib's tavern.

He still managed to arrive first. He leaned against the tavern wall, beside the sign of the Chipped Tankard, and watched Highmark Street wake up.

Livette arrived. Her smile suggested questions, but she said nothing and they fell into the familiar rhythm of opening Shib's Tavern for the day's business. The usual lot of tradesmen, mechanics, apprentices, coopers, carpenters, and tailors stopped in for a quick, fortifying tankard before beginning their respective labors. The drink of choice invariably beer. Someone ordered watered wine, Brick knew without looking he was a clerk or lawyer, maybe a student or doctor. None of these this morning, just beer drinkers. Fine with Brick. The way he felt he was too likely to conflate the wine drinker with Glum.

The morning rush faded. Brick heard doors opening and closing behind the taproom. Shib shifting some merchandise about, he supposed. Putting together funds to pay Glum and Nahl. Brick tried not to think about it. The commencement of the midday meal drinkers gave him a reason to concentrate on something else.

Kalapo didn't go in for lunch, morning and evening meals being the norm. But enough workers had time to stop in for a tankard about noon that Shib's Tavern did brisk business that time of day. Some came in bearing a pail, tasked to deliver beer to the rest of the crew on a job site. There were also the unemployed, long term or newly, perhaps even as recently as that morning. They tended to stick around for more than one drink.

Livette served a third tankard to a man in a torn and bloodied tunic. A leather apron lolled from the edge of the bar next to him, kept from slipping to the floor by the weight of the tools thrust through sewn-on loops. Brick kept an eye on him from his vantage on the stool by the front door. The blood on the man's clothes suggested that his freedom to drink away the afternoon had come at the expense of some violence.

The man drained his tankard. Livette stood at the far end of the bar, filling up a pail for an apprentice who looked too young and frail to bear the weight once Livette had brimmed it. The ex-carpenter, or whatever he was called for another round, then again louder, adding 'bitch' for emphasis.

Brick was across the taproom in three strides.

"Not the most polite way to ask for a beer," Brick said, leaning in close, well into the man's personal space, smelling sweat, drying blood, and spilled beer.

"No? Wasn't polite getting axed from putting up the new granary on Wharf Street." The man locked eyes with Brick. Angry eyes, eyes a little unfocused. "Not polite at all. Reason why wasn't too fucking polite either; godsdamned foreman wants the job for his piece-of-shit nephew." The man laying out his grievance, working himself up to some more cathartic violence. "Tell you what, I'll let you know just as soon as I give a fuck about polite."

Brick twisted his fingers into the man's hair, slammed his face against the bar top, then yanked, spilling him from the stool to sprawl amidst the bark chips. Brick stood over him, the apron bunched in one hand, raised at shoulder height, the tools dangling menacingly above the fallen carpenter.

"You give a fuck now?"

"Starting to, yeah."

"Brick, knock it off," Livette said, appearing at his elbow. "Man's had a rough day, lay off."

"Maybe so, but he's got no call talking to you like that." It sounded lame even as he said it, a whining excuse for his behavior. Livette could handle herself, he knew that. If she'd wanted his help dealing with an abusive customer she'd have asked for it. Pounding on this unlucky bastard had nothing to do with the man himself.

Brick pulled the man to his feet. "Beer's on me. Now get out of here. Next place you stop, treat the bartender with respect."

"Get ahold of yourself, Brick," Livette said. The out of work carpenter hobbled out the front door, clutching his heavy leather apron with one hand while cupping the other to his bleeding nose.

"Don't like to see you treated like that, is all."

"Sell that shit to someone who's buying. Something's eating you. That's your business. Deal with it. Customers are my business—and ought to be yours. That poor guy was just venting frustrations. He wasn't hurting anybody. Give him a few beers, a bit of sympathy, and you've got a regular. By tomorrow that man will be on with one of the crews throwing up mansions on Merchants' Reach. But now, thanks to you, he won't be spending his pay here."

Brick kicked at the sawdust, his eyes lowered. Shroud's tits. Livette had it right. He hoped Shib hadn't heard any of this.

"Brick, may I see you upstairs? That is, if you are finished beating up our patrons and giving away our beer."

Brick started. Stealthy fucking Shib.

***

Watching the big man twitch never grew old. But Shib derived less enjoyment from it this time. He let a critical eye linger on Brick before he turned to lead the way upstairs. His bouncer was on edge, that much was clear from the way he'd treated that customer. Brick was becoming unreliable. Maybe even sooner than Shib had anticipated. Brick would be the last remaining link from the Vawn job to Shib once this business concluded, and Shib had always meant to see that link cut short. Now he might need to act sooner than expected. Something to ponder.

Shib sat behind his desk, his spine rigidly straight. Brick hesitated before sliding onto the bench opposite.

"I've had a busy morning, Brick. Thus, I'm uncertain precisely how many of my customers you've thumped and tossed today. Was it more than a dozen? Under twenty?"

"Sorry, boss. Won't happen again. This shit with Glum and Nahl's got me on a low boil."

"That might be for the best," Shib said, letting out some line, playing Brick like a Port Weir bass. "A bit of pent up aggression could be useful next time we meet with those two. But—and this is important—stop beating up those customers who don't actually require your professional attentions."

Brick nodded. Shib thought he looked chastened, but that faded. "So, you had a busy morning. And you're anticipating another meet soon. You got word from Glum already?"

Shib reminded himself not to underestimate this man. Otherwise severing the link might prove a problem. "I spent the morning putting together funds to meet Glum's extortion. My supply of—second-hand merchandise—is almost exhausted. But I think I've accumulated enough. And I think you'll enjoy this: Guess who was my primary purchaser? Go on, guess."

Brick cleared his throat. Shib pushed on. "No, don't bother. You'll never guess. I sold handcart-loads of worthless shit stolen by that worthless shit Nahl to none other than—wait for it—our old friend Cester Bailick Faren."

The look on Brick's face made all the hours of hustling that morning worthwhile. "Cester? No fucking way."

"Repartee like that is why I keep you on the payroll, Brick. Thing is, I got to thinking that with Glum and Nahl holding this little job over our heads, it might do to have some insurance against official attention from the Horse Guard or the Magistrate. What better insurance than an Elector? An Elector who owes you a favor. Or an Elector you have dirt on. Either is good."

"Makes sense. Is he going to call his goons off, or do we keep looking over our shoulders for men in red?"

"The former. Or so he tells me."

"Why does he want all that garbage you sold him? And how did you get in to see him?"

"How is easy. I went to his house and announced myself. As to why, you can thank the current administration. Seems the Magistrate announced a new law outlawing the purchase of votes. But the fine, upstanding men of Clackmat who hold the franchise still cling to time-honored tradition: They expect something in exchange for their votes. That junk Nahl stole holds some value, and it isn't legal tender. An exact reading of the new law doesn't prohibit—gifting—of goods to voters. Only coin. So Cester Bailick Faren intends to offer a silver candle holder here, a pair of matched silk cushions there in return for a promise to drop his chit into the urn come next election.

"I got paid. Glum and Nahl will get paid. I'll get the medallion and the Periapt. Faren will get re-elected. Everybody wins."

Brick snorted. Shib figured maybe he should have mentioned what Brick stood to gain. Tough to do, given he meant to see Brick gain nothing but a pine box and a shallow grave. How to arrange that? Simple plans usually worked best. After they retrieved the medallion, ask him to get a keg from the storage room, follow him in and stick a knife in his spine? Burn the place down on the way out, taking the trading credentials and a bag of Petals. A few years bilking the humans in the Clackmat hinterlands, and who knew? Quite possibly he could put together a big enough poke to buy his way back within Council borders, back to civilized environs.

Shib sat, letting the silence build. Good technique to make Brick nervous, put him back in his place after that impertinent snort. But Brick only cracked his knuckles, rolled that ridiculously sized head on that ridiculously thick neck. Reminding Shib he'd need to be careful when placing the knife. Brick offered a large target, but vast sections of it were less than vital.

Shib tapped his fingers on the desk. "I received word from Nahl and Glum this morning while you were moping about downstairs."

"What, Glum send you a coded poem?"

"Nothing quite so clever. But just about as unexpected. The messenger was from Priests' Promenade. One of the Verians. Earnest, I think you'd call him. Introduced himself as Harribol Gravin, Apostolic Truthseeker of the Verians."

Brick grunted. "Yeah. Glum's mentioned him. Called him a soft touch. Easy to manipulate."

Maybe, Shib considered, he could manipulate someone into dealing with Brick for him. Cester Bailick Faren, for instance. Drop the location of the baker's shop where Brick dossed, let Faren's guild hardboys torch the place. Wouldn't be the first bakery to catch fire.

"I can believe that. Soft Touch Harribol doesn't seem the sort to ask questions. He bought whatever story Glum sold him at face value."

"So, where is the meet?" Brick asked.

"I think Glum might be the superstitious sort. Feels safe around churches. He's set the meet on Priests' Promenade. The Temple of the Entropic Order," Shib said, thinking maybe he could goad Nahl into taking out Brick during the exchange. Couldn't be too hard to instigate hostilities between those two hotheads, could it?

"When?"

Shib drummed the desktop with his fingertips. "Tonight."

***

Despite its ramshackle appearance, the temple housing the Third Iteration of the Entropic Order had struck Glum as solidly built. Nihilists they might be, but Glum guessed the members of the Entropic Order still didn't want the ceiling collapsing on them. The main sanctuary, open to the public, offered a tawdry display of decay. Leaning pillars. Sagging ceiling beams. All false, a show for the marks. Hook the disaffected, the clueless, rebellious youth and aimless anarchists. The halls beyond eschewed architecture as allegory, constructed along simple and functional principles.

Below, the subterranean fane—where Glum crouched, concealed behind an artfully gashed arras—was also solidly constructed. Had to be, given the weight of the building resting atop it. But the same interior designers—who had strewn the worship space above with fallen tiles and cracked steps leading to a shrine with a gaping split in its altar stone—had also decorated this sanctum sanctorum with suggestions of dissolution.

From Glum's hiding place he observed the cultists of the Order preparing the ritual. They'd cleared splintered benches from the center of the floor, revealing flat, smoothly mortared, and tightly fitted flagstones. Aljak Vest plied a broom, whisking away mounds of grit and debris. Another priest sat on his haunches, sketching with a lump of ochre-color chalk. A third set tapers burning in tall candle holders at regular intervals around the cleared space.

Shib ought to be arriving soon, waiting for Glum to let him in the side door. Brick too, in all probability. Glum couldn't imagine Shib would risk the exchange without his guard dog.

He ran through his plan again, searching for major weaknesses and any poetic infelicities. The main weakness he encountered was his current lack of drink. Other than a couple meager flagons about noontime, he hadn't had a drop of wine all day. A forked branch of sharp choices, that. A man could use liquid succor when piloting a risky shoal like he proposed. Yet a foggy head could see him scuttled, breaking up on the rocks. After weighing the choices, Glum decided to proceed clear-headed. Once he'd dealt with Shib and Brick he'd go on a celebratory bender. He didn't like it, though. Could almost feel the shakes coming on.

More cultists entered the sanctum until over a dozen roamed about the chamber. Some assisted with preparation, others created a human perimeter about the geometrical figures chalked on the stone floor. The chalk pattern formed an octagon within a circle. The circle touched the octagon at the vortices. The empty spaces between the octagon's faces and the curve of the circle held characters from several antiquated languages, along with symbols Glum hadn't seen before. He could barely make out the markings in the dim light, could make no sense of the arrangement. But he didn't have to. Let the experts do the work.

Glum tried to memorize the details. The scene possessed a romantic menace: The shifting shadows cast by the flickering candles, the Order cultists in their black cassocks, faces hidden by cowls, the low arching stonework of the subterranean vault, the mystic glyphs sketched on the flagstones. He'd try to work it all into verse once this business concluded. And after a judicious amount of drinking. No point rushing his genius.

Aljak finished sweeping. He leaned the broom in a darkened corner, then took his place at the perimeter. Glum wondered what the man would say if he knew Glum was watching. He doubted Aljak remembered much of the previous night. The priest might harbor a faint unease, a nagging memory of perhaps having betrayed certain confidences. Maybe. Highly unlikely he recalled the details, letting slip what the Order planned for this evening, or offering Glum a bed for the night, or sneaking him into the temple. Glum had heard neither hue nor cry that morning, so if Aljak had noticed that Glum was not occupying the nook by the kitchen stove that Aljak had shown him last night then he'd kept it to himself to avoid any awkward questions from his superiors.

Glum had waited only long enough for Aljak to sway and stumble from the kitchen before taking up the threadbare blanket Aljak had loaned him and commencing his inspection of the temple. He wasn't in much better shape than Aljak. His attempts at stealth often threatened to unbalance him. But he had reached the patient stage of inebriation and didn't mind a bit of tottering, or even a stint on hands and knees. He'd found the underground chamber Aljak had mentioned during the fourth bottle. Or was it the fifth? Finding a concealed spot to sleep it off was second nature to Glum. His current hidden position behind the arras still held the blanket he'd covered himself with, now wadded up as a makeshift cushion. It helped some, but he still had to squirm now and again, fighting off the tingling and numbness as first one asscheek then the other fell asleep.

It was, Glum figured, about time to see if Shib would show up. Discovering the discreet exit from the temple had required some time. But Glum had spent enough time in the worship halls of Priests' Promenade to know he'd find a postern eventually. Sneaking out to task Harribol Gravin with a message had been a risk. At this point, though, what wasn't? Glum's moment neared and he'd no intention of backing out now. The opportunity Aljak had dropped into his lap might never come again. This wasn't work he could manage himself, the magical heavy lifting involved required some group or other along the Boulevard of the Heavens.

Glum would creep away from his hiding place one more time, trying his nerves well out of proportion with any real prospect of detection. He levered himself up gradually. He didn't want to alert the members of the Order to his presence. Also, given what felt like an angry mob of seamstresses prodding his legs with sewing needles, he didn't want to risk any sudden movements pitching him forward onto his face. Crumbs spilled from his lap, the remains of the loaves he'd filched from the kitchen on the way back from his visit to the Verians.

He'd told Harribol to instruct Shib to arrive just before sunset. Aljak's revelation last night had included the information that the ritual would commence at sunset. All signs indicated the ritual was imminent, meaning the sun must be dropping beyond the West Hills. The question recurred: Would Shib show or not? Had he brought Brick along? Probably. He'd be a fool not to bring him along. He couldn't match Glum for vision, but he was no idiot. Lack of vision, that was the shortcoming of Sharks. Nahl had possessed barely enough cunning to plan a house burglary. Shib could put together a heist like the break in at Trader Vawn's. But neither one had Glum's genius, his vision. Shib would come to realize that soon.

If he showed up, that is.

Glum tucked the bundle of pilfered garments under his arm. He crept from his hideout—a sort of surreptitious mezzanine, neglected, forgotten, or simply of no current use—onto a landing of a back staircase leading from the sanctum below to the ground floor. He almost always found hidden passages and spyholes in the temples of Priests' Promenade. Was that reflective of a paranoia common to the ecclesiastic temperament in general? Did the hierarchs of the various organized faiths fear and suspect the lower clerical orders? Or did mysticism inspire additional layers of secrecy, a need for a mystery behind the mystery, the importance of which is reinforced by—or wholly reliant on—hermeneutic security measures?

All good questions with which to impress drinking companions.

Glum stole through the corridors toward the side entrance. He assumed all the members of the Entropic Order were below, preparing for the ritual, but so late in the game caution recommended itself.

He eased open the postern door. By the corner of the temple, a few paces into Priests' Promenade, Shib's tall, lanky frame waited next to Brick's bulky one, Brick's outline widened by a knee length cloak. So Shib had brought his guard dog along. Glum had figured he would. Pack mule too, the bouncer toting a lantern, its pierced, sheet iron sides casting dim patterns on bricks still holding faint twilight illumination.

Now for it. The game grew risky here. But the reward more than made up for the danger of the throw. The time had come to lie. Lie big and convincingly. But after all, was he not a poet and playwright? He lied professionally, no less than did an Elector, or a lawyer.

He took a half step from the doorway, keeping one foot inside, prepared to turn and bolt if Brick made a move.

"I see you received my invitation," Glum said.

Light patterns on the street twirled and swung as Brick shifted to face him. Glum felt mildly disappointed that neither Brick nor Shib so much as flinched. But on reflection, better not to start them off on a jumpy footing.

"Yes, your messenger boy was diligent," Shib said. "Now can we get on with it?"

"Did you bring the coin?"

Brick shifted aside his cloak. Underneath he wore his studded leather vest and a belt from which dangled four pouches stretched to their tolerances. Glum had doubted Brick wore the cloak for warmth.

"Here you go, Glum," Brick said. "You're a rich man. Come on over and take your wealth."

Glum laughed. "That's a charity laugh, Brick. You still have no grasp of humor. Toss a sack over here. I'm a trusting sort. A rough count will do. I don't need to pile up neat stacks of Petals and break out the number strings."

"Do you have my goods?" Shib asked, cutting off whatever retort Brick intended.

"Me? Shib, this will all proceed more smoothly if we each assume the other is not an imbecile. Nahl is holding them. If you try anything—any tiresomely stupid stunt like attacking me, or attempting to pay with pouches full of river pebbles—then you'll never see the medallion again."

"Show him," Shib said

Brick untied a pouch from his belt, worrying open the knot with one hand. He teased open the mouth of the small leather pouch and held it up to the lantern. Silver caught the light of the oil-burning flame, sending coruscating glints to dance in the air before Glum.

"*Refulgent,* wouldn't you say?" said Brick.

"Open the others," said Glum, though he began to worry this step was dragging on too long. Someone could pass through the alleyway on the way to the Boulevard of the Heavens. An Order cultist could come up behind him, on his way to fetch some forgotten item needed for the ritual. Still, the pouch in Brick's hand could be the only one containing any coin. Best to be sure.

"Shib, why don't I just chuck one of these sacks at him? I can bean him in the head from here."

"Humor him, Brick. This will all be over soon."

Glum enjoyed Brick's discomfiture. He enjoyed the sight of the money even more. Without counting he couldn't be certain Brick was showing him the precise amount agreed to. But even from the distance he could tell it was close enough. Not a fortune, perhaps. No argosy. Not wealth to beggar the imagination—certainly not his imagination. A poet can dream. Kalapo's wealthier citizens, or foreign merchants such as Trader Vawn, might consider it little enough. But a frugal man might live on this for the rest of his life. Glum figured he could live on it comfortably until he'd begun exploiting the power of the Panaegic Periapt.

"That will do," Glum said. "Let's go make the exchange. Here, put these on." He tossed black robes and cowls outside into the dust of the alley. Then, not waiting to see if Brick and Shib complied, Glum backed into the temple to don his own Entropic Order vestments. Keep moving, he told himself. Don't allow them time to stop and question.

The robe felt stiff, heavy. It constricted his movements. Running no longer remained an option. Fine. His future did not depend on running. It depended upon a poetic audacity.

He could hear Brick grumbling and swearing as he wrestled the robe over a frame larger than it had been intended to contain.

"Come on," Glum said, leading on into the main hallways of the temple, deserted now, the faithful gathered in the sanctum below.

"What's your notion, Glum?" Shib asked. "Are we to follow you into a darkened room where Nahl is waiting with his knives?" The rustling of robes ceased as Shib and Brick stopped moving.

"Tedious. We're heading for the safe anonymity of the crowd. The Entropic Order is gathered below for a worship service. We will make the exchange with about twenty potential witnesses at hand should anything go wrong. You curb your dog, I'll curb mine, Shib."

"How about this dog pisses on your leg," Brick said. "after ripping it from your body."

"Let it go, Brick," Shib said. "This is actually a well-considered venue for the exchange. You want to hunt Glum down afterwards, fine. Do it on your own time."

"If we're past the angry taunting stage," Glum said, "may I ask you to shut the fuck up? We're about to join the congregation— the anonymity of the crowd, if you recall. Silence before the curtain opens, if you please."

Metal clicked on stone, Brick setting down the light. The beams from the lantern ceased their wavering dance against the walls, resolving into a firm pattern striking lower on the wall. Glum tensed. Was Brick about to rush him from behind? Don't give him time to work up to it. Keep moving.

"This way," Glum stage whispered.

He found the main stairwell and started spiraling down, not waiting to discover if the other two were following. They had to. They were committed. Same as he.

A rhythmic pulsing from below resolved into chanting voices as Glum descended. A soft orange glow took on hues of yellow and crimson, even touches of emerald and purple. Glum hoped he hadn't delayed too long. The banter had been fun, reminding him of better times at Shib's Tavern. But the talk had been to a purpose and he hoped he'd not let nostalgia overcome his sense of timing.

Glum edged out from the back stairwell.

A circle of black-draped figures two deep swayed and chanted. The sing-song nonsense rose, rose some more, dropped, then repeated. Words and fragments of words sounded maddeningly familiar, but Glum could place neither language nor meaning. Candles formed an inner circle, or perhaps a boundary, around the chalked circle, the Order cultists keeping outside the limits thereby defined. The wicks served as core to fat flames, reaching high, much higher than the waxed twine of votive candles had any business reaching. The flames burned chartreuse, then red or green or heliotrope, without sequence or repetition. Rhythmically intoning priests scattered multi-colored powders in the air that flared when they met the queer candle flames. The atmosphere within the circle was thick with floating particles, the powders hanging in air currents, forming a dust cloud that captured the varying lights, mingling and amplifying them.

An eerie sight, one Glum wished he had more time to appreciate. But now he worried he might have brought Brick and Shib down too soon, too early in the ritual.

Glum sensed a presence nearby, looked. Shib and Brick took up positions bracketing him, both men staring rapt at the scene. Shib towered near two feet above his head, Brick not much less, the big man wedged into a robe that threatened to burst at the seams. Glum began to think he'd been too blithe regarding the religious garbs' capacity to disguise. One look at either of these specimens would arouse suspicion. So far, though, all attention remained fixed on the ceremony.

Shib leaned down to whisper in Glum's ear. "Where is Nahl? How do you propose we make the exchange?"

Glum pointed up, across the sanctum, at the arras concealing the alcove where he'd spent the night. "He's watching from up there." Improvising now, buying time. "When I give the signal he'll fetch the items. Brick leaves the money here with the two of us, makes his way up. There's an alcove behind that curtain, see. Time it takes him to get up there gives Nahl time to get your fancy necklaces from our hiding place, bring them to the alcove, and leave them there. Brick gets the goods, tugs at the curtain to let us know he's got them. You leave the money here and get out of here with your bodyguard. Try anything and you'll interrupt the religious service of these fine folk, busy working themselves into a frenzy."

He thought that sounded good, for putting together the lie on the fly.

"And what if I hadn't brought Brick?" Shib managing to make the whisper sound suspicious.

Shit.

The chanting rose again, making whispered communication impractical, and giving Glum a chance to think. Keep moving, he reminded himself, don't give them time to question. Like Shib just there. Ignore the question. Move on. Poetic audacity would see him through this, see him to his reward.

"There, did you see that?" Glum asked when the chanting returned to a more subdued cadence and the dust cloud shimmied from royal blue to deep crimson.

"See what?"

"The curtain twitched. Nahl's wondering what is the hold up. I'll give him the signal. Like you said, let's get this over with. Tell Brick to leave the money. I'll direct him to the back way up to the alcove."

It was hot down here, an oppressive combination of the flames, the heavy wool garments, the mass of cultists performing their sweaty dance. Glum hoped Shib would attribute the glisten of sweat on his forehead to the heat and not figure it for nerves. Glum had made his throw. If he couldn't bullshit Shib for whatever amount of time remained then he'd lose, poetic audacity or no.

Shib opened his mouth.

"Shroud's tits, what the fuck is that?" Brick said in a tone approaching the limits of the accepted definition of "whisper."

An ill-defined form began to take shape within the nebula of polychromatic dust. The chanting rose to a crescendo, then stilled. A hiss replaced the chanting, the hiss modulating to moan, to growl, to scream, the sounds accompanying the transformation of the shape in the circle. No, not accompanying the shape's transformation, Glum realized, emitted by it. The form grew, swelling horizontally, then expanding upwards, stretching toward the dimly illuminated vaulted ceiling above. The form uncoiled, rising onto what appeared at first to be three legs in a tripodal configuration. Then the rear leg resolved into a tail. The legs supported a

216

massive torso, flanged and ribbed. As the body stretched up through the cloud of dust, Glum could see it glistening wetly, the vertical protrusions thrust out like fins, plates of some sort of ochre-colored bone, the horizontal ribbing like black, organic metal, punching through mottled reptilian skin, and curving to plunge back into the body. Heavy musculature supported this horrific carapace or exoskeleton. Glum couldn't decide which. The extrusions exhibited aspects of both. Long arms sprouted from shoulders the size of catapult ammunition, each arm ending in a taloned hand the size of a shovel blade. A thick neck bore a head similar in both size and shape to a ram's. The thing exuded a rank musk, overpowering the sanctum's odor of candle wax, incense, and human sweat.

At last. Glum exulted. He'd delayed long enough. And now power lay within the palm of his hand, waiting only for him to curl his fingers and claim it. No, that metaphor was lame. He'd work up a more potent, fresh metaphor later when he penned the epic verse detailing his rise to glory.

A certain relief accompanied Glum's excitement. He'd feared the Third Iteration of the Entropic Order might not be up to the summoning. But they'd done it. They'd called forth a demon.

Now, one more act of poetic audacity.

He plunged forward, shoving and elbowing his way through the circle. The devotees of the Entropic Order did not hamper him, too stunned at their success to comprehend what he was doing.

"Glum, stop!" Brick was yelling. Let him yell. Glum was beyond heeding the admonitions of fools. That one he liked.

"Admonitions of fools." He'd try to remember it.

He broke through the second rank and stumbled forward, thrusting a candlestick from his path, seeing the elaborate chalk glyphs within the section of circle and octagon smudge beneath his feet. He felt a wisp of resistance, as if he'd burst through a spider web. Then he was past, into the circle. The demon loomed above him, a damp, reptilian cliff of bone, fang, and muscle. It stank and pulsed waves of heat, its pebbled skin giving off a reddish light that compensated for the candles dimming to natural levels of radiance.

Glum turned his back on it. The demon was insignificant.

He faced the section of cultists through which he'd come, seeing Shib behind them, and Brick pushing his way into their midst. Glum could see hesitant, uncertain movements, the first hint of what might turn to panic. He reached within his clothing, beneath the tunic under his stolen robe, and pulled free the Panaegic Periapt, holding it aloft on its golden chain. The gem caught the crimson light behind, throbbing a vivid maroon like a beating heart.

Glum declaimed, "Behold! The Panaegic Periapt. I claim it, and with that claim my time has come. Witness as I command this demon and know it is within my power to command all such." He paused. His voice had carried resonance and conviction. He'd worried the speech he'd composed might come off artificial, even archaic. But he thought he'd delivered it well, authoritative without being pompous.

He cleared his throat. The circle of Order cultists began to fragment, individual cowled priests backing away from their neighbors. Well, they were right to fear him. Though in the future he'd have to insist his audiences fidget less, pay his words the rapt attention they were due.

Brick and Shib stood clearly visible now in lanes opened by the parting ranks of the Entropic Order. Shib had his head tilted to one side, listening. Brick looked utterly aghast, his hood thrown back. Glum wondered what look Brick's face would carry when Glum set the demon on him. Perhaps Glum could force something other than sardonic superiority from Shib before the demon ate that fucking Shark's face. If not, it didn't much matter. Glum would still have the pendant. And the coin.

Not a bad start for the most powerful man in the Clackmat Confederacy.

"A new age is at hand, an age I shall lead. Take this historic opportunity to become the first of my disciples." Glum liked that bit, an appeal to their self-interest. He could have wished the venue more acoustically sound. Also, cooler. Sweat ran freely from his forehead. He'd grown clammy under his tunic. This fucking demon cranked out a bonfire's worth of heat. "Join me in ushering in a golden era, an era worthy of song and poetry."

Glum felt a drop splash on his shoulder. A wisp of acrid smoke rose from the heavy wool robe. He felt a sting of pain. He yelped then turned and gazed up. The demon had eased closer, its ruminant head thrust above Glum, its sour odor an almost physical affront. A green froth foamed at its muzzle, glowing as if bioluminescent. More drops fell, sizzling as they struck the stone floor. Then the jaws opened.

Glum held aloft the Panaegic Periapt. "Demon," he said, "I abjure—"

Bright green liquid jets shot from the gaping jaws above, showering Glum. Whatever other words he'd intended were lost in a debilitating moment of agony.

***

Brick watched the demon vomit a spray of acid, engulfing Glum Arent. Glum did not even have time to scream. His clothing dissolved. His flesh washed from his bones like mud sluiced from the front stoop with a bucket of water. Glum's bones clattered to the stone floor along with whatever metallic or mineral objects he'd had tucked in his pockets.

Glum, what were you thinking? How could you have been so stupid?

Brick had seen demons in action too many times. He knew the outcome. He knew he and these shit-for-brains cultists were dead men. But he'd no intention of going to meet Shroud without putting up a fight. The Fury flared within him, a rising heat.

A tall bronze candlestick stood at hand. Brick grabbed it, considering. The candlestick came up only to his chest. It wasn't quite long enough to keep this monstrosity at bay and he doubted it packed enough heft to get the demon's attention even if he wound up and put everything behind the swing. A last resort, then.

The demon snuffled and huffed over Glum's remains. Then it rocked its head back and forth, eyeing its surroundings. The cultists shuffled backwards, on the brink of panic. Through an expanding gap among the ranks to his left, Brick glimpsed the end of a bench or pew, about a third of it, the heavy oak planks anchored to a stone base. Brick pushed his way through to it, lugging the candlestick with him. His back to the circle of cultists and the demon, Brick crouched, set the candlestick aside, careful not to let it clatter and risk drawing the demon's attention.

Brick felt around the base of the bench fragment, searching for handholds. He worked his fingers into position, straightened his back and tightened his abdomen. He tensed, raised his chin, then lifted. Nothing. The bench didn't budge. Brick felt his bad leg throb, felt tendons in his forearms protesting. And he felt the Fury churn. His anger exploded—at Glum for dying so stupidly, at Shib for starting this shit, at these fuckwit cultists for summoning this demon. He reset his grip, released a scream, and heaved.

Let the demon notice. Brick wanted to draw its attention, give it a faceful of granite and aged oak planks.

The bench rose. Brick tottered upright, staggered back. He grunted, hoisted the bench above his head, the uneven balance threatening to tear the ungainly missile from his grasp. He turned, ready to stagger forward and hurl the bench at the demon, fall into Shroud's dry embrace blazing with Fury and acid burns.

The demon wasn't there.

No, there it was, nearing the opposite side of the chalked circle. Candlelight from the far side of the circle gleamed faintly through it. It looked smaller. And with each shuffling step it grew noticeably smaller and more indistinct, insubstantial. Apparently killing Glum—the one who'd breached the protective circle—had satisfied it. There was no telling with demons. They might rampage for hours, killing indiscriminately, or they might seek out only those wearing yellow, or they might wander to the nearest body of water and take a swim.

The bench wobbled above Brick's head. He could see a cowled form bent over Glum's bones. Brick figured it for Shib. But the terror stricken and mortified members of the Entropic Order were demonstrating some resilience. With the demon no longer a threat they were free to focus on other points of interest. Like the bellowing stranger menacing them with a bench.

The ranks closed again, shutting off Brick's avenue of sight to Glum Arent's remains. And Brick had more pressing concerns than whether or not it was Shib he'd seen.

"Bastards," Brick growled and heaved the bench into the advancing mass. A half-dozen cultists dropped, the weight of the bench crushing rib cages, snapping arms, and shattering pelvises. That bought Brick enough time to retrieve the candlestick. He didn't wait for the cultists to resume their advance. The Fury enfolded him in its red embrace. He waded in, candlestick describing wide arcs that trailed sprays of blood, teeth, and skull fragments.

Fists struck him. Brick didn't feel them. Knives sliced at him, gashing holes in his ill-fitting robe, gouging into his leather vest, scoring red lines in his arms. He felt them, vaguely. He didn't care. The candlestick rose and fell now, staving in heads and cracking collarbones.

Breathing space opened. Survivors stepped back, leaving Brick standing amidst a pile of limp bodies and a few fitfully stirring, curled up and moaning. He'd done some damage, no question. But the cultists still

222

had a significant numbers advantage to his lonesome self. And he could see them beginning to recognize that basic mathematical fact. The cowls had fallen back from most of the cultists. The looks they exchanged were clear enough.

"Try not to kill him," one of the Entropic Order said. "We can question him later, find out who put them up to this."

"And if we do kill him?" asked another.

The first speaker shrugged. "Entropy happens."

They came at him in a rush, Brick figuring about ten of them. He swung the dented, blood-stained candlestick again, but only connected with one cultist. The others ducked or slipped the blow. Brick's bum leg gave out as he tried to control the follow through. Brick went down beneath the scrum, absorbing fists and elbow strikes. He tasted blood. Sparks and whirling flares of blue and yellow danced at the bounds of his vision.

Some of these boys knew how to brawl. Brick got the idea that ecclesiastic disputes on Priests' Promenade might get a bit heated in the wee hours. But he didn't like the idea of going out like this. Crisped by a demon, that he could accept. Beaten to death by priests? To the Thousand Hells with that.

Brick shrugged off a punch. Then he surged up, throwing off two cultists, and rolled to his knees. His momentum sent the money pouches tied to his belt slapping against him. Brick yanked down on the pouch at his right hip, snapping the laces. He swung upwards, backhand, the silver-stuffed bag connecting with the jaw of a cultist who was attempting to launch a looping roundhouse. The man's jaw dislocated and several teeth sprang free.

Brick wheeled, swinging the other direction. The pouch proved itself a more than adequate cosh, slamming solidly against the temple of another cultist who fell backwards against two more, the trio sprawling on their asses.

The rest stepped back again.

"Anyone else want to question me?" Brick asked. "No? Well, if you change your mind, ask for me at the Clackmat Drayage and Cartage Guild."

Two of the Entropic Order stood between Brick and the stairs. He eyeballed them, the sturdy leather coin purse in his right hand dripping blood. He gave it a moment, then stalked forward. The two backed away to either side, leaving the path open to freedom.

***

Once he'd left the well-lit vicinity of Priests' Promenade behind him, Shib entered the intermittent darkness of Kalapo at night. That troubled him little; Haptha eyes saw better at night than did humans'.

Shib discarded the cowl and too-short robe, dropping the garments in the darkened recesses of what looked to him like more an accidental gap between adjacent buildings than an alley. He patted a pocket sewn inside his tunic, feeling the reassuring hard lump of the trading credentials. And next to it the almost cylindrical form of the pendant. He'd taken the extra moment to snatch that bauble up from Glum's smoldering bones. It was a pretty enough thing and might fetch fifty or sixty Petals.

Not much good against Outside Powers, though. Poets. Fools would believe anything. They wanted to believe. Anything. Shib hadn't even had time to construct a good story when he'd decided to mess with Glum, not intending any more than to have a little fun at the human's expense, maybe see how far he could push it before Brick or Livette called him on it. He'd not needed to push it. Those few words had nudged Glum onto this fatal path. Curious, gullible, greedy. Probably on the verge of alcoholic madness. The dumbshit had invested the amethyst with powers of his own invention and had died for it. His own imagination had killed him.

That little outing had been a near thing, closer than Shib liked. But it could hardly have worked out better. He had the medallion. Glum Arent presented no further problem. And given that the poet had possessed the goods, Shib had to assume he'd somehow disposed of Nahl. Leaving only Brick. And last Shib had seen, Brick had his hands full dealing with enraged Entropic Order fanatics.

Pity Brick still had the money. A pittance, compared to the amounts he'd rake in posing as a Credentialed Trader. But a good stash of silver like that made for good seed money.

Brick *might* win through. Wouldn't surprise him. The man was absurdly tough. Would Brick head directly to the tavern? Probably. All for the best. Shib had to return there himself, pick up the remainder of his travelling money, grab his bug out bag, and buckle on his sword. He'd allow enough time for Brick to arrive, say a couple of hours, give the man time to walk off a concussion, limp back on that bum leg. That still left Shib plenty of hours until daylight, plenty of time to run a sword through the bouncer a few times and still be miles from the city by sunrise.

If Brick didn't return? Well, Shib would have to stick around, make inquiries. He couldn't risk Brick informing Vawn who held his credentials. The Trader had enough juice with the Magistrate to set what passed for Clackmat law enforcement searching the Confederacy for a Shark passing himself off as a Credentialed Trader. That would put a crimp in Shib's plans, no question.

Shib crossed a brightly lit stretch of Market Street lined with public houses and the residences of moderately successful merchants and professionals. Two blocks later he'd only starlight for visibility.

That allowed him sufficient light to see the knot of men—no, boys, rather, a year or two shy of manhood—congregating on the front stoop of some sort of business. Shib's eyes weren't quite keen enough to make out what image the sign depicted. He could barely make out that there *was* a sign. A giant tooth, maybe, indicating a dentist's practice? Or was it an enormous glove? No, too far from Garment Street. Didn't matter. He was glad enough he couldn't see the building itself. Likely a typical Kalapo box of wood and stone, nothing like the edifices of marble, concrete, or colorful glazed tile that adorned Port Weir. But what Shib could see—and count—were the boys, could see them pass around a bottle, see a red point brighten as one of them drew in smoke from a smoldering weed of some sort.

And he could see that they could see him.

A bit early for Kalapo's street gangs to be out. They did not usually materialize until the eating shops and taverns closed or slowed for the night. But there weren't really rules. Kind of the point of a gang to begin with, dispensing with rules.

The red dot hit the ground, disappeared beneath someone's heel. The gang sauntered Shib's way. Playing it cool, drawing out the fun, a gang of cats toying with a captured mouse. Shib stopped in the middle of the street, let them come to him, surrounding him in a loose cordon.

"Lost, sir?" one of the boys asked. "May we assist you with directions? Help you carry a package?" The others chuckled, enjoying the droll wit of their leader.

"Boys, I'm in a hurry. Do you mind if we skip the bullshit and move straight on to threats?" Shib shifted his stance, testing the footing of the dirt road surface.

"Have it your way. Drop everything you're carrying or we'll tie your guts around your throat. Might do it anyway, just to practice our knots."

"Not bad," Shib said. "I admire the creativity. But I meant my threatening you."

Shib couldn't make out facial features, but turned heads and shuffled feet suggested confusion. What could give this mugging victim the confidence to brazen it out like this? Was he bluffing? Or just drunk and stupid?

They settled on bluffing.

"Fuck him up," said the leader. Bored with it already, a world weary sixteen.

Must have appeared to the kids like a street magician's prestidigitation, the knives appearing in Shib's hands miraculously. He didn't wait for the circle to close. He darted left, crouched, and spun. His knives traced deep cuts in two gang members, eliciting shocked profanities that would soon shift to screams when the pain struck.

Shib could have slipped through the gap he'd cut in the line and hoofed it. There was no way these boys—these human boys—could keep up with his speed. But the lack of respect they'd displayed rankled. And he was still a bit on edge from Glum's stunt, glad for an excuse to vent.

The wounded kid on his right slumped to his knees. Shib stepped over him, leapt up and drove a knee into the chest of the next gangbanger in line. As that boy fell back, Shib brought his other leg up, planted a foot on the boy's shoulder, and pushed off. He launched, knife points first, into the two rushing up in support. His knives—forged in Port Weir from alloys these backwater humans had yet to develop, strong, flexible, and capable of holding an edge a razor would envy—plunged into flesh, helping Shib arrest his dive. He swung his legs forward, feet into the two torsos in which he'd jammed his blades, riding the bodies to the ground.

"He's a fucking Shark," said one of the remaining boys.

"Scatter." Shib recognized the leader's voice and pivoted to face the direction it came from. The kid had his arms pumping and legs driving already. The rest of his gang followed his example.

Shib rotated the right-hand knife about his palm, taking the blade between thumb and first two fingers. Hard to judge distance and target speed in the dark, and he was out of practice. He flipped the knife. If his instincts remained reliable, the blade would make three-and-a-half revolutions, and then

. . .

Shib heard the knife blade sink home. His instincts remained reliable. Comforting. It increased his confidence in his ability to deal with Brick. While the man was as big as three of these punks combined, he was probably less nimble, slowed by his bad leg. No way he could match Haptha speed.

With Brick out of the way, he'd leave Kalapo a vision fading in the dust of the next mule cart out of the city. Shib didn't much care where it would be headed. Kalapo, such as it was, represented the jewel in the crown of the Confederacy. The next jumped-up village fancying itself a city would be even worse. But five years, maybe a dozen, spent separating the local merchants from their coin ought to bring in the fortune he'd need to sneak back into Port Weir, reestablish himself with a new identity. It would be worth the continued sacrifice. And what was a decade or two to a Haptha still more-or-less in his prime?

Shib retrieved his thrown knife, then returned to the Chipped Mug to await Brick.

Chapter 11 - Sweeping Up

Dahlia fidgeted with the buckle of her sword belt, the buckle inscribed with a prayer for victory to the warriors' patron, Vivek. The leather about each notch hole was embroidered by her mother with a single word invocation to the five primary Leyvan gods of battle. Dahlia's bunk in the barracks beckoned, promising the comfort of sleep. Trel Minton had pulled night watch in Vawn's chambers, so Dahlia was off duty for the rest of the night. But she felt restless, her mind too active to allow her to sleep. She thought she'd reconciled her guilt, at least enough to continue working for Trader Vawn. But that was only one aspect of the issue. One other unresolved item nagged at her. Brick. Dahlia couldn't stop wondering about his culpability in Heareld's death. Had he killed the guard? Or directly assisted? Or was he an indirect accessory like Dahlia, perhaps bearing the same sort of remorse as she?

A simple, direct course of discovering the answer suggested itself. Go talk to him. Shib's Tavern should be open for at least another three or four hours. Plenty of time to walk down.

Why not? If she didn't she'd just toss and roll in her bunk, obsessing.

The night air held a pleasant coolness and the descent from the West Hills toward the river was mild, with the exception of a few steep slopes. She could almost enjoy the walk. She wouldn't, of course. Enjoyment dulled the wits. Even in the generally safe environs of Merchant's Reach it paid to stay alert. And heeding that advice held even greater value upon reaching the narrow dirt streets and alleys nearer the Mette. Dahlia kept hands near hilts the entire way.

Light from the windows and open doorway of Shib's Tavern illuminated bright geometric patches of Highmark Street. Dahlia glanced inside. The taproom wasn't buzzing, only three of the tables propped up dedicated drinkers. The bartender in the low-cut blouse was running a rag along the bar top. No sign of Brick.

Dahlia entered. None of the patrons so much as glanced up from their tankards, men with a purpose.

She walked to the bar. "Hi, I don't know if you remember—"

The bartender set down her bar rag and straightened up, looking Dahlia in the eyes. "You're the Trader's bodyguard, Dahlia. I remember you. A woman wearing that leather and metal ensemble is memorable."

Dahlia was uncertain if that remark was meant as a slight, a compliment, or simply a neutral observation. She bobbed her chin at the bartender's bust. "In my business, I can't get away with a neckline like that."

The other woman snorted a laugh Dahlia read as one-half cynical bitterness and one-half genuine amusement. "In my business, it's essential. I'm Livette. I assume you're not here for a drink. Looking for Brick?"

"Is he working tonight?" Dahlia asked.

"If so, he's not working here. Shib just got back from whatever hush-hush shit they are up to and think I don't notice. Brick is still out."

Dahlia leaned against the bar. "Could be a wait, then. Still have any of that brandy?"

"Willing to wait? And at this hour." Livette brought down a bottle, splashed a dram into each of two mugs. She handed one to Dahlia and kept one for herself. "The big guy has got your attention, doesn't he."

Dahlia hid her face behind the cheap, poorly thrown ceramic mug. The vapors from the brandy reached her nose and she felt her eyes begin to water. "He does draw the eye."

"No question. Hard to figure how he gets those shoulders through doorways. Women like a bit more grace, know what I mean? All that muscle is a turn off. Still, he's got a certain charm about him."

Dahlia didn't respond. She agreed with Livette about the charm, but not with her assessment of Brick's physical attractions. Dahlia, at least, found the muscular development . . . intriguing. She didn't want to argue with Livette. She'd felt some apprehension that the bartender and Brick had an understanding. Livette's confession inclined Dahlia to a more charitable attitude toward the woman. Living in the barracks with the other guards, Dahlia had little female contact and no girlfriends. She sipped at the throat-warming brandy and kept silent.

Livette came around from behind the bar to attend to an empty tankard. She returned and picked up her brandy, Dahlia watching her, appreciating her utter assurance maneuvering through the tables, seeing a woman completely at home in her surroundings. It inspired a certain confidence, though she couldn't say why.

"You're saying Brick and Shib were up to something?" Dahlia asked.

"Yes. Ever since Trader Vawn—and you—stopped in, the two of them have been as thick as thieves. Though, I'll tell you this: I've never seen Brick look so rattled, so

232

unsure of himself. Whatever he's been up to with Shib, he isn't happy about it."

"And Shib came back by himself? Did he say anything about Brick?"

"No. He came in and started banging around in storage, then upstairs, making a very un-Shark-like racket. And look at you. You're worried. Worried about Brick. You like him."

"Fine, Livette, I admit it. From the moment I saw him taking on those red tunics, not showing even a hint of hesitation, he had my attention. Even though the gods have dragged my life through three, maybe four of the lesser hells since that day . . . Livette, if you get me going on my family drama, not to mention work stress, I'll be bending your ear until that bottle is empty. But through all the shit and drama I still had Brick in my thoughts. Yes, I like him. Or I think I might, given the chance."

"Well, keep it to yourself," Livette said, nodding toward the front door, "or he'll have the upper hand from the start."

Brick stood in the doorway. Even in the dim taproom light Dahlia could see he looked battered, face and neck darkened with smears of dried blood. He did not step inside. He gestured and Dahlia felt something tighten within her and felt her cheeks grow warm thinking he was summoning her. Then she saw Livette sashay around the bar again and realized Brick had gestured for the bartender, not her at all. She felt as if she were falling, as if she'd sat down on a stool without looking only to discover it wasn't there.

Stupid, she told herself. Grip reality, Dahlia. You've met him a couple of times and exchanged—what, twenty words? You can't expect Aphalia to cast her silk net about him just because you like his looks.

Brick and Livette were holding a tense, whispered conversation in the doorway. Livette pointed back, toward the door behind the bar. Brick glanced that way. Dahlia met his eyes. A smile cracked his blood smeared face. Then he crooked his finger, beckoned. There was urgency in the gesture.

Dahlia set down her unfinished brandy. She tried not to hurry as she crossed the narrow taproom to the doorway. She ignored an angry grumble from one of the tavern's customers after the hilt of the dagger on her hip grazed him. She brushed her fingers along her icon bracelet. She caught Livette's smile as the other woman passed her going the other way.

Then she was facing Brick, looking up into his broad, abused face. Dahlia found her hand reaching up to touch his bruised cheek and she forced it back to her side.

Brick grabbed her by the wrist and tugged at it gently. "Come outside," he said, voice rising barely above a whisper.

Dahlia allowed him to lead her onto Highmark Street. "What is it?" she asked.

"Shib can hear bat wings from across the Mette. I don't want him to know I'm back, or even alive."

"Alive? What happened?"

"We're still too close. Let's walk and I'll tell you."

Dahlia didn't hesitate. She'd come here uncertain whether or not Brick had helped kill Heareld, maybe killed the boy himself. Now she was wandering off in the dark with him.

With the unhurried stride of those with no particular destination, they walked south, following Highmark Street toward its distant terminus where it would merge with three or four other north-south city thoroughfares and join the Clackmat Highway. Dahlia found herself edging close within Brick's protective ambit. She had no need of protection. Sword and dagger swung at her hips, and she was armored in leather and in steel rings. She was more than a match for Kalapo's night predators. But nonetheless she felt reassured by his solid presence.

Silence built for several minutes. Then, "Glum's dead," Brick said.

"How? Killed? Who did it? Was it that Shark you brought to the compound?"

"It wasn't Nahl. I think Nahl is dead too. And I think Glum killed him. At least I hope so; Nahl deserved killing. It was that fucking Shark stuck a knife in the guard. Murdered him for no reason."

Dahlia traced a finger along her bracelet, listening to the icons tinkle. This was precisely what she'd hope to hear. Assuming Brick was telling the truth, he hadn't killed Heareld. It had been the scarred, frankly terrifying, Haptha. She wanted to believe Brick. Truth was, she did. He exuded a bluff honesty. That could be a front, a lie to sell a lie, but Dahlia didn't buy it. Brick might be a killer but he wasn't a knife-in-the-dark throat slitter. "And you think Glum killed Nahl? Why? A falling out over money? Did they kill each other?"

"I don't have all the answers, but I can tell you they didn't kill each other. I don't know exactly how Nahl died. I can't be certain he is dead, but I doubt even he was stupid enough to involve himself in the stunt Glum pulled. My guess is either Glum tricked Nahl into disappearing for a few days or—and this is where I'd put my Petals—he stuck a knife in Nahl's back to get him out of the way."

"What stunt? You're not making any sense."

"Sorry, Dahlia. What I saw tonight doesn't make any fucking sense. Glum—that dumb, arrogant, poetry-drunk son of a bitch—snuck us into a demon summoning. Then the stupid fucker broke the summoning circle, trying to boss around the demon. Poor bastard's body dissolved. The flesh slid off his bones before he could even scream."

"What? That's . . . Which of Mertonic's ninety-nine delusions would make him think he could command a demon?"

"Well, I don't know which of the ninety-nine. I don't even know who Mertonic is. Sorry. I assume he's a Leyvan god, right? But it wasn't one of Mertonic's tricks that fooled him. It was one of Shib's."

"Shib convinced Glum he could command demons?" Dahlia was perplexed. This story grew increasingly more bizarre. And Brick wasn't much of a story-teller. Unlike, apparently, the man he was telling the story about.

"Not exactly. Remember that purple stone on a chain we stole from Trader Vawn?"

"How could I forget it?" Dahlia asked, disliking the reminder.

"Well, Shib led Glum to believe it was some sort of magic necklace with power over summoned beings. I told Glum that was a wagonload of horse shit, but he wanted to believe it. And anything anyone said about it just strengthened his conviction."

"And he just had to find out."

"Looks like. Tired of writing about the deeds of others, I suppose. Wanted to be worthy of a poem himself."

"Maybe he is, now," Dahlia said. "But tragedy or farce?"

"I don't know. If I live through the next couple of days, maybe I'll give it some thought."

"That's right. You were worried about Shib hearing you at the tavern. And Livette said Shib was out with you, but returned first. What happened? Are you worried about Shib?"

"Shib left me to fend for myself against a pack of very pissed off demon summoners. He snatched Trader Vawn's medallion and purple necklace from Glum's bones and ran. The odds were for shit, but get a Shark fighting at your side and suddenly it doesn't look like such a bad bet. The demon disappeared after Glum died, so all we had to face were pasty religious types. Sure as Shroud's cold embrace, Shib knew the two of us could fight our way out together. But he left me there. What does that tell you?"

"I don't think he had your best wishes at heart, that's what it tells me. What are you going to do?"

At some point—Dahlia couldn't remember exactly when—they'd taken a side street and started east, toward the river. A chill mist swirled at their feet, climbing up past their ankles as the street dropped them nearer the Mette. The glow of banked embers seen through gaps in a shuttered window lent the mist an eerie solidity. She discovered that she'd moved even closer to Brick, his right hand occasionally brushing against the stiff leather vambrace on her left forearm.

"I'm not sure what I'm going to do," Brick said. "Shib has been good to me these last few years. Only one who'd give me a chance. That's got to count for something, doesn't it?

He brought me in on this Vawn business. Shows some confidence in me. He might have always meant to double cross me. Might have planned to kill me all along. The chance to get me beaten to death by the Entropic Brotherhood was just a happy accident he took advantage of. But how can I be sure?"

"Sure? What is sure besides the gods?"

"Philosophy and theology. Thanks. You're picking up the slack for Glum."

Dahlia eased a step away, slowing her pace. That dismissive tone hurt, coming from Brick. She'd expected better from him, though she supposed she had no real reason to.

"No, wait," Brick said. "I'm sorry. I didn't mean to sound so asshole-ish. I'm seriously asking for your opinion. What do you think I should do?"

Dahlia stopped. Maybe her instincts weren't so bad after all. She took Brick's hand in hers and he swung to face her, his wide face dimly visible above her. She said, "Someone—someone I once held great respect for—told me that sometimes a man must do what is best for himself, even if it means cutting longstanding ties. And I think those words hold true here."

"That why you do what you do? Yeah." Brick nodded. "Why you strap on swords and armor instead of being a good Leyvan girl. You're doing what's best for yourself."

"I never really thought of it that way. What's best for me?" Dahlia noticed she still held Brick's hand, that he'd twined his fingers through hers. "Didn't start that way. I suppose it started as a daughter mimicking her father. My father is in most respects the most conventional of fathers. You want to talk Leyvan customs? My father follows them all. Almost. He thought I might follow him into the apothecary trade, become the first Leyvan woman to take up the profession."

"No one back home would ever know, right?"

"Right. That was my assumption. He never openly talked about it. Unfortunately for him, I never developed an interest in tinctures and herbal concoctions. Also, unfortunately for him, I used to watch him practice the sword forms. I was fascinated. I wanted to do it too. And here he broke from tradition again. Maybe because he had no son, but he indulged my interest and taught me the forms. I never outgrew my— unwomanly—interest in the sword."

Dahlia absently let her fingers play with Brick's sausage-sized digits. "Is that the best thing for me? Maybe not. Maybe following my mother's example would be. She's always seemed happy. And she's a wonderful woman. I love her. I even respect her. But how she lives isn't how I want to. You understand? I don't know if, in my case, what is best for me and what I want are the same thing. But right now, we have to figure out what is best in your case. This thing with Shib, we're talking life and death, aren't we?"

Brick offered one of his deep grunts, the sort that could mean anything or nothing. She could see the steady glitter of his eyes appraising her. Seeing, what? Then he said, "How about first I do what makes me happy, put off doing what's best for me until tomorrow." His free hand, the one that wasn't locked with hers, slipped around her waist. Dahlia felt leather and metal bunch up as he pulled her in close.

She didn't resist. She didn't want to. Her head tilted back and her lips met his. For the first few moments anxiety gripped her, worry that her lack of experience would tell, that Brick wasn't enjoying this and would step away. Then she stopped worrying, stopped feeling anything except pleasure.

After some minutes—a period at once timeless and too brief—Brick lifted his head. He did not release his embrace.

"My lodgings are five minutes from here," Brick said.

"I'd love to see where you live," Dahlia said, then laughed at the absurdity of the euphemistic half-truth, neither of them willing to speak bluntly.

Brick joined the laughter, and his laugh seemed to possess the same self-conscious tone. Keeping her hand in his, he led on.

Chapter 12 - Steel Resolution

It took Brick a moment to understand what troubled him about his attic chamber. It was the light passing through the gaps in the wall boards. It was too bright, the light of morning, not of dawn. Brick could not recall the last time he'd slept past dawn, the last time dreams of blood, terror, screams of pain, and the roars of rampaging war demons hadn't forced him awake before the sun cleared the horizon.

He lay on the rope mattress, staring up at the ceiling beams. He could see his breath plume, the chill, early autumn air rising from the river penetrating the thin walls (long due for re-chinking) and the even thinner blanket. Thinking back, he couldn't recall any nightmares from the night's slumber. Utterly dreamless. How many years had it been since he'd enjoyed a peaceful night?

Brick stretched, luxuriating in the unaccustomed contentment. He heard a muffled complaint, like a kitten whining at the disturbance of its laptop rest, and he felt a body shift next to him. He looked over at the form sharing the blanket. Moving with deliberate caution, Brick raised himself on one elbow to gaze down at Dahlia sleeping by his side.

Her dark hair fanned over her face and across one of Brick's tunics, rolled up to serve as a pillow. Her smooth flank rose and fell in a peaceful rhythm, the curve of one pert breast visible between her arm and the faint outline of her ribcage. Brick lifted a finger to trace the rise and fall of the ribs, then checked the motion, happy enough simply watching her sleep.

He could hear the baker's wife clattering around below. Brick wondered what she'd make of Dahlia coming down the stairs. And then he wondered what *he* would do after he came down the stairs. What was his play?

Letting his gaze remain on Dahlia, Brick worked through the problem. The shafts of light crept along the room, over the pile of Dahlia's discarded armor and clothing intermingled with Brick's vest and clothes, while Brick thought about Shib, and Trader Vawn, and Vawn's medallion, and about poor, stupid Glum.

At some point Brick realized Dahlia eyes were open and fixed on him.

"Good morning," she said and smiled, a curve of lips and rising color in her cheeks suggesting mingled shyness and joy.

Brick was captivated. "You'll get no argument from me," he said.

Dahlia slapped him playfully on the shoulder. Then she yawned and stretched, arching her back and spreading wide her arms. She sat up and blinked away some sleep. She frowned at the bars of light on the wall.

"It's morning," she said.

"We covered that. A good one, to be precise."

"I'm late. I've got to run." She tossed aside the blanket and rose. "Help me suit up,"

Brick got up to help. "Not as much fun putting it on as it was taking it off."

"You'll get no argument from me," Dahlia said.

"Don't rush to a conclusion. We ought to repeat the process a few times, just to be sure."

She pulled his head down to hers, delivering a lingering kiss that, in Brick's estimation, showed dramatic improvement from their first attempt the previous night.

"If I don't have chamber guard duty, maybe we can try the experiment again tonight," Dahlia said. She pushed him away.

They busied themselves separating his garments from hers, then set to encasing her in gambeson, leather, and steel. Brick knelt to strap on her weapons belt.

"You're headed immediately back to Vawn's, right?" Brick asked, craning his neck to look up at her face. "There's something I'd like you to do for me."

***

Dahlia paused a few steps from the front door of the baker's house. She slipped her icon bracelet from her wrist and fingered through the bangles. She stopped at the tiny brass lozenge depicting Gerihu, the personification of fathers. She worked the icon free and held it close, examining the fine engraved detail, the upraised rod of authority, the absurdly long and bushy beard, the rather phallic corona of red enamel backing the figure.

A noise from behind her caused Dahlia to face about. The baker's wife emerged from the house, a bucket in her hands. Brick had created some anxiety in Dahlia about meeting this woman and he'd led the way downstairs to run interference. But the look she'd given Dahlia had been more appraising than disapproving. Now she offered Dahlia a faint smile before dumping the refuse from the bucket onto the midden pile heaped in the street. The coming rains would soon begin to erode the pile, washing the detritus into the Mette, but by the end of spring next year the midden would begin growing again. Nothing in this city ever stayed pristine.

Dahlia returned the smile before the baker's wife returned inside. Then she took the icon between thumb and forefinger and flicked Gerihu into the garbage heap.

She sorted through the gods again, locating Erisala, the Mother. She plucked it free and considered it for a long moment before reattaching it to the bracelet. No need to go crazy.

Dahlia turned her attention to the rise of the West Hills, picking out the distant compounds studding Merchant's Reach. She commenced a slow trot westward. She had a message to deliver.

***

Shib heard Livette enter the tavern, her softer, shorter step clearly distinct from the thumping limp he'd been listening for. Well, let her work if she liked. Though she'd seen her last payday from him.

Shib swung open the concealed locker behind the bottle rack for the third time. He gave the interior another thorough inspection, looking for a stray Petal or even a tarnished copper bit. Once again, he failed to find anything. He'd already cleared it of valuables. And the valuables were all neatly stowed away for his departure. Shib was ready to go. Had been since about midnight. But he was reluctant to leave while the one thread tying him to the Trader Vawn heist remained uncut.

If Vawn grasped hold of the thread he wouldn't let it slip from his fingers until he'd traced it all the way to Shib. A real son of the

Haptha Council, Vawn. He'd feel it his duty to see 'justice' done. Had his head stuffed with all that shit in Port Weir, made him a true believer. The sort who thought that while making his pile here in Kalapo he was also doing some good, enlightening the savages with the Haptha way. Instead of fleecing the ignorant bastards like he should be doing. Shib considered it too dangerous to have someone like that on his back trail. That thread had to be either nipped or tied off.

So instead of running, what Shib did was spend the hours pacing, unpacking and repacking, scouring his office and the storeroom for any portable wealth he might have missed. And waiting for Brick. Mostly waiting for Brick.

There was, Shib reflected, one other thread. That woman. But she was complicit, and her self-worth too tied up with her job to risk losing her position. Brick, on the other hand, assuming he still lived, couldn't be counted on to understand his own best interests. Out of spite, a temporary bout of stupidity, or some irrational code of honor, he just might implicate Shib even though it meant admitting his own role in the heist. Too much was riding on this to hazard an uncertainty factor like Brick. If Brick had survived the cultists he must be dealt with.

Shib closed the bottle rack and dropped the latch, paced to the door leading to the taproom and listened: Livette piling up tankards by the wash tub. Shib spun on his heel and strode to the back door, looking over one more time the stacked crates, chests, and satchels he hoped to have loaded on a mule cart before too long. They appeared precisely the same as the last time, marshaled by the door. The door beyond which his erstwhile customers were wont to relieve themselves. The door through which his true sources of income entered, bringing the middling-value swag Shib fenced. The tavern was half latrine, half-petty larceny clearing house. Be good to leave this place behind, move on to bigger things. He checked the ride of his sword belt on his hips and the fit of the blade in the scabbard. Still comfortable and smooth. He considered another inspection upstairs.

The steps of a large man with a hitch in his gait crossing the sawdust covered floor told Shib that Brick had arrived. About fucking time. Shib's sword was halfway out of the scabbard before he even turned to face the taproom door. Then he let the blade slip back home. If he killed Brick in the taproom he'd have to kill Livette as well. Needless and messy. Patience. See how this played out. Brick was smarter than he appeared, but couldn't compare with the cunning of a Haptha. Maybe Shib could still use Brick, let him live. Doubtful. But the point was to pick his moment to dispose of the bouncer. This was Shib's show. He'd direct the action.

Shib heard Brick exchange words with Livette. Then the door creaked open.

"Boss?" Brick stuck his head in the door, saw Shib, and came in. "Wasn't sure I'd find you here."

"No?" asked Shib. "Where did you think I'd be?" He shifted his stance, more edge on to Brick, letting his offhand fall unseen toward the scabbard. The fingers of his sword hand drummed the air, preparatory to grasping the hilt.

"Upstairs in your office."

Shib relaxed. "Sometimes a business owner needs to get his hands dirty, step away from the office. This storeroom has seen me perform more manual labor this morning than it has the last couple of years combined."

Brick nodded toward the stacked goods. "So I see. Anything I can help with? Moving stuff around is one of my more useful skills."

"Brick, you are a man of many useful abilities. Why I hired you. Why I promoted you." Shib backed away, took a seat atop the chest of ready money he'd unbolted from his office floor and dragged thumping down the stairs a couple hours before dawn. "In fact, I've been thinking about increasing your responsibilities. It's become clear to me you're wasted doing nothing but tossing drunks."

Brick folded his arms, leaned against the wall beside the taproom door. "Oh?"

"Oh, indeed. I have been considering asking you to manage the Chipped Mug. On a trial basis."

"While you take a little vacation?" Brick asked. "That's a lot of luggage."

Shib weighed his answers. He was opening a second tavern. Across the river. Plausible, could work. He'd need operating capital, fixtures, and inventory. A reason for the pile by the door. But Brick already had it in his head he was taking a voyage. So, play off that. Less resistance.

"Vacation? Hardly. Think business trip. Did I ever tell you about my old business partner, Plose?"

Brick shook his boulder of a head.

"No? Well, Plose and I owned a small chandlery in Port Weir. I emphasize 'small.' We weren't outfitting the big merchant caravels or the fast frigates of the far-ranging merchant adventurer types. Showy bastards, the lot of them. No, we catered to a more—circumspect clientele. It's a chancy place, the sea. All manner of calamities and unfortunate events arise. Confusion and misunderstandings can lead to cargoes that were once on one vessel ending up in the hold of another, the kind crewed by men with flexible commercial scruples. You follow me? Our chandlery specialized in supplying the latter type of ship. And brokering the sale of those mysterious cargoes. That's where the real money came from. You with me?"

"I followed Glum's rambling stories, I can keep up with yours," Brick said.

"Right," said Shib, not entirely liking Brick's tone, the hint of cold menace he thought he detected. Well, the spacing remained to his liking. He could stand, draw, and skewer Brick before the big man could push himself straight and uncross his arms. No need for concern. "One day the captain of one of these plucky, daring craft came in. I was out, so Plose dealt with him. Told me the story later. Seems this captain had brought in a sextant or some other bit of navigational gear. Doesn't matter which one, I don't think the Confederacy has developed it yet so you could hardly be expected to know what it does anyway. The point is the thing was worth its weight in Petals. And this captain wished to use it for barter, equip his ship with hawsers and candles and hard biscuit, and the like. Standard, you understand? Except for the offer to pay with the navigational instrument. Plose and I adhered to a strict cash only policy."

Brick shifted. "Glum's stories were usually more entertaining by this time."

"Patience, and all will stand revealed. The captain promised the sextant—"

"Or whatever it was."

"—or whatever it was, represented merely a down payment. He offered Plose a percentage of his next haul if he'd only accept the offered barter. No deal. Plose stood firm."

"We are getting to the moral of the story soon, aren't we?"

"There is a lesson to the anecdote, my impatient friend, but I wouldn't go so far as a moral. What happened was the captain found an alternate outfitter, set out to sea, and returned—surreptitiously—with one of the most extravagant prizes in the history of piracy. Of which neither Plose nor I saw one pence."

"Meaning we're now willing to accept payment in kind for beer?"

"A deliberately obtuse manner is the height of wit. Hilarious. No, Brick. The lesson is to never spurn an opportunity. Always say yes."

"I see. What opportunity are we talking about?"

Brick had straightened. But his arms remained crossed. Shib still considered him unthreatening. He heard footsteps in the taproom, and a faint, almost musical tinkling. Early for customers, but coin is coin. Not that he should care whether or not the Chipped Mug ever earned another, but habits die hard.

"The opportunity," Shib said with exaggerated patience, "that requires my absence and this stack of luggage. I have a chance to buy a popular tavern in Matila, front another enterprise similar to what we're running here. I've got operating capital and inventory so I can hit the ground running."

"What about this tavern?"

Time to bait the trap. "I was circling back to that. How would you like to run the Chipped Tankard during my absence?"

"The tavern and the—other enterprise?"

"You've proved you have the aptitude. And I know you have the brains for it." Season the bait with a bit of flattery.

"Aptitude? You mean that recent job? About that, do you still have the goods? You want, I can try to find a buyer for that purple stone, get a feel for the work."

The trap snapped shut. Got you, Brick. You'll never know how close you came to bleeding your life out right here on the storeroom floor. Shib dug beneath a smock and two layers of tunics. He lifted free the trading credentials and the amethyst pendant that hung from chains about his neck.

"I do, Brick. But it's probably best you start with something less valuable, less recognizable. Besides, I need these to get the business started in Matila."

"That's fine," Brick said. "It isn't me who wants them anyway." The bouncer half turned his head and called out over his shoulder, "Dahlia."

The taproom door opened. That Leyvan woman stepped through—Vawn's bodyguard. The source of the tinkling. He should have known that. He was getting sloppy, too anxious to leave. What did she want? He made to tuck away the medallion and necklace, then checked. She knew he had them. Some sort of extortion attempt? He might have to do some killing this morning after all.

"Shib," she said. "There's someone here to see you."

* * *

Brick had maintained the Fury at a low simmer throughout his interview with Shib. It threatened to boil once or twice, but he'd had an unexpectedly easy task of keeping it in check. Now it dropped to quiescence as Dahlia ushered in Trader Vawn.

The trader looked dapper in his tight, parti-colored getup, punctuated by the hat with the absurdly long feather. In comparison, Shib came off rather shabbily in his low-key tradesman's attire. But both Sharks boasted long swords, of the narrow-bladed Haptha variety, belted about their waists. Trader Vawn held the height advantage, but Brick knew Shib was agile and he couldn't discount his cunning.

"Ahh, Shib," said Trader Vawn. "I have been looking for those two baubles. How convenient that you have both of them dangling about your neck."

Shib tucked the two chains back beneath his tunics. "What brings you to my establishment so early? Needing another bottle of the Wisterian?"

"As delightful as I found the brandy, thirst did not motivate my visit. The simple truth is that I owed Brick a favor and he called it in, Dahlia serving as his messenger."

"Brick called in a favor?"

Brick noted Shib dragged out his words. The Shark's eyes shifted. Brick could imagine the calculation going on behind them. Shib's stance widened, his right leg shifting to the fore, as if casually getting comfortable for the conversation.

"Yes. I was indebted to him for his valor on my behalf. Dahlia told me he was 'calling in his marker' and requesting only that I come meet him here immediately. One might almost suspect our man Brick of possessing a devious streak."

"One might," Shib said.

Brick felt comfortable interpreting the look Shib sent his way as hate. No question that Shib would kill him if the opportunity arose.

Shib opened his mouth again, but Vawn overrode him. "Please spare me the lies and excuses, Shib. I am not sure they are beneath you, but they are beneath my notice."

"That's a relief," Shib said. "I can get on with killing you." He swept his sword free of the scabbard and stepped into a lunge with an eyeblink speed that shocked Brick, though he'd seen it before and was half-expecting it.

Trader Vawn apparently had expected it as well. Unlike Brick he was not shocked. He leaned aside, letting Shib's thrust slip by a finger's breadth from his torso. Then his sword was out and on guard before Shib recovered to a ready position.

Brick felt an anticipatory grin tug the corners of his mouth. He'd fought Sharks during the war. He knew how quick they were. But those battles were mass engagements, in close and without room to maneuver. No fancy one-on-one duels, but brutal face-to-face hacking and stabbing and hoping. This bout between Shib and Trader Vawn promised something different. And as a bonus, this time Brick wasn't an immediate target of Haptha steel.

Not an immediate target, true, but he remembered that look of Shib's and shuffled a step closer to the taproom door. No point in letting himself become a temptation should the fight bring Shib within sword reach.

Brick brushed against Dahlia, glanced down and saw a smile akin to his own. Figured she'd enjoy this. Probably a connoisseur of duels. He resisted the urge to take her hand. She might need it free if this plan of his turned sour.

The scrap didn't look like much to Brick at first. The two Sharks poked their swords out, points crossing, the blades scraping with a metallic susurrus. A bit of shifting back and forth, the sword blades moving hardly at all. Bit of a disappointment really. Brick risked another look at Dahlia, saw the rapt expression on her face. Maybe there was more going on here than he understood. That didn't come as a great surprise. He'd been taught how to thrust a spear and block with a shield. Practical training and useful in a battle line. But it didn't necessarily translate to appreciation of this sort of overgrown knife fight.

Then Shib jabbed at Vawn's face. Brick realized it was a feint after Shib dropped the point and thrust at Trader Vawn's leading leg. Vawn must have realized the same thing much sooner. His parry looked almost lackadaisical. But his riposte was pure Haptha, lightning with greased axles and a fresh team pulling. Shib brought his sword back in line to turn the counter, but barely. Brick took a moment to absorb the fact that Shib stood unscathed, he'd been sure he'd see the bloody point of Trader Vawn's blade erupting between Shib's shoulder blades. Instead, Shib skipped back and moved laterally.

"Such speed," Dahlia said. "I never imagined."

"I didn't either, first time I saw them," Brick said. "More fun to watch than to face, believe me."

Trader Vawn pursued Shib across the storeroom. He put on a burst and attacked, the movement unexpected—one moment his pursuit patient and relentless, the next he'd closed the gap and lunged. Shib spun away from the attack, and changed course, edging along the back wall. He snatched a bottle from the rack behind him, a mediocre red from a vineyard a couple days' journey south along the Mette, a bottle Shib marked up tenfold and sold as a prestige wine to the occasional nouveau riche who came in—accidentally, one presumed—and pretended some knowledge of viniculture.

Shib flung the bottle at Vawn's head. The trader ducked. The earthenware bottle hurtled, end-over-end, toward the taproom door from which Brick and Dahlia watched. Brick threw up a hand. The bottle smacked into his palm and his fingers wrapped around it, the catch utter chance from a purely reflexive defense.

"Drink?" he asked Dahlia.

Shib used the distraction to move away from the wall to the center of the store room. Trader Vawn flourished his sword, saluted. The two Sharks engaged again, their blade work a blur, the action proceeding too fast for Brick to follow. The sound of metal ringing on metal echoed in the confined space. Then Shib stepped back, slapped his free hand up to his ear. The tip of Vawn's sword beaded with wet, red drops.

"I learned during my service in the Hierocracy that the Leyvans sentence a thief to have his ear notched for the first offense," Trader Vawn said. "You stole two items from me, Shib. Shall I demonstrate the penalty for the second offense?"

"Hardly an inspiring choice of last words," Shib said. He feinted a lunge, then spun on his heel and sprinted the few steps to the stairs. He stopped halfway up and turned.

Trader Vawn followed, engaged. The swords flickered again. The upper half of the feather in Vawn's cap drifted to the floor, the shaft cleanly severed. Shib was holding the high ground.

Vawn attacked again, but it became clear even to Brick that Shib's advantage would tell soon enough. The trader's breathing grew labored enough that Brick could hear it during a lull in the fight.

Dahlia left Brick's side and climbed up to the lowest stair. She drew her parrying dagger and gripped it lightly by the tip. "Your off hand, sir," she said.

Trader Vawn extended his left hand, palm up, while continuing to deflect a flurry of thrusts and cuts from above. The hilt of the dagger slapped into his hand. He faced Shib now with two blades and went on the offensive, driving Shib back one grudging step at a time.

Brick joined Dahlia at the base of the stairs for a better view.

"Can we not be reasonable about this?" Shib asked. He was nearing the last step. "What if I tell—"

Trader Vawn caught Shib's blade with the quillons of Dahlia's dagger and twisted it to the side, leaving Shib's torso exposed. Shib's last words ended in an explosive wheeze as Trader Vawn rammed his sword into Shib, the point plunging in immediately below his sternum then punching out through his spine. Shib coughed, a pink froth appearing at his lips. Trader Vawn swiveled toward the wall side of the staircase. Shib vomited up a gout of blood that just missed Vawn, then he was sliding off the end of the sword, tumbling down the stairs to the storeroom floor. He lay crumpled at Brick's feet, eyes staring up unblinking, Brick thinking he looked even more like a shark with his dead eyes and bloody mouth.

Trader Vawn descended, winded, his arms hanging limply. At the bottom, he sucked in a great lungful of air, let it escape slowly with the look of enjoyment of a man sipping his first glass of the day.

"Thank you," he said, handing Dahlia her dagger. He stooped over Shib's corpse and worked the two chains free over Shib's head. "And thank you. You will not be needing these any further, I trust."

Brick laughed. Wasn't that funny of a remark. A laugh of relief, he supposed. He had trouble believing his scheme had actually worked. Yet there sprawled Shib, no longer a threat.

"Have I paid my debt?" Trader Vawn asked. "Or am I once again in a deficit? Your message has seen the recovery of my credentials." He wiped his blade clean on Shib's smock.

"We're even. You owe me nothing," Brick said. "Even" probably wasn't the right word. He didn't want to begin calculating the extent of his debt to Trader Vawn.

"As you say. What will you do now? May I point out there is now a tavern in need of a publican."

Brick pondered it. Shib had asked him to take over management. As far as he knew no one would question the change of ownership.

So long as the Magistery received its yearly tax payment, and the occasional Horse Guardsman or Elector got his palm greased, there shouldn't be any problems. A big step up, completing the rise in fortunes that Shib had promised him. And well ahead of schedule.

He looked down at Dahlia, who was inspecting her dagger for nicks, likely calculating how much time she'd have to spend honing them out. She caught his gaze, smiled at him, though with a quizzical quirk to one eyebrow. And Brick wasn't so sure running the bar was what he wanted. Did he want the day-to-day responsibility? Did he want the reminder of Shib constantly about him?

Trader Vawn retrieved Shib's sword from where it had clattered to a stop against the stacked boxes by the back door. He offered Brick the sword, hilt first. "You know, Brick, as it happens I am looking to fill a guardsman position."

Brick considered the sword. "I don't suppose you know anyone could teach me how to use this toothpick," he said.

Dahlia jabbed an elbow in his ribs. "A sword is a weapon for the refined. I doubt anyone could teach an oaf like you. But it might be fun trying."

Brick had to admit that hiring on as one of Trader Vawn's bodyguards held promise. An elegant solution to a sticky ethical dilemma. He felt some responsibility for the death of Heareld, though he knew the immediate blame fell on Nahl—now presumably dead by Glum's hand—and the ultimate blame fell on Shib—now dead at his feet. With Glum dead, that left Brick the last of the crew. Taking Heareld's place could serve as an act of atonement. Little good that did Heareld, true, but he could only do what he could do.

Then there was Dahlia, looking at him expectantly. The thought of spending every day in her company sweetened Vawn's offer considerably. He felt a serenity in her presence. He could get used to it.

Brick took the proffered sword. "We'll need to discuss salary."

"I think we can reach an accommodation," Trader Vawn said.

"What about the tavern?" Dahlia asked.

Brick grunted. He walked into the taproom. Livette stood on the customer side of the bar, a barrier between her and the recent commotion in the back room. A stack of heavy wooden tankards sat near to hand, ready to throw, and she clutched a bodkin in a grip that betrayed only a slight tremble.

"Livette," Brick asked, "how'd you like to own a tavern?"

The End

About the Author

Ken Lizzi is an attorney and the author of an assortment of short stories and novels. When not traveling—and he'd rather be traveling—he lives in Oregon with his beautiful wife Isa and his delightful daughter V.V. He enjoys reading, homebrewing, and visiting new places. He loathes writing about himself in the third person.

Visit him at:
http://www.kenlizzi.net

www.ingramcontent.com/pod-product-compliance
Lightning Source LLC
Chambersburg PA
CBHW021118110726
47900CB00007B/2245